HOUR
OF THE
ASSASSIN

Also by Matthew Quirk

THE NIGHT AGENT

DEAD MAN SWITCH

COLD BARREL ZERO

THE DIRECTIVE

THE 500

"The action never ceases in Quirk's story, and you'll find yourself reading way past your bedtime."

—*Star-Ledger* (Newark)

"This one is a gritty, intense political thriller, filled with nuance and dire exploits. Totally entertaining. A treat from start to finish."

—Steve Berry,
author of *The Malta Exchange*

"Quirk's *Hour of the Assassin* feels tailor-made for the big screen and reads like a blockbuster from beginning to end. Trust me, if you're looking for a great thriller to sink your teeth into, this is it. Quirk brings his very best here, delivering a stunning, page-turning reading experience that's not to be missed."

—TheRealBookSpy.com

Praise for

THE NIGHT AGENT

"*The Night Agent* rocks. Fast as hell, especially with Quirk's steady hand in control. This story is impossible to put out of mind once you enter this look-over-your-shoulder shadow world. Relevant and revealing, this is one of the best thrillers to come along in years."

—Michael Connelly

HOUR OF THE ASSASSIN

A Novel

Matthew Quirk

wm

WILLIAM MORROW

An Imprint of HarperCollins*Publishers*

HOUR OF THE ASSASSIN. Copyright © 2020 by Rough Draft, Inc. All rights reserved. Printed in the United States of America. No part of this book may be used or reproduced in any manner whatsoever without written permission except in the case of brief quotations embodied in critical articles and reviews. For information, address HarperCollins Publishers, 195 Broadway, New York, NY 10007.

First William Morrow mass market printing: January 2021
First William Morrow international paperback printing: March 2020
First William Morrow hardcover printing: March 2020

Print Edition ISBN: 978-0-06-299161-4
Digital Edition ISBN: 978-0-06-287554-9

Cover design by Jae Song
Cover photographs © Doug Armand/Getty Images (Capitol building);
© Liderina/Shutterstock (man)
Author photograph by Mark Finkenstaedt

21 22 23 24 25   CPI   10 9 8 7 6 5 4 3 2 1

For Eileen and Rick

1

ASSASSINATION IS A tense, sweaty business. So Nick Averose found it odd, as he sat inside this bush for the fifty-third minute, how cozy his spot had become. Berry and pine scented the air, and the little enclosure reminded him of childhood games. He could almost forget the Smith & Wesson hanging on his hip and the knife sheath in a horizontal draw on his belt.

The air shook with the sound of a heavy V-8. Nick pressed his back against the brick wall at the base of the fence. The six-bedroom mansion was all stone with slate roofs, fit for an Ivy League campus, though its perimeter was more appropriate for a military installation. It seemed unbreachable without raising the alarm.

But every defense had its weakness. Nothing was perfect. No one was safe. Nick had to believe that, to prove it tonight and every night.

As the black Chevy Suburban pulled up the driveway, Nick stole toward it. The faint blue glow of a cell phone lit the interior and the face of his target, Malcolm Widener, the former director of the CIA. The job was simple enough: kill him with no trace.

Once Widener had commanded an army of spies and paramilitaries, and a round-the-clock detail from the agency's Security Protective Service had lived on this property. Now he worked for a global hedge fund, trading on what and who he knew. His company provided him with the best guards money could buy.

There were a few ways to get through that fence, but the easiest was the most obvious and the most dangerous: the front driveway. All Nick needed was a stalking horse and some way to open the wrought iron gate. Widener's own vehicle would do both.

Nick waited, taking measured breaths as the gate rattled back. When the Suburban rolled forward, he stepped onto the driveway and walked toward the car's rear right tire, moving in a fast crouch in its blind spot.

Getting through that gate was the crux of the entry. He knew the compound's layout by heart. Once inside, he moved in a careful choreography: dart right into the blind spot of the southwest corner camera, sprint to the hanging vines of the pergola, duck behind the stonework of the outdoor kitchen, then wait one hundred and forty seconds. He stared at the faint green glow of his watch, cupped in his hands, while a drop of sweat rolled down his lower back. Footsteps hushed across the lawn. A flashlight's beam swung toward him and glinted off the grill.

It lit up the grass behind him and the other side of the stone wall where he had taken cover but left him in a long shadow. The light swung away. The guard moved on, barely a minute off schedule. The security, armed with SIG semiautos, worked methodically through any spots the cameras wouldn't touch.

Nick waited ten seconds, stood, and continued on, his eyes on the guard's back, staying fifty feet behind him, relying on the fact that the man's attention would be focused ahead. If he turned around, he could easily put a pair of nine-millimeter holes in Nick's heart.

He stalked in the man's slipstream toward the rear of the house, then cut under the south portico and took up a post next to a door of breakproof glass. He could see inside, down a long corridor lined with landscapes, family portraits, and a few classical pieces in marble.

His fingers closed on an acrylic box the size of a pack of cigarettes in his pocket. He stood close to the white circle next to the door, where access cards were swiped. Widener came around the corner at the far end of the hall and walked straight toward him.

Nick waited, calm. Because it was dark outside and light within, he knew that Widener could see only his own reflection, but that did little to kill the eerie feeling of staring eye to eye at his target.

Widener came closer, until he was six feet away, then turned right down a hall as Nick pressed a button on the side of his device. It was a Proxmark amplifier—he'd built it himself—that boosted the signal between the key fob in Widener's pocket and the receiver by the door. The lock slid back with an expensive, beautifully engineered silence.

Nick opened the door an inch, waited a few seconds, then entered, trailing Widener on the long runner across the herringbone floor. He was moving away from the living room toward a set of stairs that led to the upper floors, where Widener would be most vulnerable.

Nick followed him as he went upstairs and disappeared into the bedroom suite. Nick didn't enter, just listened to the sounds of running water as he continued to the top floor and turned left into Widener's office. An antique desk commanded half the room, facing the windows and a sitting area with two club chairs, a sofa, and a wall-mounted television.

Moonlight filtered in. Nick looked over the frames on the wall. There were class portraits from St. Albans and Georgetown, and shots of Widener with the past two US presidents, with prime ministers, with senators. These were real photos of friends, of intimates, not staged handshakes at fund-raisers.

Nick had spent a decade in the Secret Service. He had once protected men like this, which had taught him how to get to them. He crossed the room and tucked into a dark nook where a copier and office supplies were stacked.

Through a window, Nick had a view of the driveway and the staff cars parked beside the garage. The wife was in New York. He could see everyone coming and going, would know when he was alone with Widener, when no one would be around to hear him call for help.

Widener entered, now without his jacket and tie, and switched on a lamp. He poured himself a small glass of scotch and added a few drops of water, as he did every night. A man of routine.

It would be easy enough to do it now. Killing wasn't the difficult thing, though it was harder, louder, and shabbier than most suspected. Killing and getting away was the true test.

Widener sat at his desk, his back to Nick. He flipped

on the TV, tuned to a Hoyas basketball game, then pulled his laptop toward him and set to work.

Nick stepped out of the shadows. One turn, one careful look, and Widener would see him. But people so rarely stop to examine the familiar world around them. We walk blindly through this life.

This was the most difficult part: to hold, silent and still, in the same room as the mark, even as the adrenaline raced through his body like flame up a fuse.

Time was his weapon, isolating them. Nick watched through the window as the housekeeper pulled out in her Honda.

Malcolm Widener would have a place in the history books. But at the end of the day, he was just a man, sitting alone and vulnerable. Following someone this closely inevitably created sympathy. Nick used it as a tool to put himself inside a target's head. Now he tuned it out. This was a job, and he was a professional.

The gate opened and closed. One guard remained on the property, finishing his patrol before he went to check the security feeds from a post inside the pool house. There were no cameras here. Nick was inside the sanctum. It was time.

He closed on Widener with silent steps, stood behind him, and touched his fingers to the sheath.

Nick didn't draw a knife or gun. In his other hand he held a small envelope marked "Indicator of Compromise." He laid it on the ground a few feet from the chair and stepped back into the shadows.

Tonight everything was real but the killing.

2

NICK WAITED FOR his moment, with Widener's eyes fixed on the game, then slipped through the side door into the back hall.

He took the rear stairs down and crossed to the front door, double-checking for the guard, timing his exit.

Heavy steps sounded from the top of the main staircase. He turned and saw the former CIA director staring down at him, holding his drink in one hand and Nick's letter in the other.

"So you're the red team?" he called down.

"Yes, sir," Nick said, doing his best to keep the smile off his face.

"And I'm dead?"

"In this scenario, yes."

Widener took a sip of scotch and raised his glass.

"Well roll away the stone. Come up here."

Nick was a security consultant. He posed as a threat in order to find the weaknesses in anyone's defenses, testing systems under real-life conditions, as he had done tonight. The profession was known in its different varieties as red-teaming, security auditing, or penetration testing.

Nick had worked protective details as a marine before he joined the Secret Service, where he had learned to put himself into the mind of the adversary, to live the part.

Clients normally needed to be handled with kid gloves, but Widener was oddly unfazed. He'd run the agency. He was used to living in a bubble of guards and bug sweeps and assuming everyone around him was watching and listening.

"We don't have to go over everything now," Nick said. "I don't want to put you out."

"Any more than breaking into my house and killing me? No, come on up. I want to know how you did it."

Nick climbed the stairs and followed Widener into his office. He sat behind his desk while Nick stood in front.

"I got the email from Aegis saying they'd be testing security," he said. "I didn't expect anything this intense." Aegis was the company that handled Widener's protection and employed the guards Nick had slipped past.

Widener looked over the letter. It was proof of a successful break-in, lovingly known as the "you're dead" letter.

He studied Nick's face. "Have we met before?"

"Not formally. I was Secret Service when you were the president's briefer."

"You were on the West Wing detail."

"That's right."

Widener sat back, his shoulders relaxing. Nick could see that had won him some trust.

"What's your name?" he asked.

"Nick Averose."

"Malcolm," Widener said, then stood and shook Nick's hand across the desk, his palm like leather.

Nick was impressed. Guys like him were often invisible to someone at Widener's level, just part of the scenery. When he'd first seen the former director, a man with the natural dignity of a weathered elm, he'd imagined he'd be reserved and a little haughty, but face-to-face he was all old-school establishment charm and ease.

"And now you work for Aegis?" he asked.

"I contract with them," Nick said. "You should have been briefed on the scope of tonight's test. I have the paperwork here." He pointed to his pocket.

Widener nodded. Nick slowly pulled out a second piece of paper, a letter of authorization. He passed it across the desk. Red-teamers always carried a contract with the client's signature, just in case they ever ran into trouble with the law and needed to prove they were on a security audit. The industry shorthand for it was "a get-out-of-jail-free card."

Widener looked it over.

"The guard outside?"

"I made it past him. He's still there."

"Are you armed?" he asked.

"An unloaded pistol and an empty knife sheath. Everything is as realistic as possible."

"Show me."

Nick cocked his head and considered the request. It felt intensely wrong to draw the pistol, even unloaded, on a man like Widener.

"Slowly," Widener said. "Just finger and thumb on the grip."

Nick showed the sheath and then reached inside his jacket and brought the gun out like a cop holding a piece of evidence. He laid it on the desk.

Widener nodded gravely, then checked that the chamber and magazine were empty.

"And how do you go about it? Killing me?"

Nick weighed his answer. There was a danger in getting too real with a client.

"Indulge me," Widener said. "Surely you know how it's done." He took a sip and waited.

"The knife," Nick said.

"To keep it quiet?"

"Yes."

"Odd way to make a living," Widener said, his eyes on the gun. "Why did you leave the Service?"

"I got married. It was time."

Widener nodded. It's hard to be a family man when your job is catching bullets. "So my company spends whatever ungodly sum of money on all this security, and I'm still dead."

"The system is one of the best I've seen on a private residence."

"Then—no offense—why are you sneaking up on me with a gun?"

"Nothing is perfect and no one is safe."

Widener regarded him, and Nick realized he had spoken it like the article of faith that it was.

"Your setup is damn close."

"What needs fixing?"

"This may sound odd, but I would encourage the guards to be a little less punctual."

"Too predictable?"

"That's right. And there are some firmware updates you can make on the access card system."

Widener looked Nick up and down, noting the dark pants, the running shoes, the button-down under his jacket.

"I was expecting . . ."

"A black turtleneck? Fatigues?"

Widener laughed. "I guess so." He pointed to the gun. "Those guards could have killed you."

"It's a real-world test. And that's why I don't wear the turtleneck. No one gets shot to death in business casual."

The other man nodded, seemed to appreciate the point.

"I'll send a report to Aegis covering everything in detail," Nick said. "A few tweaks and no one will be able to get to you."

Widener narrowed his eyes. "You will."

Nick took a moment, trying to get a read on him.

"I'm fucking with you," he said, and tapped the signature on the contract. "Do you have the email for this woman from Aegis? Alexandra Hart."

She was the company lawyer who had contacted Nick and arranged this test.

"Sure. You didn't talk to her?"

"No."

Nick crossed his arms. That wasn't right. She'd said she had cleared this with Widener personally. He took a step back and looked out the window.

Tss tss. The noise came faint through the window on the other side. It sounded like a rattrap snapping, but Nick knew it in an instant.

Silenced shots.

Nick turned and rushed to the other window as time seemed to slow, the seconds like minutes, his vision narrowing to a tunnel as he scanned the yard.

A still form lay on the ground. The guard was down.

3

NICK FELT HIS stomach turn as he moved toward Widener.

"Sir, call the police."

"What?"

"Someone else is here."

"You're joking."

"No."

The former director went to say something, then stopped, his face tightening with fear. He lifted the phone on his desk.

"Do you have a gun, any kind of weapon?" Nick asked.

"No. But the guard does."

Nick took his empty pistol off the desk and holstered it, then strode through the main door. "Lock both doors behind me and don't come out."

He moved along the corridor, then down the stairs to the ground floor. At the landing he scanned the entry hall, then crossed the marble tiles toward the front door. He paused by a window, approaching it from the shadows to avoid being seen, and peered through.

A silhouette shifted in the dark. Someone was out there. Nick stepped back and took out his phone. *No signal.*

He muttered a curse and watched the figure passing along the fence. The training took over. *Protect the principal. Get a weapon. A kitchen knife. The guard's gun.*

The doors were locked. He couldn't let the threat inside, no matter what it took.

He crossed the living room and caught movement in the side yard through a window. The attacker was circling him.

Pacing toward the rear of the house, Nick felt a draft run over his skin, as if a door had been opened. Someone was already inside.

How many of them were there? Dread washed through Nick, left an acid taste in his throat.

A faint noise near the back stairs: footsteps. Nick stalked closer. It was an echo from above.

Two low thumps sounded through the ceiling, somewhere on the upper floors, between him and Malcolm Widener. Nick's breath caught. It felt for an instant like all the air had rushed out of the room and there was nothing to fill his lungs.

He sprinted to the stairs and climbed, then edged into the hallway that led to Widener's office, scanning in both directions. The office's side door was open.

Nick moved toward it, the adrenaline pushing him forward like an automaton. He pressed against the wall, left side, then right, buying as much of a vantage on the room as he could.

He saw the desk, the back of Widener's chair, a still hand palm-to-ceiling on the armrest.

Fast through the door. He blew into the room and circled. A glossy red-black puddle inched across the floor. He stepped to the side and saw Widener, sprawled across the chair, his clothes slick as a barber's gown, wet with his blood.

Nick scanned the room. No one else was here. His eyes went back to Widener's throat. Whoever had done this was a professional, moving quickly with no sign of hesitation.

Pressure. Airway. Breathing. Circulation.

Nick took two long strides toward him and clamped his hand over his neck. He felt for a pulse. It was there.

No. That was his own. Nick's heart banged against his chest like an unbalanced dryer. He looked into Widener's eyes, searching for a spark of life, but they were like glass.

A knife lay on the floor. Nick knew that blade. He crouched and reached for it, felt the blood drip down his fingers. He lifted it and examined the weapon, the tip rounded from resharpening, the handle worn, smooth and shining where the index finger would rest, with a large chip missing near the lanyard hole. It wasn't just the same kind of knife. It was *the* knife, his knife.

Nick had left it at his office two hours ago.

His face felt hot, fevered. *Now would be a great time to wake, Nick.*

He regripped the knife and spun. He was still alone. He looked on the desk for the letter of authorization. That document would prove he was no criminal. It was gone, along with the other papers.

Whoever had killed Widener had taken them.

Nick held the knife and looked to the body, then the blood on his hands. He understood the scene, the simple story it told. Nick Averose, who could get to anyone, anywhere, had murdered the former director of the CIA.

4

HOW DID THAT night go so wrong? Through the next desperate hours, the question wouldn't let go of Nick as he picked apart every moment that had brought him to Widener's office, looking for some way he could have known, could have stopped it all.

But the day that ended with Nick holding that knife had started ordinarily enough, or whatever passed for ordinary in Nick's world.

Many former Secret Service agents go into corporate security, guarding VIPs and managing risk for multinational companies. But Nick had his own shop that he ran out of a converted carriage house in the Shaw neighborhood of DC. He liked working for himself and setting his own hours. His reputation brought in more clients than he could handle, and he could afford to pick the more interesting challenges.

That morning he'd come in early with breakfast sandwiches for himself and Delia Tayran, the twenty-seven-year-old engineer who handled the IT and technical side of the business. She was Nick's only employee, though she was more like family.

They'd finished going over the plan of attack on Widener's residence for a third and final time by eleven.

By eleven thirty, Nick was in handcuffs, his arms bound behind his back. Delia had locked him up like a pro. They were taking a break, messing around with a strange pair of cuffs, seeing if Nick could pick his way out of them. Locks and safes and restraints were all part of the trade. Delia always seemed to know when Nick could use a respite from the tunnel vision of plotting a job and the role he played.

He worked against his linebacker's build, trying to pass the cuffs under his legs and in front of him. He hopped and tugged and felt them budge against the back pockets of his jeans. They moved an inch farther, but that threw off his balance and he had to lean against the wall.

"Mercy?" Delia asked, standing in front of him with her hands on her hips, laughing.

"Never. Who made these?" He slid his fingers over the metal, feeling along the hinge, looking for the keyway, trying to angle a bent pick inside.

"The Stasi. Some hacker guy I met at a conference let me borrow them. Don't scratch them."

Delia looked to her side and her jaw dropped slightly. Nick craned his head back.

A woman stood in the open door of the shop, arms crossed, a mix of apprehension and wonder on her face as she took in the scene.

Delia leaned down and fumbled with the key while Nick smiled at their guest. Her name was Alexandra

Hart. She was a lawyer for Aegis, a high-end executive protection firm based in London and New York. They handled Malcolm Widener's security and had hired Nick to run an audit at his residence that night.

Hart wore a tweed dress with short sleeves that showed the upper arms of a dedicated athlete. Her hair, her mouth, her posture—everything was pulled tight in a determined beauty.

"Be with you in a minute," Nick said.

The cuffs released. Nick rubbed his wrists and held his hand out. "Alexandra, come on in."

She tucked her small attaché under her left arm and shook his hand while eyeing the red marks from the cuffs.

"Escaping illegal restraints," he said. "Part of the portfolio."

"Of course," she said primly, and brought out a file. Nick always signed the letter of authorization in person. They executed three copies. After Nick did tonight's job at Widener's house and saw just how vulnerable the former director was, he would document any weaknesses and report them back to Hart.

"I'm eager to hear your findings," she said.

"I look forward to it," Nick replied, and puzzled over his own formal diction. He was too old and too married and too professional to be thrown by a gorgeous woman, but there was something else about her his attention kept snagging on, something beneath the all-business exterior.

Nick watched her walk out and turned to see Delia looking at him. She rolled her eyes. Nick checked his watch. They were way ahead of schedule. He pointed to the cuffs.

"One more go," he said. "I was close, right?"

Delia squinted and seesawed her hand in the air. "'Close' would be generous. I know we've been over this before, but I have one word."

"Don't."

"Yoga," she said, and closed the cuffs around his wrists.

He was out of them in eight minutes.

That was it. A regular day. A good day. No sign of the storm to come.

At six o'clock, Delia went home after they finished prepping gear. Nick liked to do his final run-through alone, sitting in silence, going through the whole operation second-by-second in his mind.

He was ready. He drew his knife from the sheath and put it in the top drawer of his desk, then went out to the cabinet safe where he kept his gun. He checked and rechecked that the Smith & Wesson magazine was unloaded and the chamber clear. He placed the ammo in the safe, along with a copy of the letter of authorization in case anything went wrong.

He put the paperwork in his pocket and—armed with an empty sheath and gun—locked up and went outside. His truck was parked in the front. He started it up and headed for Malcolm Widener's house.

NOW NICK STOOD over Widener's body on the top floor of that home, anger and pity rising in him in equal measure. The presence of death seemed to fill the room, lingering in the air like smoke.

He lifted the landline on the desk. No dial tone. His cell still had no signal. He heard rustling through the window, in the side yard, then the softest whisper of a step in the hall.

He crossed the office with silent paces and sprinted through the main door.

He saw the blow coming, a blur at the edge of his vision. A man, pressed against the wall just outside, thrust his hand toward Nick's face.

It was blue. A surgical glove. Nick halted, leaned back as if slipping on ice, and the glove passed an inch from his jaw.

Nick seized the wrist and drove his fingers and thumb

like a C-clamp between the radius and ulna, where the nerves ran.

A short, vicious punch from the man's free hand caught Nick in the temple, but Nick stayed up, wrenched the arm, dragged him toward the floor.

The attacker leaned to the side, trying to relieve the pressure on the joint, and Nick pushed him over. He crashed, twisting, to the ground, and Nick let the wrist go, then kicked him hard in the stomach, the head.

The man raised himself with one arm and brought his feet beneath him, but as he stood, his face went slack. Nick noticed a substance smeared across his cheek and lips that looked like petroleum jelly.

The man looked at the glove, the palm coated with the same oily material, then fell to the side. He didn't move, didn't even try to check the fall.

Nick edged toward him and snatched the gun from the man's holster. No response. He had tried to hit Nick with whatever was on that glove. It must have been some kind of paralytic.

Nick checked the pistol. A round was chambered. The mag was full. He started down the hall, then froze. Doors opened and closed in the front and side of the house.

He moved toward the rear stairs and heard more people coming.

He stepped back into Widener's office. He was trapped. The one with the glove had been in the lead. The others downstairs sounded like they were moving in from the exits, closing a noose around Nick to make sure he couldn't escape.

Blind them. You need the dark.

He slipped the knife blade through the cord of the desk lamp. A blue spark leaped out, and the room went black. The metal in the knife short-circuited the wires and tripped the breaker. That was what he had hoped for. The hallway was dark, too. The same breaker fed this wing.

Surprise them. Get to their backs. Knife in hand, he went to the window, saw a figure moving across the yard, and crossed the room to the other side. There was a circular window at the end of a dormer. It looked onto the peak of the roof below. It was high up with steep slate on either side, but he could see a way out: along the spine, down to the roof of the sunroom, and then a twelve-foot drop to the back lawn.

His mind worked coldly, methodically, focusing on each move, each next step, holding back the panic and shock.

He looked for a latch to open the window, but there was none. He brought his elbow back and drove it into the frame. The glass shattered, and pain shot up his forearm. He ignored it as the night air rushed in.

GRAY CROSSED THE entry hall of Malcolm Widener's house, calm amid the violence. Men with pistols drawn followed him like a pack of dogs.

The lead man had taken down Widener quickly and cleanly. He excelled at stealth and so had gone in first. Now all Gray needed was Nick Averose, dead in this same house, to complete the story. They had him surrounded, all the exits blocked.

He heard glass shatter above and vectored on the noise, his body tensing. He raced up the stairs. Moving down the hallway, Gray held his flashlight beside his gun, checking every door, every corner, as he passed. The men fanned out, searching, closing in on Widener's office.

Gray stepped inside. The flashlights illuminated the director's body, the finger-streaked blood.

A draft streamed into the room, and they fixed on a circular window, its frame and glass busted out.

Gray moved toward it, looked through, and saw the shards glittering along the roof.

"He's gone," his deputy said quietly, peering over the backyard.

"Go." Gray flicked his head toward the window. The man climbed through, broken glass crunching under his legs, hissing in pain but saying nothing.

Gray approached the desk with his light and glanced over Widener's body. The knife was gone. That was only the beginning of the evidence he needed to complete the frame. He had plenty. But he also had Nick Averose armed and on the loose.

He needed to take him before he made it over that fence.

7

NICK PRESSED HIMSELF against the panel, deep in the kneehole under Malcolm Widener's desk, pulling back from the light as if it, in itself, were lethal. A man moved a few feet away.

The blood had pooled here, lukewarm and tacky, clinging to the soles of Nick's shoes and his hand pressed against the floor. That meant more tracks and more prints, but right now that was the least of his concerns. He felt like he had stepped outside his body and was watching it all happen, a nightmare so lucid it shocks you out of sleep.

But there was no waking from this. He forced himself to slow down, to breathe. His forearm started to cramp and he eased his grip on the knife. The nearest man moved closer, stepping around the blood. Nick narrowed his eyes against the light.

They would find him. He had no chance. He was going to die in this room, on this floor. The thought nearly broke him, left him numb and unable to move, but as he faced it, he found an eerie calm in the center of the fear.

He wouldn't go quietly. He flipped the knife into an ice-pick grip and tensed, stomach tight, ready to lunge as the man came closer.

"What is it?" someone asked.

Sudden dark. The light moved away. Voices spoke, but they were farther off and he couldn't make out the words. Footsteps moved out of the room. He heard a tile skitter and fall. Nick had heard the sounds of more glass breaking. Now he understood. Someone had gone through the window and was on the roof. These men were following the false trail he had left.

He waited, then slipped forward on his elbows. The room was empty. He stood and stole toward the side door, and saw men walking down the back hall. One spoke quietly into a radio mic connected to an earpiece. They were headed for the stairs in the rear of the house, going toward the route he would have taken if he had escaped through that window. Nick went out the office's other door and took the hall to the house's main stairs. He stopped halfway down the last flight leading to the ground floor.

Boot soles creaked faintly on the marble below. Someone had new footwear tonight. A mistake. New rubber on smooth floors would often make a sound. Nick moved closer. The guard waited near the landing. Nick wanted stealth, wanted to get out of here without bringing hell down on himself, but he didn't have time to hold until that man moved on. He took the stairs one by one, weight on the balls of his feet, testing for noise before he committed to each step.

The blood pumping through his body made the growing bruise on his temple ache with every beat. How long had it been, before tonight, since he had last been in a real life-or-death fight? Not since the Service.

The figure was side-lit and looking toward the back of the house, where they were hunting Nick. Nick noticed a scar on the man's neck. Nick had his knife and could have taken him quietly, but he wasn't going to kill anyone if he didn't have to. Step by step. How close until the target heard the rustle of fabric? Heard him breathe?

Close enough. The man turned but Nick was already in motion. Sweeping his arm through the air, he caught the man in his windpipe as he pivoted, and brought him down hard on his back as if he had slipped on black ice. He was out.

Nick crouched by the wall, put the tip of his knife in an outlet, then kicked it in, breaking the plastic and shorting the circuit with a bolt of blue lightning. Another breaker tripped. Nick picked up the knife and moved through the blackness.

GRAY STOOD ON the back deck of the house and watched the lights sweeping the yard.

"We don't see him," said a voice on the radio.

He heard a crack from inside, then turned and stepped back into the house. He tried the lights. Nothing.

He raised his pistol, held his light beside the barrel, and advanced.

Kitchen: clear. Living room: clear.

He spoke into his radio. "Is he inside?"

"He must be. We have a man down by the front door."

"Dead?"

"No, jacked up proper, though."

"I'll come to you and we'll clear it room by room."

A sound like a right cross to a heavy bag, leather pounding leather. It was hard to place it with all the echoes in the hall.

"Copy?"

No answer.

"Copy?"

Another man down. Gray spun, his flashlight circling like a lighthouse beam.

Averose, where the fuck are you?

9

NICK CROUCHED OVER the man on the ground, the second he had taken down, just inside the front door. He patted his pockets, looking for a wallet or keys or an extra magazine for the gun.

They were empty except for a set of Chevy keys. Nick eased open the door and stepped outside. He could see people moving at the side of the yard and lights crossing the entry hall, coming after him.

He ran and ducked behind the hedges. A Chevy Suburban was parked on the street, but there was no way he could get to it without going through those men.

He took his own keys out of his pocket and pressed the small red button. After two seconds, the horn sounded and lights flashed behind the house, the alarm on his own truck. The flashlights broke away, fixed on the source of the noise.

"Out back!" someone yelled.

Nick sprinted to the fence along the front of the property, leaped high, and dragged himself over. He landed on the far side and came up half stumbling and half running. He went to the driver's door of the Suburban, put the key in the lock, and opened it, avoiding the fob so that no lights or horn would give him away.

He jumped in and started it. The engine roared to life, and he took off, flashlights arcing toward him. He rolled the window down, the night air cool against the sweat on his neck and the blood drying on his skin.

Two lefts on country lanes. A right. A highway. A two-lane road with no lights. A pitted street.

He tried to power on his phone, but it was dead, the screen smashed when he went over the fence.

He checked his mirror. He was clear, for a moment at least.

And now?

His knife was the murder weapon. His fingerprints were at the scene.

Nowhere was safe.

BREATHE. JUST BREATHE.

Nick loosened his grip on the wheel. The dread had worked into every muscle like rigor mortis, but he forced his shoulders back and filled his lungs.

There was sympathy for the dead man in the chair, rage for his killers, fear for the future. They competed in Nick's mind with a thousand possibilities of what had happened and *what next what next what next,* not thoughts anymore, just a maddening noise like a kennel full of barking dogs.

Breathe. One step at a time.

Finding calm in chaos. It wasn't bravery; it was a tool he had learned to use like a gun or a Kevlar vest, a skill he had come to depend on and had practiced so long he could call it up even in the middle of all this.

What now? he asked himself.

Go to the police. You have done nothing wrong. Tell the truth.

But those were desperate thoughts, naïve and hopeful. His mind flashed back to the blood painting the dead man's skin, streaked with Nick's hand- and fingerprints.

He couldn't go to the police until he had the contract, the whole paper trail showing that he had been authorized to be in that house.

He shouldn't have touched the body or the knife. But even as the blood flaked from his hands, he didn't regret trying to save that man.

The former CIA director. God, what was Nick into?

He forced his breath to come slow and even, ordered his thoughts, and took a careful route on winding roads until he was sure that there was no one tailing him. He was in McLean, Virginia, a wooded enclave of wealth and power across the Potomac River from DC.

At least he had stolen that man's keys. The SUV Nick was now driving might tell him who was behind all this. He flipped open the glove box. It was empty except for the registration and proof of insurance. He pulled them out and glanced down. They were both in the name of a limited liability company: ARC Leasing.

This was a well-orchestrated execution. The theft of his knife, the team at the house, the kind of people with the wherewithal to frame someone and the need to kill a CIA director. Thinking of it made the hair on his arms and neck bristle.

They wouldn't want him running loose. He was a capable man. They had meant to kill him then and there. That would have been the cleanest way to set him up.

That would explain whatever drug was on that surgical glove: it was a way to take Nick down with no sign of a struggle so that they could stage the scene. They could have made it look as though he and the guard had killed each other as he tried to escape.

He couldn't see anyone following, but that didn't mean they didn't know where he was. The Suburban might have some kind of GPS beacon; fleet vehicles often did. He didn't want to be stuck on foot, but he needed to get rid of it.

But first the blood, dry now, stiff on his clothes. He turned the wheel to the right and saw a simple wooden sign he knew well: "Lewinsville Park."

He used to coach soccer here, pacing up and down the sidelines, shouting and cheering with the moms and dads.

The bathrooms were locked, but the water fountain outside ran. He took off his jacket and shirt, both stained with blood. His undershirt was clean. He rinsed the soles of his shoes, then leaned down and splashed water on his face and his neck and his arm, washing the last of Malcolm Widener's life onto the sidewalk.

Tires hummed along the road. He lifted his head, wiped the water from his eyes, and saw headlights slashing through the trees.

He walked back to the SUV, climbed in, and sat low, his eyes fixed forward as the lights swept toward him, that brightness all he could see. He waited, chest still, as the lights passed. A patrol car. It moved on, toward the baseball fields.

He looked at the soccer nets, swaying in the wind, and savored a long breath.

11

NICK PULLED THE Suburban into the parking lot of a Metro station on the Orange Line, with trains running along Interstate 66. The roar of traffic washed through the night as he went past the sign for "Kiss and Ride" and parked in a short-term spot. He took the registration and insurance papers and left the vehicle behind.

Taxis were hard to come by in the suburbs, but there would be some here. There was a good chance that his office was being watched, but Nick knew how to watch, how to spot a sentry.

He flipped the bloodstained jacket inside out and carried it in a bundle with the guns and his knife and his button-down inside as he approached the line of taxis.

He knew he looked off, walking around in his T-shirt despite the chill. He came at the cab from the passenger side, its blind spot. It's harder to say no to someone who's already inside.

He opened the door and landed on the vinyl seat. It wheezed from its seams as he put the jacket on the floor.

The driver didn't say a word. Nick glanced at his ID badge; a Serbian name. He regarded Nick suspiciously.

"Going into the city," Nick said. "Just head for Logan Circle."

The man's eyes drifted toward the Metro entrance. No one took a cab back into the city from a Metro stop in the suburbs. From here they took a cab to their warm little houses on cul-de-sacs, to their families.

He should have been at home now, lying in bed with a history book propped on his chest while his wife, Karen, turned over, furling the covers around her shoulder.

"That's a long way," the driver said, perhaps trying to buy time to take Nick's measure.

"I know." Nick lifted his wallet, held out three twenties.

The man locked eyes with him in the rearview, body still, hands resting on the wheel. "Cold, isn't it?" His gaze moved down slightly, and Nick followed it. A mottled pink spot stood at the end of his sleeve. He had missed it at the park, but it was easy to catch here under the lights of the parking lot.

"Yeah," Nick said. "Can't wait for spring." He sat back and looked out the window—indifferent, untroubled.

The man put the car in drive. The engine groaned to life, and Nick gripped the door handle as the taxi pulled out and headed for the city.

12

GRAY STOOD ALONE in the office with Malcolm Widener's body. He turned, eyes skimming over the blood, poring over every detail. This man was a Washington titan. Now he was two hundred pounds of dead weight.

The room had been arranged as carefully as a Renaissance painting. Any trace of Gray or his men was gone. Nick's fingerprints were everywhere, and his vehicle was still parked down the street. He would be the only suspect.

Nick Averose. Malcolm Widener. Two men. One secret. They had both gotten too close to the truth, even if they didn't fully understand the game they'd been drawn into. They both needed to go away. The past needed to go away.

"Dust to dust," Gray whispered.

He raised his cell phone and tapped out a message in code.

13

DAVID BLAKELY'S PHONE vibrated twice in his pocket. He ignored it as he put his hand on the senator's arm and whispered in his ear.

"It's time."

Senator Sam MacDonough smiled at him and squeezed his shoulder as he rose from the table and strode across the marble floor toward the front of the room. Outside the windows, the moon hung low, a white sickle over the Washington Monument.

David slipped along the side of the room, around the assembled dinner guests, then stood with his back to the wall. He wore a bespoke navy suit by Gieves & Hawkes, outrageously and invisibly expensive with its Milanese stitches and a silk latch hidden behind the lapel.

His eyes were narrowed slightly, as if scanning the horizon on a sun-bright day. He pulled his shoulder blades back and down. His bearing gave David, at five foot eleven, the impression of being taller.

That was practiced. Everything was practiced even now, thirty-five years after he had arrived as an outsider in this world. David was an investor. Once he had financed real estate development, then whole industries through private equity, but all of his successes, all of his wealth—numbered in the billions and held mostly offshore—ultimately came from staying close to power. In the end he invested in men, men like Senator Sam MacDonough.

The servers walked out of the room. The doors closed. The senator arrived at the front of the salon with his dog, a Rhodesian ridgeback named Theo, padding along beside him.

MacDonough didn't wait for quiet. He simply began to speak, and the room hushed in an instant. He moved loosely over the tiles, his blue eyes flashing from one listener to the next. This room—the former officials, the top donors, the party elite—felt as natural to him as a gathering of lifelong friends. This air of great and responsible men at the helm of the nation was the air he had been breathing his whole life. Sam was a senator's son.

David didn't need to listen. He already knew every word Sam would say. It was more important that David watch the faces of the guests at the tables, reading them one after another. Because these thirty people had a rare power.

Who picked the president in this country? Forget what they taught in high school civics. It wasn't the voters. It was this room.

Welcome to the money primary, the invisible primary. The real election wouldn't take place until next year, but before a single citizen cast his or her ballot for the leader of the free world, the candidates had to win the only contest that mattered—the contest for the favor of the party machine. The people gathered here would anoint a front-runner after a series of one-on-one talks and dinners in homes and clubs around Washington and on jets streaking in and out of the private terminal at Dulles. Money and endorsements would herd around their favorite, giving him an advantage that in most years would be impossible to overcome.

These insiders controlled the primary rules and the convention. They were retaking control of the party, prepared to shut out any outsider candidates, insurgents, and wild cards who could steal power away from them. Sam was one of three serious competitors for the nomination, an early favorite, though some thought the fifty-year-old senator needed to bide his time, wait his turn. Sam had to move quickly, to lock the key players down before the other candidates could strike their own deals.

This was the back room full of smoke, the oldest American tradition. The founders had nailed the windows shut in Independence Hall one sweltering Philadelphia summer so that no one would hear the deals they struck as they laid out the Constitution in absolute secrecy. Now those kinds of talks took place here in the salon of an eight-bedroom Queen Anne, once an embassy, now a private home.

This was American democracy at its finest, no real democracy at all. Whichever candidate the VIPs in this room chose would have a wide-open lane. Their party was the opposition. The incumbent president was polling in the low forties and the stock market was down 18 percent this year. The Oval would belong to whichever man they nominated.

The chair of the national finance committee finished his glass of Dujac premier cru and sat back. A swing-state governor whom David had never once seen put down his phone now rested it on the table.

Their eyes all went to Sam MacDonough as he spoke with that easy smile and the skeptical, slightly amused tone he so often used, like he and his audience were all in on the same joke. A golden boy. Trite, but politics was a trite business and it really was that simple. You could spend half a million on pollsters and image consultants, but in the end it came down to the schoolyard, to the hardwired logic of the tribe.

When five people tried to talk at once, everyone would turn to Sam. David had first seen it when they were in prep school at St. Albans, on the sports fields and at the keg parties behind McLean mansions when he and Sam were kids. Lacrosse captain then, president-in-waiting now. It was the same shit. Built as solid as a column, Sam had his own gravity, drew people in, engulfed them with charm.

It made you want to hate him at first, give in to the jealousy, look for the smugness, the prick vibes, and that was the worst part. There were none. Sam MacDonough wanted to know how you were doing. He would invite you along, even if you were David Blakely, a St. Albans boarder from New Jersey with no class whose father was in the construction business. Sam was really fucking nice. He didn't work at any of it. Too nice, perhaps.

He was second-generation-Washington soft while David Blakely was first-generation hungry. That was why they needed each other.

The room was small enough that Sam required no microphone or podium, and Blakely had had the property swept for any other kinds of mics. For tonight, he wanted a private residence—so hard to wire up, so few staff who could be compromised, not like a hotel or club.

A leak from inside this room could be fatal. This was no ballroom or banquet hall or prime-time debate. That would all come later, during the public campaign. Tonight was thirty people in someone's home, a real dinner. No stump speeches or poll-tested messages. These were friends, old friends. This was real talk, the one time in MacDonough's campaign when he wouldn't be delivering overworked bullshit.

Tonight the donors' money was on the table. They could speak frankly about what they would give and what they expected from him, always dancing at the edge of an explicit quid pro quo. The promises now would be policy later, and everything in between—the campaign that the rest of the world would see—would just be tactics, a performance to get from one to the other.

Sam's dog wandered toward David, nuzzled its head against his leg, and David gave it a rub behind the ears as he scanned the room. These people all had their needs: a ban on online gambling, a cabinet post, a little break on the media monopoly rules for the big merger. The host was in it for an ambassadorship, a good one: western Europe or the Caribbean.

David knew each of these players, what they wanted,

what they feared. He knew how to prod them, how to build heat around a moment like this: get the money thinking that the party folks are already going for Sam, get the party thinking the money's already in motion. David whispered in their ears, stoking this fire, playing on everyone's fear of missing a moment they'd write histories about, like Franklin Roosevelt in '32, Nixon in '68, Reagan in '80.

This wasn't about a president. It was a realignment. It was the work of David's life. He had poured tens of millions of dollars into MacDonough's campaigns, starting with his first House race, had blocked and tackled for him since they were in high school. After each day at St. Albans, Sam would go back to his family town house on Capitol Hill, and David would return to his bunk bed in the dorm rooms with the international kids and the other boarders. Now he was Sam's chief financier and ran a network of political action committees. His little empire had paved the way for Sam's rise from congressman to Senate cardinal to presidential front-runner.

David turned to the front of the room and listened as Sam MacDonough's voice grew grave.

"I know what every one of you has at stake in this election," Sam said. "And I don't need to convince you that I will take care of you and your issues, because you know me. Most of you have known me for decades. But this is about more than any one cause.

"That's thinking too small. This isn't about me. That's too small. This isn't about the presidency. That is too small. Locking down the White House"—he raised one finger—"is step one, our beachhead, our D-Day, the crucial battle in a larger war. We're not stopping until we have everything. You've seen the money

I give to vulnerable candidates. You know I can win unwinnable races. If you give me your support, we can take that wide. I'm talking about the Senate, the House, the statehouses, the governors' mansions. I'm talking about building a wave from the bottom up."

Sam's eyes met David's as he glanced around the room.

"Elections like these only come every ten years. A census year. Which means we redraw the districts after we win. I will lead the charge. I'm talking about permanent control, a permanent majority, and now is your chance to get on board."

Sam stopped. No blandishments, no needy applause lines, no thank-yous. David crossed his arms, concerned for an instant that this kind of naked confidence wouldn't play.

The crowd didn't clap. They stood and moved toward Sam, surrounded him, a polite little mob. They could've been back on Steuart Field at St. Albans after a win, except now they were playing for the highest stakes. Sam had the shine of the inevitable, of a man on the cusp. Everyone wanted a piece.

Sam looked his way, and David gave him a nod. He'd been building up to this moment for twenty-five years. He could win this election before it even began.

David had sold his soul so long ago for a night like tonight. He needed Sam MacDonough to win. He loved that man. He would do anything to protect him. It was about politics and power and money, sure, but there was something deeper, hungrier, in David. It was about his own survival.

He stepped out, crossed the hall to the library, and shut the door. He took out his second cell phone, unlocked it with his fingerprint, then opened an encrypted-messaging app.

"319," it read. It was a message from Gray. A code. It referred to Genesis, chapter three, verse nineteen. "For dust thou art, and unto dust shalt thou return."

Ashes to ashes, dust to dust. It was done. Malcolm Widener was gone. The secret was safe.

14

NICK STALKED DOWN the alley toward his office. He'd had the cabdriver drop him four blocks away, and then he'd spiraled in closer to the carriage house, sticking to the shadows, searching out every hidden place where someone might be waiting, watching.

He saw no one. That didn't mean they weren't there. It was a risk he had to take. He needed to prove he was allowed to be in that home tonight, that it was all an exercise.

He took out the loaded pistol he'd pulled from the man who attacked him at Widener's house and held it low in his right hand. He carried his bundled jacket in the left.

With a last look down the alley, he closed toward the entrance to his office. He put the jacket down, unlocked the door, then sprang inside, cutting sideways. He reached the corner and looked into the shadows, sliding around furniture by memory.

All he heard was the clink and sigh of the heating system over his own rapid breathing.

His office was empty, and he opened the desk drawer where he had left his knife. Gone, of course. But he needed to see it.

He quickly cleared the rest of the shop, working his way toward the back room with its bins of gear and finally the bathroom. No one.

He walked back and brought his jacket inside, then went to the cabinet safe and dialed in the combination. The door slid back, silent and slow. The steel shelf was bare where he had left the signed letter of authorization.

His shoulders drew back, and he let out a long breath. He shoved the panic away.

In his office, he checked his desk for the files on Widener. The plans were there for the attack he had so carefully rehearsed, but the copy of the contract was gone, along with anything that would prove he was working for a client.

He opened his laptop, logged in with his fingerprint, and pulled up his email. He searched for Alexandra Hart's name. How many times had they met? Twice. Had they written? Maybe six. That was enough. That would tell the true story.

They were gone. He checked again, and then looked through his sent emails. Nothing. Alexandra Hart had stood in this room earlier today, but now any trace of her had been erased.

A bead of sweat ran down his ribs. What was happening? It was like he was diving down, the water pressing on his chest, his lungs, his eardrums, a killing pressure.

How much else pointed to him as the murderer? He

couldn't go to the police now, not until he understood just how deep he had been buried.

He went back to the safe and pulled out two boxes of Winchester rounds along with two extra magazines in a belt holster, then walked into his office. He pulled down the backpack he used for work trips, which already held his entry kit and the basic tools of his trade, and put his jacket with his knife and gun inside.

In the back room, he picked up a work shirt, a cheap smartphone, and a few prepaid SIM cards still wrapped and fixed to plastic cards.

He took a half step away, then went back and grabbed the medical kit.

He marched out and stopped in front of the open door to the bathroom. In the mirror, a smear of blood showed behind his earlobe.

Nick stepped inside and looked at his face, which was spectral, with a growing bruise staining his temple. He lifted his hand. Dried blood circled the nails.

The hot-water spigot on the sink turned with a creak. He needed a shower, needed to get clean, to wash away any trace of this blood and its old-penny smell, but not here. They might be back.

He scoured what he could from under his nails and washed his face and neck, then headed to the front room.

A shadow moved across the window. He waited for it to keep going, to see it pass the window on the other side of the front door. It didn't.

Someone was here.

He had needed to come here. He'd needed those papers, this gear. But there was another reason. Part of him was straining toward the threat like a dog at the end of its leash. He wanted them to come, wanted to close in on whoever was behind all this and tear the truth out of them: *Who are you and why are you fucking with me?*

He stole toward the front door, staying close by the wall, moving silently. He didn't stand in front of it. He knew a mining executive who had gone to answer a door in Medellín and was shot twice in the head by a cheap *sicario* before he even had a chance to open it up.

The knob rustled, then turned. The door opened. Nick aimed the pistol, looking through its sights, eye to eye with a woman, young, as she gasped in fear.

It was Delia Tayran.

FOUR OF THE ASSASSIN

DELIA STEPPED BACK, hands rising, as he lowered the gun.

"Are you all right?" he asked.

Wide eyes and a silent nod.

"Here," he said. "Come inside."

She entered without a word, and Nick shut the door.

"Jesus, Delia. I'm sorry."

"Who were you waiting for, Nick?"

He stared at the window.

"What the hell is happening?"

"I'm handling it, Delia. You should go."

"I didn't hear from you after the job, Nick. You didn't answer your phone."

"The job got complicated."

"I drove to Widener's street. I've never seen so many cop cars in my life. The FBI was there, and a bunch of other feds I couldn't even identify. What happened?"

Nick ran his hand along his jawline, felt the stubble

scratch. "It was a setup, Delia. An ambush. Malcolm Widener was hurt very badly while I was there. Whoever did it is trying to make it seem like I'm responsible. I know that sounds crazy but it's the truth."

Delia brought her hand to her chest and said nothing for a moment, just looked at him. "We need to go to the police. We have the letter."

"The letter is gone. Someone broke in here. They took every copy. They took anything that made it look like I had a legit reason to be there. Even the emails are gone. This is deliberate. Everything from that house points to me."

"What?"

He didn't answer.

"You said they tried to make it look like you're responsible. How?"

"By planting my knife there."

Delia braced herself against the desk. That made the violence real.

Her eyebrows drew together, and he tried to read her face: concern, sure, maybe disappointment. She looked like a kid who had just found out her parents were human beings after all. And there was something else. Was it fear?

"There has to be some kind of trace. Some proof. That woman. Alexandra Hart. She can vouch for you," Delia said, and went toward the computer.

He heard sirens in the distance and looked to the windows. Light moved across them.

"Delia," Nick said. "We need to go. It's not safe here."

A car door closed outside.

"It can't all just disappear."

"Now," he said. "Out the back."

Her eyes met his, and she nodded. She grabbed two laptops and a bag from her desk, and he led her out the rear door.

Nick covered her with the pistol as headlights approached and they circled to her car.

Nick drove, speeding out of the alley. He took a winding route, eyes on his mirrors, looking for anyone following.

"Why don't we call Alexandra Hart?" Delia asked.

"Give it a try." She was the only real connection he had to whoever had set him up.

Delia looked up her number and dialed. He could hear it ringing. A soft prerecorded voice came on the line. "We're sorry, you have reached a number that has been disconnected or is no longer in service."

She ended the call. Delia flicked through her phone. "I'll get her other number. She was on the Aegis directory." She pressed her lips together. "Her page is gone. I was looking at it yesterday."

Delia tapped her screen. "The LinkedIn is gone, too." She turned to him. "What the fuck, Nick? How does someone just disappear?"

"I don't think Alexandra Hart ever existed."

16

NICK DROVE EAST as Delia kept searching for other traces of the woman who had come to their office.

He needed to find someplace safe where they could start tracking down the real Alexandra Hart, where he could get cleaned up and breathe easy long enough to figure out what to do next.

He passed over the railroad tracks north of Union Station. Every year the line between rich and poor pushed farther out in this direction as new development turned over more of the city: the old warehouses near the train yards, the vacant buildings along New York Avenue. Cranes towered over them as Nick drove on through the night.

Delia saw it ten minutes later: a sign for a hotel that said it had HBO and color TV. "Just pull in there," she said.

It was exactly what Nick wanted, an uncared-for and uncaring place. He could have gone to his house, but they would be looking for him there. Karen was on a business trip in Chicago. The only grace in all this was that he didn't have to worry about her at home.

They checked in. The night clerk barely looked away from the TV that sat on his desk blaring out canned laughter. He didn't seem to notice that their only luggage was two backpacks.

The hallway was painted in strange orange and brown tones. Through thin walls, Nick picked up the nighttime chorus of car subwoofers and raised voices.

They put their gear on the bed, and Nick bolted and chained the door.

He sat at a small table, logged into his laptop, and began to type, his eyes on the keyboard as he picked out the letters. He looked up to see Delia staring at him, pained.

He slid the computer toward her and gave her the chair. Her fingers danced over the keys. He watched her do something to the location settings on the laptop and then connect to the web using a VPN, an encrypted tunnel through the Internet.

"So what *do* we have?" Delia asked.

"There are the security cameras at our office. That's all in the cloud, right? There might be backups of her emails. Any info from the headers. Can you get—"

"IP addresses. Maybe."

Nick stepped to the side of the blinds and peered out. A gray Dodge Charger idled at the far end of the lot, smoke rising from its tailpipe.

Delia took in a sharp breath. He turned and walked toward the computer. A folder was open on the screen, full of images of Malcolm Widener. There were telephoto shots of Widener at breakfast with his wife, of him beside his bed, and a slightly out-of-focus picture taken through a bathroom window of him swallowing pills.

Nick had cased Widener's house, but he hadn't taken any of these. They went beyond anything he would need for a security audit. These were a stalker's gaze.

Delia had a web browser up on the other side of the screen. She had typed in one word, "how," and Google had filled in the rest as a suggestion, the text blue, indicating that it was one of his previous searches: *How to clean DNA from a knife.*

"What is that?" Nick asked.

"Your search history."

"But . . . I never wrote that."

She stood aside as Nick came to the table and pulled the computer toward him. He cycled through the images in the folder, then the searches in his history: killing and extradition and covering tracks.

Nick noticed a bookmark at the top of his browser. He had never seen it before. "Mail 2." He clicked it, and it went to a web email provider. Nick had never heard of it, but the menu bar read: *Free, anonymous email.* He was somehow already logged into an account. He looked at the messages.

Each of them was addressed to Widener's work email, and they carried no subject lines. He selected one.

Leave her alone, it read. He opened another message: *I can get to you. I can get to anyone.* A third email read simply, *No one is safe.* It appeared as though Nick had sent them all to Widener.

Nick had seen thousands of messages like that, from the stalkers and psychopaths who swarmed the famous and the powerful. That last email used a phrase that

Nick said often. Whoever had set this up even knew how to sound like him.

The laptop was an assassin's bible. Anyone who got their hands on the computer or subpoenaed his online history would have to conclude that he was guilty.

It was like he had blacked out, actually done the killing himself, and only now saw the traces. The walls began to waver and pulse, and pressure built in his temples.

He put his hand on the table, took a deep breath, and looked to the side. Delia stood halfway between him and the door, all the blood drained from her face. Her eyes moved back and forth between Nick and the evidence staring back at them from the screen.

The photos. The searches. He had known her for most of her life, had looked out for her like a father after her parents passed, but that didn't mean she should ignore what was right in front of her eyes. She had to believe she was in this room with a killer, and he couldn't blame her.

He raised his hands. "I know how this looks, Delia. I don't know what's happening, but none of this is mine."

It sounded so false coming out of his mouth, like the words of a con in the back of a police car.

"What happened at that house, Nick? You can tell me anything, you know that. I need the truth."

"Someone killed Malcolm Widener. It wasn't me."

She took a step back, and her eyes went to his gun.

"I understand if you don't believe me," Nick said. "I wouldn't."

17

DELIA LOWERED HER head. Her hand covered her mouth. "No no no," she said, and took a few paces away from the door.

She looked up at him. "God, Nick. This is so bad. This"—she pointed to the computer—"is next-level, like NSA or foreign intel. I believe you. Of course. I saw her. I saw those papers. But no one else in the world will. Why didn't you tell me he was dead?"

"I didn't want to drop too much on you at once. You should go. I don't want this coming back on you."

"Tough. After everything you did for me, for my family, I'm not going to bail on you in the middle of all this." She tried for a smile. "And I've seen you type."

She tossed her phone on the bed and sat at the laptop. "There might be a way to turn this around on them."

She opened a command terminal on the screen and began typing. A moment later she glanced at the clock, and then to Nick, studying his face.

"You know what we need?" she said.

"Shoot." He moved toward her bag.

"Food and caffeine."

An hour later Delia was hunched over the computer, finishing her second waffle. Nick's burger was already gone. Most tech people he knew ran on energy drinks or Mountain Dew, but Delia's preferred brew was insanely strong green tea.

They had ordered delivery on her phone from the chain diner across the highway. Delia was her mother's daughter in that way; she thought all problems could be solved by an enormous meal. The coffee and the hot food and Delia's presence offered the first respite he'd had since he had heard the gunshots at Widener's house.

He used the second laptop to check the security camera at his office. The footage of Alexandra Hart had been deleted.

Nick still had the registration from the Chevy Suburban he had taken at the house. That was his most solid link to the killers. He searched for any public information related to the leasing company, but that only led to a registered agent, a limited liability company out of Delaware. Its owner was another LLC, out of Nevada.

Shells within shells. It was effectively anonymous. That LLC could be held by another one in the Caymans or Luxembourg. There were ways to pierce the veil, but it meant days if not weeks of work. Everyone makes mistakes, uses the same address twice, leaves a real name on a registration.

He showed Delia what he had found.

"We can pattern match," she said, peering at the screen. That meant looking for shared addresses, other shells linked to this one, finding any lawyers or banks they held in common.

"I've done it manually," he said. "But it takes days, at least."

"I don't do anything manually," Delia said, and he handed her the computer.

Nick stood up and went to the window, searching for a hint of dawn.

He shut his eyes. That woman was real, even if everything about her was a lie. She was out there in the world, and she must have left a trace. He put himself back in that moment: Alexandra Hart signing the papers, tucking them in her attaché, and walking out, Delia rolling her eyes at him.

He listened to his breath coming and going, and replayed the scene in his head, looking for any detail he could exploit. He remembered a few stray white hairs he'd noticed near the hem of her dress: a dog owner, maybe.

He came back to one instant. The carriage house had a good view of the street across a church parking lot. He'd seen Hart once more, or thought he had, driving by after she left, just a flash. He didn't know how useful that would be. He wasn't even certain of the make of her car. But as he thought about it more, he realized that it might give him what he needed.

"She drove a silver car," he said. "Alexandra Hart."

"Did you get the tag?"

"No. But she went by right after she left. Unless she ran, she was parked on our block, to the west."

Delia nodded. "If we had the security camera footage, maybe we could get a shot of her license plate, but the footage is gone, right?"

"Ours is, but the other stores have cameras." There were two or three businesses between them and the corner that would have eyes out.

"Right. We can get a shot of her coming and going, maybe the tag on her car. It would be proof at least that she existed. You can ID people from an image, too."

She came toward the window and stood beside him. "We're going to find whoever did this, Nick." She looked up. "Nothing is perfect."

18

DAVID BLAKELY PULLED his Audi over on C Street Southeast, a block up from Sam MacDonough's town house. He killed the engine, a five-hundred-horsepower twin turbo hidden under the sedan's unassuming black exterior.

Sam MacDonough sat on the passenger side, and his dog brought its head out from the back seat as if it wanted in on the conversation. David rubbed the sleek fur of the ridgeback's neck. It twisted against him and then lay down in the rear.

"Sam," David said. "I want you to be prepared. You're going to hear about it soon, and you should hear it from me."

Sam shifted in his seat.

"Everything is taken care of," David said.

"With . . ."

David raised his hand. He didn't want Malcolm Widener's name spoken out loud.

Sam put the back of his hand to his mouth. He looked away, out the window at the cranes towering near the old Union Station railyards.

"So he's . . ."

David nodded.

"Christ," Sam said. He shut his eyes and pinched the bridge of his nose. *Killing.* He mouthed the word, his lips barely moving as he shook his head.

After a moment, he brought his hand down and turned back. "That isn't me, David."

David looked at him squarely. "Isn't it?"

Sam leaned closer, his face hard with anger. *Was that a threat?* he seemed to be asking. But it wasn't. It was just a stark reminder of the stakes they were playing for, the facts they needed to deal with.

"When we talked about this," Sam said, "this isn't what I wanted."

"Come on, Sam. You wanted me to handle it. It's handled. There was no other choice. You don't have to pretend with me. You knew what you were asking for. That's why you're only having a ministroke right now."

MacDonough let out a long breath.

"I know you, Sam. I'm the one person who really knows you. I can protect you from all this. I have for twenty-five years, and we only need a few more days."

Sam ran his hands along his thighs, saying nothing. David wondered if he might break. It would be understandable.

But when Sam turned back, he just nodded his head twice and looked as if the conversation had never happened. He was a politician. The mask was back on.

"The only way out of this is through, all right?"

David said. The safest place for Sam MacDonough was in the Oval Office.

David had left behind almost every mark of where he came from as he assumed the ways of Washington. Within a few weeks of arriving at St. Albans as a teen, he had dropped the faint North Jersey accent he didn't know he had and started saying "water" instead of "wood-ur." But one trait never left him: he looked out for his friends, no matter what. It was a rare thing here, and it had served him well.

Sam reached for the door handle.

"Are we all right, Sam?" David asked.

Sam's eyes opened a little wider as he thought about it.

"Of course." He patted David twice on the leg. "Thank you. For everything."

19

NICK AND DELIA worked through most of the night. She caught a couple hours of rest, but there was no chance of Nick sleeping in the middle of all this. A little after five A.M., they drove back to her apartment. She was going to start tracking down anything she could find on those shell companies and the other leads.

Delia had set up the smartphone for Nick so that he could call and message her securely. Calls to his regular number would forward to the smartphone as well.

He told her to keep her head down. She would work this from behind the computer, and he would handle anything on the street.

"What if the police call or come by?" she asked.

"Don't lie to them," he said. He didn't want this coming down on her. "But you don't have to talk to them either."

"So don't answer the door?"

"For anyone," he said.

He put his hand on the doorknob, preparing to go, but he noticed Delia looking down. Something was sitting wrong with her.

"Why did they choose you to set up, Nick?"

"Because I could get to him."

"I don't know. All this work. The way they targeted you. Those messages. It all seems so personal."

He nodded. He'd been thinking the same thing all night. Nick couldn't shake that question—*Why did they choose you?*—as he left her apartment and walked through the predawn gray toward Shaw.

Their work truck was parked in an alley, a rented space a block down from the carriage house. They used it on bigger jobs when they had to carry a lot of gear. He made sure no one was watching it, then got in and headed for home.

The sky was turning red as he wound down a tree-lined street and parked in front of his house. A few lights flicked on in his neighbors' homes. A minivan cruised by. The *Post* lay in its plastic wrapper on the driveway.

For an instant, Nick could pretend everything was normal. He could imagine himself inside, a cup of coffee warm in his hand as he split the paper with Karen.

The night had been hunting and being hunted, a thousand questions, the desperation of escape. But now he stepped back.

They had planned to kill him at Widener's house. He was certain. What could be worth that risk? Worth murdering the former director of Central Intelligence?

He thought of those messages they had planted to make it look like he was threatening Widener. They were dated from a month ago, and he had no idea if they had really been sent then or had just been somehow placed in that account and backdated.

Leave her alone, the message had said.

They made it seem like Nick was a stalker, that he had some grudge against Widener because of a woman. Why would they choose that motive to connect him to Widener? Nick was crazy about his wife. He never strayed.

He looked at his home, perfect as a photo on a real estate agent's flyer, and Karen's garden. His eyes lingered on the driveway, the front door, the picture window with a clear view into his living room.

There was only one reason that he could think of. It had happened a month ago, here at this house. A woman he had once known well had come to him with a secret and then disappeared.

Her name was Emma Blair.

20

EMMA SHOWED UP at Nick's home unannounced on a cold and cloudless Saturday.

He had just parked his truck in the driveway and was walking to the front door. Karen was out with a friend. He heard footsteps behind him and turned to see Emma Blair coming toward him on his front walk.

She was Nick's ex and, like Malcolm Widener, a child of the Washington establishment. She and Nick had dated for a year, had been practically living together for part of it, but that had been a decade ago.

He was surprised to see her. They didn't talk anymore, though he had run into her once or twice in Georgetown. Those encounters had been cordial enough, not much more than a few pleasantries and a goodbye. Everything between them had ended well. It was all in the past.

As she came closer to him on the path, he noticed her tentative steps and the way her eyes never stopped moving, scanning. She was afraid of something.

It wasn't unusual for people to seek out Nick when they thought they might be in danger. His friends knew the kind of work he did.

Emma started out talking too fast, apologizing for just showing up, saying something about not trusting the phones or email.

"It's all right, Emma," he said, speaking calmly, holding his hands out. "Just tell me what's going on."

She looked up and down the quiet street, and then at him.

"I need you to protect me," she said.

"Come inside."

Nick led her to the living room and Emma sat on the couch, perched on the edge, all restless energy.

"Is someone threatening you?" he asked, standing by the coffee table.

"Yes. I mean, no one has said anything to me, but I've seen them at night outside my house, and black trucks behind me on the road, following me."

"Do you have any idea why anyone might be after you?"

"It's something that happened a long time ago. It was really bad, Nick. I never talked about it, did anything about it until now. I started trying to make it right, and it got all fucked up." Panic edged into her voice. "And now the people who did it—"

She took a deep breath in and ran her fingers under her eyes, then went on, calmer now.

"Please, Nick. I'm scared. I just need you to look out for me for a little while."

It hurt him to see her, or anyone, this upset. He wanted to sit, to comfort her, but that didn't feel right with just the two of them in the house.

"Everything's going to be okay, Emma," he said, his voice soft. "Don't worry. Who are we talking about?"

"It's serious, Nick. It's DC, it's this whole town, the people I grew up with. I should have left years ago."

"Can you give me a little more than that? Anything you tell me stays in this room. Did someone hurt you back then?"

"I don't want to get into the specifics. I don't want you to feel like you have to do something, to take it all on. I know how you are, how you don't let things go. I just need you to watch out for me while I figure out what to do next. It won't be long."

Nick checked her eyes. They were clear. Emma had her issues. She drank. When they were together, she had tried to play it off like some high-class bohemian jazz-age charm, all classic cocktails, but he saw it for what it was. That was a big part of why he'd left her. She wasn't ready to stop, or accept help, though he'd heard that in the years since she'd been in and out of recovery places in New England and out west.

"I can find someone to look out for you, Emma." He couldn't guard her himself. He didn't do that work any-more and it was too intimate a job to do for someone he'd been involved with.

"No. People said you were the best, and I need some-one I trust. You were always so good to me, Nick. You're not part of the world I came from. That's what I need."

Her father had been a cabinet secretary, and she'd grown up with too much money and too little attention, attended private school with the sons and daughters of the big names. Those kids ran the town now. They'd inherited it from their parents.

Emma looked up. Her attention fixed on a photo on

the wall, a portrait of Karen with her mother and father. She stood and walked toward it.

Karen had also been raised among the elect and had gone to National Cathedral School with Emma. It was the sister school to St. Albans, their campuses side by side surrounding the cathedral and gardens on one of the highest points in the city, Mount Saint Alban.

Emma took a step and peered into the den. A few photos there showed Karen with clients of her PR firm—a governor, the CEO of a tech giant.

She turned back and examined one of the framed shots in the living room. It showed Nick and Karen on their wedding day, walking down the aisle in a field surrounded by friends and family. They had just beaten the rain.

"She's still close with everyone from school?" Emma asked, her hand inching toward her collar.

"Karen?" Nick said. "A lot of them, sure."

"Are you?"

A car pulled into the driveway. Nick looked up to see Karen stepping out of the passenger side of her friend's Mercedes SUV. Karen looked through the window, a smile dawning on her face as she saw Nick, and disappearing just as quickly as Emma came into view.

"Did you ever think you had it backward when you were in the Service, Nick?" Emma asked, watching him carefully. "Guarding all those politicians? Did you ever think you should be protecting us from them?" She took in this perfect Craftsman house and the furniture Karen had inherited from her family. "Or are you part of it now, too?" Emma looked down. "I'm sorry," she said, her face reddening. "This . . . I should go."

"We'll get you some help, Emma. I know a lot of good people. You don't have to be afraid."

She broke away, shaking her head. Nick followed her as she marched toward the door and passed Karen without a word. He stopped beside his wife, her face full of puzzlement and hurt. She didn't need to say anything. Her look said it all. *What the hell is this, Nick?*

Emma got in her car and drove off.

He should have followed her. He should have found a way to protect her. Now he knew that.

Because he had never seen Emma again. As far as he could tell, no one had ever seen her again. Nick had called to check on her that night, and a few days later. He knew what real fear looked like. He'd seen it in her face.

She didn't answer the phone. He found out later she didn't show up to work that Monday. One of her coworkers eventually called the police to report her missing, and they went into her house. She was gone, with no sign of foul play. By the night of Widener's death, Emma had been missing for a month.

It wasn't totally out of character for Emma to drop off the map. She would go off on retreats—Costa Rica, Peru—always looking for answers, for an escape. But she had left no trace of any plans for a trip.

After the way she came to him, Nick couldn't let it go. He felt an obligation, a duty, guilt. She had asked for his protection.

He went looking for her, trying to find anyone who might know who was after her or why she was so afraid. He talked to her friends and coworkers, and some people from her AA meetings. Emma had always been troubled, but she had seemed so clear that day she came to him. She was eight months sober, starting step nine. She was making amends.

As he had searched for her, he'd noticed them every so often in his rearview mirror: black SUVs keeping their distance. He would ask himself if they were following him, if they were pros. Or if maybe Emma was just paranoid and had run off somewhere, and the paranoia was starting to infect him, too.

Nick didn't find her. He didn't find the answers. But now he feared the worst: Emma carried a secret worth killing for.

He'd been targeted. Maybe someone thought Emma had shared what she knew with Nick, or thought he was getting too close to the truth. Someone powerful. The kind of person who would have the resources to pull this off and would need to take out a CIA director.

21

NICK STEPPED THROUGH the front door to his house, drew his pistol, and started going through one room after another, clearing them. He'd learned it at Camp Pendleton and mastered it at war. He'd never thought he'd be doing it in his own home.

Karen was due back sometime today. They both traveled constantly. She was a communications consultant and had her own firm. There had been times recently when it felt like they were just regulars at the same hotel.

Part of him hoped that the people hunting him would come here, that they would be waiting. The simplest way out of this would be to haul whoever had really killed Malcolm Widener in to the police.

But the house was empty. He went to the master bedroom and his closet, where he kept a small safe beside his shoe rack. He dialed it open and put a stack of cash into his wallet and his passport in his pocket. Then he took out the Glock 19 and its accessories. He placed them into his pack, along with some clothes.

He still had his knife, with blood dried on the blade and handle, wrapped in a plastic bag he'd taken from the ice bucket at the hotel. He laid it carefully on top of the other items and zipped shut the backpack.

A car engine purred up the street, coming closer.

He went to the window. It was Karen, pulling into the driveway in her Lexus. He shouldered his bag, went downstairs, and met her outside as she stepped out of the car.

"God, it's good to see you," he said, spreading his arms and wrapping them around her, holding her close.

After a moment, she stepped back and looked at the bruise growing on his temple. Her eyes widened with concern. "What happened?"

"Work." He waved his hand. "Just a bump." He reached into the back of the car, grabbed her suitcase, and led her inside, putting her bag and his backpack down as they walked into the kitchen.

"How was the red-eye?" he asked, and started the coffee.

"Magical as always."

He looked over her face, framed by dark curls laced with gray she felt no need to cover. Every year she seemed more beautiful, confident, at ease. She laughed and gave him an odd look. He realized he was staring at her, smiling like a kid on a first date.

"What's going on with you?" she asked.

He felt high, flooded with relief. He was home. She was safe.

He wanted to ask her whether she knew if there was a connection between Widener and Emma Blair—they might have known each other from attending neighboring prep schools—but for now he was happy to wait and draw out this moment as if last night had never happened.

"Tell me about your trip. Chicago, right?"

"Oh, the usual," she said. "Surrounded by saboteurs. But everyone pulled together and we got it done."

Nick put a cup of coffee with cream beside her on the counter. She took a sip and rolled her shoulders.

"No fun at all?" Nick cocked his head.

She shook hers, the corner of her mouth ticking up. "Are you trying to charm your way out of the doghouse?" she asked. Things had been rocky between them this past month, ever since Emma had shown up at the house and Nick had started looking for her. Karen's late first husband, a law partner and political fund-raiser, had been unfaithful. She had a hard time with trust.

"Just glad to see you."

"We went to karaoke," she said, relenting a little. She took out a plate, then pulled an orange from the bowl on the counter and started to peel it.

"What did you sing?"

"Nick. I appreciate all this, but I'm really tired."

" 'Sweet Caroline'?"

She nodded. It was her go-to.

"I bet that *crushed*," he said.

"You bet right," she said, the peel one long unbroken strip in her hand. She put it on the plate, pulled the fruit into two halves, and handed one to him.

"Are you sure you're okay?" she asked.

He wanted to tell her everything, but he checked himself. This was all too dangerous to bring her into. "Yeah," he said, and touched her arm. "Thanks."

She ate a piece of orange. Images from last night crowded into Nick's mind, dark snapshots from the scene of Widener's death. He thought of Emma Blair. He knew that talking to Karen about her now wouldn't go over well, but he had to find some way to understand what was happening.

"I need to ask you something," he said. She looked at him out of the corners of her eyes, the concern coming back.

"What is it?"

"Did Emma Blair know Malcolm Widener?"

"Nick, please." She put her hand on the counter. "Can you just drop this Emma thing? It's bad enough you're always going out there, hung up on it, talking to people about your ex. But at least leave me out. I'm so damn tired of it."

"Karen, it's important. I may have found something."

She looked at him sharply, then sighed. "Why are you asking about her and Malcolm?"

"Did he know her?"

"Yes. Their families were close. He was like an older brother to her, back in school at least. I can't imagine they talk anymore, though. Different paths." She put her hands on both sides of the coffee cup. "I think Malcolm was in love with her back then, actually. Like every other guy in her life."

"Would she have gone to him for help?"

"Recently?"

"Yes."

"I don't think they were close like that anymore, not unless it was something specific."

"Do you talk to Malcolm?"

"No. I haven't seen him in years."

"Thanks," he said, and raised his hand. "That's it." He had already asked her a dozen times about Emma and why she might have been so worried when she came to Nick for help. He glanced out the window and saw a sedan parked across the street. He put down the orange and moved closer to the panes.

"What is it?" Karen asked.

"Nothing."

She slid her cup away, ceramic scraping against the countertop, and faced him. "What aren't you telling me?"

"What do you mean?"

"I know you, Nick. I can tell when you're . . ."

Lying? Hiding something? But she didn't go that far.

He hated deceit, with Karen most of all, but he wasn't going to drag her into this, not after what had happened to Emma, and to him.

"I'm just working too many nights," he said. He looked back to the window and watched the car pull away.

Nick's phone buzzed in his pocket. He glanced at the screen. It was a message from Delia: *Call me.*

"Sorry, I need to take care of this," he said, and walked toward the front door. He was just out of the kitchen when he heard a tearing sound. He turned and saw Karen unzipping his bag, about to see the knife.

"Stop!" he shouted. The command echoed through the kitchen.

She froze.

"What?" she said, and pulled her hands back. "I just need a charger."

He always carried one. She eyed him, then glanced down at the bag. The zipper was only open a few inches.

"I have gear in there. It's dangerous."

"Then why is it in the house?" she said, raising her palms. "What is going on with you these days, Nick? Why are you obsessed with that woman?"

"She asked for my help. That's it. I take that seriously."

"The police can handle that. You knew it bothered me, you going out looking for her all the time. It's pretty simple, Nick, between the two of us. You pick your wife."

"It's not that, Karen."

She held her hand up. "Whatever it is, I don't need you snapping at me. I have to get ready for work, and I just need a break. Okay?"

"Sure," he said. He didn't argue, didn't press. The kindest thing he could do right now was leave her alone and keep all of this away from her. "I'm going to head out."

She pursed her lips and nodded.

NICK PULLED OUT and parked down the street, still watching the house. He wanted to make sure no one was coming for him while Karen was home.

He lifted the smartphone and started a secure call to Delia.

"Nick?"

"What's up?" he asked.

"Alexandra Hart. I have her license plate."

"How'd you find her?"

"You were right about the cameras. The lady from the bakery let me check out her security footage. I got the tag on Hart's car and a half-decent shot of her."

"I thought I told you to keep your head down."

"I was getting cookies. It just came up."

Nick smiled. Everyone in that neighborhood loved Delia. An Ethiopian family ran the bakery and made some of the best Italian pastries Nick had ever tasted.

"You should be able to do a public records search

on the plate number," he said. "That will give you an address or a name."

"I'm on it. I'll keep you posted."

"Thanks."

Nick saw Karen walking out to her car. She pulled out, heading in the other direction. He took a last look at the house and the front walk where Emma had approached him.

Now at least Nick understood the connection between him and Malcolm Widener. They both knew Emma. She might have gone to Widener for help, too. She might have told him more than she told Nick. Maybe that was why someone had decided to get rid of Nick and Widener in one go. Somehow, they were both too near to the secret she kept. There were a dozen other possibilities, but it was a start.

Delia called back a few minutes later with an address on Capitol Hill.

"I'll keep looking," she said, "and try to find her real name based on that. What are you up to?"

Nick was already driving. "I'll go say hello."

23

GRAY WALKED THROUGH David Blakely's underground garage, past the Mercedes SL and the Audi. The door to the house opened ahead of him. David stood wearing a Georgetown Track T-shirt damp near the neck from exercise.

He waved Gray in.

"You're clean?" David asked.

"A hundred percent."

David worked his secure phone as they passed the theater, went down a long hall, and turned right into a gym. The house was a modernist masterpiece in glass and concrete, all hard edges, set on a steep hill in the woods overlooking the Potomac.

David shut and locked the gym door behind them. Bloomberg played on one TV, CNN on another. A third showed financial data streaming down over a black background.

David crossed his arms. Gray had never seen him out

of a suit and was surprised by his strength, the muscles of his arms standing out like steel cables.

"Everything is set with Averose's computers?"

"Yes. No snags."

He and David had planned for every eventuality, even Averose's escaping Widener's house alive. They had all the leverage they needed on him, and his fleeing, his last desperate moves, only made him look guiltier.

Gray didn't think Averose would approach the police, not with all the evidence against him, and that wasn't in Averose's nature. But he and Blakely had sources inside law enforcement. They would hear if he made an approach. There were ways to get to him even if he went that route.

"Where does he go next?" David asked.

"He'll try to find Alexandra Hart. That's the only connection between him and us. She's not at the apartment."

David scrolled on his phone. He turned it to face Gray and tapped the screen. A video played. It was security camera footage showing the interior of a luxury apartment.

Gray watched as the woman who went by the name Alexandra Hart strode out of the bedroom toward the front door with a large purse over her shoulder. Once she'd been an actress, but now she worked for David Blakely as a kind of spy. She had a talent for gaining people's trust.

David paid her through one of his shell companies, part of a network of dark-money groups and political action committees and limited liability companies that made up his political machine. He had put her up in that apartment.

Gray looked up from the phone. "When was that?"

"Midnight."

"Is she going to be a problem?"

"Maybe. After the news breaks about what happened to Widener, she'll know what she's a part of. It all depends on how strong she is, how much pressure she can handle."

"Does she need to go away?"

David considered it. "We'll see. She comes and goes. She tried to call me. I'll talk to her and get a feel for it. She's too smart to go against us."

David's phone buzzed. He held up his hand and stepped to the side to check a message.

Blakely could make Alexandra disappear. He could make anything go away. That was the source of his power and the reason why his candidates always won. He was so much more than a fixer. He was a kingmaker. Because he kept their secrets. He could make the past vanish, or he could use it as a weapon to destroy his opponents. That was why he kept a woman like Alexandra on retainer. She was able to get close to anyone, become their best friend, their fantasy, whatever it took. David's work wasn't blackmail but its opposite: loyalty and protection.

Gray was fascinated by it, studied it, wanted a piece of it for himself. He had once questioned how much money one man could possibly need, how many houses were enough. But that kind of wealth wasn't about luxury; it was about power, like David had, the absolute power to do whatever you want, take whatever you want, free from consequence.

He watched David at work, standing by a bench. Nick Averose was just another task to be handled by dawn, taken coolly, step by step.

Blakely had his army of eight-hundred-dollar-an-hour attorneys, his fortresses built from nondisclosure agreements, decades of carefully collected secrets. He could pressure or buy anyone's silence. He had his allies high in every media empire who could help him kill a story or turn one against an adversary.

As a last resort he had Gray, the human delete key. Because some people won't play the game. People like Malcolm Widener, who could never be brought to heel. Or Emma Blair, the woman who had started all of this, who had threatened to topple the empire David Blakely had built over the past twenty-five years.

Gray pictured her as clearly as if she were in the room with them now. She probably stood five-five in her bare feet. One fifteen on the scale. But she had nearly broken his goddamn nose when he came for her.

Emma Blair. Malcolm Widener. At times the threat alone would be enough to silence someone, and at times only the knife would do. Some refused to compromise. That made it hard to survive in this town.

David slipped his phone into his pocket and turned back to Gray. "What's next?" he asked. "I've got to get moving."

"Averose will do anything to find Alexandra Hart. We can use her."

"To flush him out?"

Gray nodded. "As soon as you find out where she is, let me know. I'll stay close, keep my eye on her. And if she sees anything, have her call me, send up a flare. But I have other ways to get to him. I'll handle this."

"Whatever you do, we need it clean."

"It will be."

24

NICK STOOD WATCH around the corner from the address Delia had given him, eyes out for white dogs and Alexandra Hart.

He had already circled the apartment building twice. He scanned the windows and watched as a UPS deliveryman entered the lobby. Only one apartment on the third floor appeared to have someone at home, and it was on the far right, the end unit. Given the size of the building, he guessed the apartment Delia had given him, 304, was probably in the middle, where he saw only darkness and drawn blinds.

Nick kept his head up, confident, as he climbed the stoop of the building and slipped through the door as the UPS guy left. He crossed the worn linoleum floors. It had once, probably half a century ago, been a high-end building. Now there was no doorman to question him, just the call box outside the main entrance.

He took the elevator to the third floor and turned

left. Hers was the second apartment down. He walked up to it and knocked, then knocked again, though he didn't think anyone was inside. If she opened the door, he would start with questions. He felt his pulse quicken, tick by tick.

No response. He didn't know how much time he had. A last knock, and then he pulled his entry set from his pocket, drawing a snakelike W pick and a tension wrench. He raked the lock toward him, bouncing the tumblers, and it let go on the third scrape.

He twisted it open with the wrench and stepped in.

A combined living room and dining area stood straight ahead, and a hallway on the side led to what looked like a couple of bedrooms. Oversaturated travel photos—Morocco, Indonesia—covered the walls. He was looking for shots of her, to confirm this was the right address, the right woman. He was looking for mail, to get a name.

A low throaty sound came from one of the rooms. A white cat slipped around the corner and twined between his ankles.

Classic guard cat behavior. He had noticed white hairs on the hem of Alexandra's dress and was relieved that she didn't have a dog, raising hell and barking.

"Who is she, huh?" he whispered, and went toward the open living area. The kitchen was a small alley. If the mail wasn't piled beside the front door it would usually be on the table or counter. People rarely had their act together enough to get mail to a desk.

He approached a two-seat dining table, bare except for an empty mug, with a faint lipstick stain on the tan ceramic. He touched the side, felt the last trace of warmth. A half hour, maybe?

When he turned, he saw it: a letter torn open at one end, tossed in the corner of the counter next to the toaster oven.

Clara Marzetti.

Same address.

It was from Comcast, a bill.

"Clara Marzetti," he said, and took in the room. He walked through the living area, scanning for any photos of the woman he knew as Alexandra Hart.

Nothing. He went down the hall. The door to the first bedroom was halfway open. He memorized the angle out of habit, so he could replace it exactly as it was. On certain jobs, Nick would carry a small bag of dust to cover up his tracks after he left.

The door's hinges squealed as he pushed it. The room was furnished with cheap bookshelves and a couch. He looked at a mark in the carpet, a long depression. It might have been from the support of a foldout bed. The cushions on the couch were stuffed in at odd angles, replaced in a rush, and on the side table there was an envelope that someone had used to leave a note. The words were scribbled in red ink.

Clara—
Had to run. Thank you for everything.
—Ali

A few quarters and dimes lay on the side table. He knelt over the wastepaper bin and pulled out two crumpled receipts, both for payments with cash. He put them in his pocket, then stood still.

The front door creaked open.

25

HE STOLE TO the left and pressed against the wall beside the light switch. That kept him out of view of anyone passing in the hall. The door to the room was still open.

A woman's shoes clicked along the hardwood floors, louder and closer with each step. The figure passed the door, and, looking over his shoulder, he saw her from the back: chestnut hair, tall and thin.

That wasn't Alexandra Hart. She crossed toward the other bedroom, then made a few kissing noises as she murmured something to the cat.

Claws skittered across the hardwood, growing louder. The cat peered through the open door. He ducked back, and it raced toward him, entering the room and looking his way with a purr.

"Patches!" she called.

The woman he knew as Alexandra Hart must have been staying here as a guest. She'd used the name Ali on the note. So now he had simply broken into a bystander's apartment. He wouldn't confront her. She wasn't the one who had wronged him, and he wasn't about to scare an innocent woman or have her raise the alarm.

But if she came in, he would have a serious problem.

The cat pressed against his ankles.

Click click click. The footsteps were quieter now, muted by distance and a rug from the sound of it. She was in the other bedroom. He looked around the door frame—clear—then slipped into the hall and made for the living room. He was halfway across it, hoping to get to the front door, when he heard her coming back.

She would see him in an instant. He cut right into the kitchen and heard a tapping sound, typing on an iPhone, just around the corner. She took another step into his field of view. He was looking right at her, though she was oblivious, staring at the screen.

The muscles in his chest tightened.

She walked away.

He shot toward the door, then paused. The phone was sitting on top of a set of low shelves, plugged into a charging cable, the display still glowing. It sounded like she was near the bedrooms.

He turned back and tapped the contacts button on the phone. He glanced down the hall and could see her shoulder through an open door. He scrolled through the names in her phone address book, looking for Alexandra. Only one entry matched—Ali Waldron—and Nick memorized the associated cell phone number.

Footsteps coming toward him. He was in the open, nowhere to hide.

"What's that, girl?"

She crouched over the cat near the closest bedroom, and Nick slipped out the front door. He went down the hallway, back to the elevator, that name seared in his mind. There was a good chance he had found out Alexandra's real identity, but where was she?

He stopped and waited for his pulse to come down. Then he turned, marched back to the apartment door, and knocked three times.

26

AS NICK WAITED outside the door, he felt like he had a "guilty" sign hanging around his neck. But this was worth the risk. This woman might know where to find Alexandra or Ali or whatever name she would use next, and he wasn't leaving any answers behind.

There were a dozen pretexts, a dozen people he could impersonate. But as he thought them through, they all seemed too contrived, too unlikely.

Most people look for the obvious. Most people are shy and deferential to any hint of authority and take what they see at face value.

He was a hard-looking guy in a jacket. Karen used to tease him when he would fall back into the old postures of a bodyguard without even thinking of it: hands ready at his waist, eyes always searching. He might as well use it.

She opened the door twelve inches.

"Yes?"

He waited for the bolt of recognition, for the shout, for any sign that she recognized him as the man who had just sneaked into her apartment.

"I'm here to pick up Ali," he said. He stayed well back from the door, didn't want to spook her.

He thought through the next couple of lines—just a driver out on a call—but she didn't even bother with questions.

At the mention of Ali's name, anger crossed her face. "She's gone."

"I was supposed to pick her up. Do you know where she is?"

The cat poked its head around the corner, looked up at him, and purred. Clara eyed him, sharper now. "No. And I don't want to."

"Damn. The number I have for her doesn't seem to work. Any idea where I might find her?"

She retreated into the apartment a few inches, put her hand on the doorknob, and narrowed the opening.

"You're one of them, aren't you?"

"Who?" he asked.

She shook her head, nose wrinkling with disdain. "Who is she working for? What is all this?"

"Sorry. I'm not sure what you're talking about."

"Coming and going all hours of the night, black trucks, tinted windows, guys like you. What is she into?"

She knew as little as he did. When he didn't answer, she let out a weary laugh.

"If you find her, tell her to lose my number."

She shut and bolted the door.

NICK WAS GLAD he had gone back to the apartment. That was no performance. She didn't know what Alexandra was involved with, only that it seemed dangerous. He took his phone out, added a new contact, and typed in Alexandra/Ali's number from memory.

He wanted to call her now, but it might be better to wait, so that she didn't know how close he was getting, and how much he knew. Perhaps there was a way to use that first call, while her guard was down, to trace where she was.

He couldn't stop thinking about what Clara had said: *black trucks*. He'd seen SUVs on his tail when he was searching for Emma and stolen one from the attackers at the house where Widener was murdered.

He crossed the street and circled to his work truck, checking the windshield for a ticket. It was a DC instinct. There were usually a half-dozen conflicting parking signs on any given street in Washington.

He swung open the door, stepped in, and slid his key into the ignition.

A woman paused on the corner a block down, her ash-blond hair pulled into a bun, a bag over her shoulder.

He leaned toward the wheel.

It was Alexandra Hart. She crossed the intersection and took her phone from her pocket.

He climbed out and started walking toward her at a normal pace. He wasn't sure if she had seen him and wanted to get close without drawing her attention.

She took off around the corner, raising the phone to her ear. He raced after her, shoes pounding against the red-brick sidewalk.

At the intersection he turned left onto a one-way street. The traffic around the Capitol was so bad he was better off on foot. There were crowds ahead, closer to the Senate office buildings, but he thought he'd caught sight of her.

He kept on, darting along the curb to get around a crowd of interns who looked like kids wearing their parents' clothes.

At the corner of First and Constitution, he looked over the vehicle barriers and guard booths that led to the Capitol grounds, the long hill down to the Mall, and Union Station's classical facade to the north.

Which way?

He searched every figure, every face. Ali had a head start and may have doubled back or disappeared into one of the buildings along the way.

A woman walked through the park toward the Capitol. He caught a glimpse of her from the back: the hair, the bag over the shoulder. He chased after, past the Capitol Police standing post with their automatic rifles and guard dogs.

She turned and lifted her phone, snapped a photo of herself. It wasn't Ali.

He started back north, then stopped by the intersection. He turned full circle. The Capitol, the Supreme Court, the Senate office buildings spun past.

Who did she work for? Why had she run *here*?

"Sir, can I help you?"

He turned and found himself face-to-face with a twentysomething Capitol Police officer kitted out for battle, an M4 rifle on a sling across his chest.

Nick was breathing hard and carried a fresh bruise on his face. He knew the air he must be giving off: a maniac.

He didn't need attention. Not here. Not now. Not with a pistol on his hip this close to Congress. The police could already have connected him with last night's murder. After a final glance around, he said, "I'm fine. I thought I saw someone I knew."

He smiled and strolled away, past the families in freshly bought tourist kitsch, past the staffers with cell phones glued to their ears, past the blast barriers.

And all around him, rolling out from underground garages and through police checkpoints, were black trucks, traveling in packs, protecting the powerful, their passengers invisible behind tinted glass.

28

GRAY HIT THE brakes on the Chevy Suburban and stopped in front of the traffic light. It was green, but the cars ahead were stacked up all the way into the intersection. He didn't want to get stuck in the middle and attract the attention of the Capitol Police. He had two unregistered handguns in the vehicle and a short-barreled rifle hidden under the back seats. He checked the mirrors for any sign of Nick Averose in pursuit.

Ali Waldron sat in the passenger seat, her right hand gripping the door handle so tightly that her knuckles paled.

"How did he find me? What if he's following me now?"

"I'll take care of it. You're safe, Ali. You can relax."

It was the same script Gray used with every potential victim. Calm made everything easier.

Ali was safe for now, as safe as any of them were. Nick Averose was loose, connecting dots. Not one day after the killing, and he had found the right thread, twined it around his fingers.

She turned and considered him. "Are you new?"

"Old." Gray smiled.

He looked at her warmly, and she seemed to relax. Kindness was a tool like any other.

As they drove on, Ali sat back, closed her eyes, and took a few long, deep breaths.

Gray was supposed to be insulated from as many witnesses as possible, but the normal, carefully rehearsed rules of this operation were bending hour by hour.

He and Blakely had arranged Ali's part in luring in and framing Averose, but she had never seen Gray.

Ali looked down at her wrist. Gray had grabbed it as he pulled her into the car. She flexed it and winced slightly.

"Are you okay?" he said.

"It's fine."

"Averose was parked on the next street over?"

She nodded. "I think so. He was in a white pickup."

"You saw him get out of it?"

"Yes."

Averose would be back. He needed his truck. Gray stopped at an intersection. He had a chance to take his man down now.

He palmed the wheel to the left and drove in the direction of Averose's vehicle, but he didn't go down the street where it was parked.

"It's that way," Ali said, pointing over her shoulder.

"I know," Gray said, and pulled over in a loading zone. He was just around the corner from the truck. He wouldn't get too close. He was going to wait, like a hunter in a blind, for Averose to walk into the kill.

"Sit away from the window."

She pressed herself against the leather while he examined the street. The setup was not ideal, but it was manageable.

"You should get in the back," Gray said. He put his finger on the stalk coming out of the steering column that controlled the wipers, pressed the tip of it in, and held it for three seconds. A soft pop came from under his seat, and he reached down and pulled out a zippered nylon bag.

He opened it and took out a pistol and suppressor.

"You're going to *kill him*?" she asked as Gray threaded on the suppressor. "In the middle of the street?"

That was how it worked sometimes, when things were moving too rapidly for weeks of planning. Stroll up behind, two pops, heart and lungs from the back, then one in the head on the ground, all without breaking stride.

You could be around the corner before any passersby managed to gather themselves enough to react. But that was an ugly option. Gray looked at the truck in his rearview. Better to simply roll by and do it through the window. The Suburban couldn't be traced.

"That man Averose is very dangerous, Ali. He's a murderer, and he would take your life without a second thought. Now get in the back."

She clambered over the console, into the rear seat, and pressed herself into the corner. Gray waited, gun in his hand, eyes on Nick's vehicle.

29

NICK WALKED DOWN Constitution toward his truck, hands in his pockets, a light coat of sweat on his palms. It was just around the corner.

The adrenaline was slow in burning off. Every sound seemed extra sharp, extra loud, like he had turned the volume up on the world.

He wanted to chase down Ali, wanted those answers now. She was gone, but he was getting closer. He had a name and number, something that could pierce the fake persona she had been using with him. He would track her down. It was a small victory, and as he neared the intersection and saw his truck, he felt the muscles in his face and neck relax, his breath come a little easier.

He stopped hard on the bricks. Someone bumped into his shoulder, and he spun toward him. It was just a staffer in a suit, his credentials dangling. He looked at Nick nervously, and Nick deserved it, standing here, blocking the way, scanning the street like a hunted man.

He turned and walked the other way. Ali had seen him get out of his truck and then gone for her phone. If she had called in the encounter to someone, they would be watching his vehicle. They would ambush or track him. It was what Nick would have done.

He needed to put distance between himself and his last observed location. He held his hand out toward a red and gray cab.

He climbed in, and the driver looked at him expectantly.

"Just head down Pennsylvania," Nick said. "I'll give you the address in a second."

He looked back and watched the Capitol shrink in the distance.

30

SAM MACDONOUGH STROLLED through the rotunda of the Russell Senate Office Building. Theo loped beside him on the left, and Sam's chief of staff kept up on the right while tapping on his phone.

He turned down a hall. A Capitol policeman stepped into his path, leaned down, and rubbed the dog's flank.

"Williams, how's your daughter doing?" Sam asked.

"Better. Much better. Thank you for the help."

"If you ever need another referral or anything else, just come by the office and talk to Tim, okay?"

He pointed to his chief of staff, who lowered his phone, then gave Sam the look. Sam was always talking to everyone, always late.

"I will, and . . . uh-oh, sir," Williams said, and pointed down the hall. "I think they're onto you."

MacDonough looked across the rotunda and saw a pack of reporters moving toward him with their rumpled shirts and lanyard credentials. They were brandishing iPhones and recorders like the spears of a hoplite phalanx.

MacDonough winked at him and started walking, following the lead of his chief of staff. He knew why they were coming. Good news entirely.

After three weeks of failed negotiations, MacDonough had just forged a breakthrough on the spending bill that was paralyzing Washington. He made it into his office before the reporters caught up to him. The staffers started clapping as he entered, and his legislative director gave him a squeeze around the shoulders.

MacDonough looked at the TV mounted near the reception desk. A CNN reporter spoke into the camera, staked out in the hall in front of this office.

His deputy chief of staff leaned in. "How'd you do it?" he asked.

Sam couldn't tell him the truth: that he'd met David Blakely early that morning. As they'd walked through a cold fog outside the botanic gardens just down the hill from the Capitol, David had told him that the opposition was secretly desperate to make a deal. They had been standing firm publicly, with the president threatening to shut down the government, but David had gotten his hands on their internal polling and strategy memos. It showed them bleeding support among their constituents. When Sam had gone into that room to negotiate, he'd known the other side would cave.

"There's always common ground," Sam said in mock solemnity. "A win-win."

"Like we get everything we want, and you might give them their balls back?"

"Exactly." Sam smiled.

There was a new ABC News/*Washington Post* poll

out this morning about the upcoming election, far too early but still telling. Sam led the pack of primary candidates by eight points, and his favorability was twenty points higher than that of the president he would be challenging.

That and the spending deal had the reporters drooling outside the office. He looked up to see a new shot on CNN: it was Malcolm Widener's house, surrounded by the police and FBI.

"Congratulations, Sam," someone said, but the voice sounded distant, underwater. "All the press are here now. I think it's time."

"Sam?"

"One minute," he said as he stepped into his inner office and shut the door.

He sat down on the sofa and brought his hands over his mouth and nose as if breathing through a mask. The walls seemed to waver. The overhead light doubled in his vision. His heart was a balled fist inside his chest.

This was real. The FBI was onto Widener's murder. What else would they uncover?

Sam's secret had been safely buried for decades, and then Emma Blair had come along. She'd started asking questions about one night twenty-five years ago, a party at a country house on the Fourth of July. They were dangerous questions, and David Blakely had done what he did. He'd made it all go away. He hadn't even told Sam about it then.

That was the beauty of David. He operated invisibly, on his own initiative. Sam didn't know the full extent of David's work on his behalf. He didn't want to. He was glad for the help, and distinctly uncurious about how everything always just seemed to break his way.

But Emma had talked to Malcolm Widener about that party. She and the former director had been close friends in school, and she had gone to him just before she went missing a month ago. Emma thought he had been upstairs at that house that night years ago, and asked Malcolm if he had seen Sam MacDonough and David Blakely upstairs, too.

He hadn't. Widener was a busy man and had let it drop—he probably thought it was just Emma being Emma, on some new kick, stirring up trouble.

But after Widener found out that Emma had disappeared, he approached Sam. He wanted answers. He talked about how somber Emma had been when she came to him with those questions and the fear in her eyes at the mere mention of Sam's name.

That was the first time Sam had heard about any of this. His stomach writhed like a tangle of snakes, and he thought he might be sick right there in front of Widener.

"What was she so afraid of, Sam?" Malcolm asked. "What really happened that night?"

Sam managed to put him off that day, to talk his way out of it, to buy time. He went to David Blakely.

David knew that Widener would be a problem. The former director had come up as a prosecutor, was relentless, and still had breakfast with the attorney general, an old Georgetown roommate, twice a month. David did what he did and saw that Widener wouldn't let this go until he found the answers. He and Sam had no other choice.

That country house. That Fourth of July. That night twenty-five years ago. Sam MacDonough's mind went back: the flowers on the wallpaper, the piss taste of light beer, the room upstairs full of silver light.

Three knocks sounded on the door, and Sam flinched. He looked up as his chief of staff stepped in.

"Are you ready to take some questions?" he asked, his voice bright as a bell. "We should really make the most of this."

Sam stood and walked toward the door, saw the half-dozen reporters and the network cameramen setting up just outside the office with their Porta-braces and lights, ready to go live. The news of Widener's death still played on the television. His tongue was as dry as sand. It was too much. There were too many eyes on him. This was insanity.

"Sam?" his chief of staff said.

You can handle this. David had told him that this morning, his hand on Sam's back. He'd been handling it for twenty-five years. They could lock up the major donors by tomorrow night.

Sam walked out. The lights hit his eyes. The shot was live.

He had this.

Sam tugged his cheeks into a tight little smile as Theo slipped through the reporters' legs, drawing a few grins. The first two questions were about the appropriations deal and Sam fed them some boilerplate about reaching across the aisle.

An Associated Press reporter shoved her way between two cameramen. "When are you going to announce, Senator?"

"Announce what, Kasie?"

"Your candidacy for president."

"Is there an election coming up?" he said, and glanced at his chief of staff. "You're supposed to tell me about these things, Tim." He let the laughter roll on for a second and then pointed to NBC. "Mark, go ahead."

31

NICK SAT IN the back of the cab going up Seventh Street. He'd checked in with Delia and was on his way to meet her in Shaw. He looked at his phone and saw there was a new message waiting for him, a voicemail. He hit play.

"Hey, man, it's me. A detective called, asking about you. Hit me back, all right? I'm worried about you."

Nick knew that voice well. It was his friend Jeff Turner. They'd been in the marines together, came up through the infantry and then worked personal security details for generals and other VIPs, running them through combat zones in armored convoys. Nick had trusted Jeff with his life for years.

Now they both had their own security consulting businesses and often worked together. The ultimate test for any protection that Jeff set up was hiring Nick to try to slip through it.

He could use Turner's help now. Jeff had a better network. If Nick was going to turn himself in to law

enforcement, Jeff could connect him with a good lawyer, make sure he approached the police or the FBI the
right way.

Nick looked at the number. His thumb hovered over
the call button for an instant, but then he put the phone
down.

Not yet. He didn't want to bring anybody else into
this, not until he fully understood the risks. Jeff could
be relentless, and Nick wasn't sure how he would react.
He might try to force Nick to go to the police, or even
insist on helping Nick go after the people behind this.
Nick wasn't about to screw up anyone else's life.

He would wait. He had a name and number for Ali.
He was getting closer to the answers, to having solid
proof of what really happened last night. He would call
Jeff when he was ready to talk to the law.

32

NICK MET DELIA outside a coffee roaster in Blagden Alley. She handed him a paper cup.

"You look like a guy who deserves a five-dollar coffee," she said.

"No one deserves a five-dollar coffee, but thank you." He raised it and took a sip, then checked himself in the window, his face like wax from the lack of sleep.

They walked out of the back alleys of Shaw, past the murals and art galleries. This neighborhood of Victorian row houses had been home, along with the U Street corridor, to an African-American renaissance that predated Harlem's. Langston Hughes and Duke Ellington walked its streets and the Howard University campus stood at its edge.

After the 1968 riots, it took decades to recover, and over the last ten years the auto repair shops and old boxing gym had been replaced by beer gardens and craft cocktail bars as the luxury developers moved in.

Nick looked for a quiet spot where they could talk and settled on Delia's car, parked a block down. They got in and shut the doors.

"I think I have a name for the woman who set me up," he said.

"Is it Clara Marzetti?" Delia asked.

"That's the woman renting the apartment. Our lady was just staying there. I think her real name is Ali Waldron, though that might be an alias. I have her cell number."

"How?"

"It's probably better you don't know." He gave her the number. "Can you get a location from that?"

"Maybe. It'll take some time, though. I'm making progress on the shell companies. No eurekas yet, but I've found some overlaps that might connect us to real-world people. There's a lot of offshore, and anonymous corporations in Nevada and Delaware."

Nick nodded. It was one of the open secrets of the banking world: there was no place better and easier for hiding money than American anonymous corporations and real estate. It was where the rest of the world off-shored their money.

Nick took her through everything he knew about the connection between him, Emma Blair, and Malcolm Widener. He had a sense of what he needed to do next. He wanted answers about whatever information Emma had and who would be willing to kill to keep it from coming out.

Delia already knew about Emma and how Nick had been looking for her after she disappeared. He ran his best theory past Delia: Emma Blair had gone to both him and Malcolm looking for help, and someone had tried to get rid of him and Malcolm last night to keep them from finding out or sharing Emma's secret.

"So they went after you because of what you knew," Delia said. "But you don't really know anything." She shook her head.

"No specifics," Nick said.

"When you were out looking for her, did you find anything at all? You must have been getting close to something so they had to shut you down."

"Maybe. Or I was just a good guy to set up. I had the right skill set and was connected to Emma so they could make it look like I was some kind of obsessive, a stalker, crazy. They were going to kill me at that house, probably make it look like a guard shot me or, I don't know, stage it to seem like I committed suicide in the office."

Delia's lip curled. "No one gave you any leads?"

Nick shook his head and looked out the window.

He had been thinking through everyone he had talked to as he tried to find out what happened to Emma. He'd asked them if she had ever mentioned something painful that happened to her in the past, any hints of crime or tragedy, any information that might have made her a target.

Emma had never said anything like that to him before the day she showed up unannounced at his house a month ago. It was odd: even with all the time they had spent together, he never had a sense that he really knew her. There was a part she always kept hidden, even during those moments, lying together in bed with the lights out, when it felt like you could say anything.

What had drawn him to her in the beginning—the wit, the worldliness—by the end had seemed like a kind of performance. She was always on to a new passion or hobby or cause, always ready with a bit of gossip or some erudition she'd picked up from an obscure book or journal, always primed to dive in on any subject but herself.

There were small signs every so often, after she'd had too much to drink and everyone else had gone home, moments when he found her looking into empty space as a darkness came on, buried anger, perhaps, or well-covered depression. But no matter how safe he tried to make her feel, she would never talk about it. Given everything that had happened over the last month, he was beginning to understand why.

He felt a heaviness in his chest as he turned back to Delia. "Nobody gave me anything solid," he said. "Emma said she never told anyone about it. She and I were close, really close, a long time ago, and she never said anything to me. She kept it a secret all those years, until now."

"No one knew anything, or no one would talk to you?"

"That's the question," he said, and took a long sip. There was one run-in that he kept coming back to: an old school friend of Emma's who had acted strangely when Nick asked him about her. "One guy shut me down really quickly," Nick said. "Eliot Hopkins. He was at St. Albans with Widener when Emma was at National Cathedral, and he and Emma went to Princeton. I met him a couple of times when Emma and I were dating, though they were more acquaintances than anything else."

Nick thought back to the night he'd talked to Hopkins. He'd run into him at a fund-raiser for Georgetown University Hospital at the Washington Hilton. Nick was there with Karen. He remembered that Hopkins had known Emma and went up to him in the foyer as he came back from the restroom. Nick chatted him up for a while and then began asking him about Emma.

"Hopkins said he hadn't talked to her in years," Nick said to Delia. "I asked him if he had any idea what might have happened to her back in the day or who she might be afraid of. He said he didn't know anything and gave me the brush-off. I would have thought it was the typical DC thing where he saw someone more important he wanted to talk to. But something was off. He was scared."

"Did he know she was missing?"

"I told him. But I think he might have already known." Nick remembered how Hopkins's shoulders rounded slightly at the mention of Emma's name, how his brow came down. Nick knew fear, could read someone's emotions at a glance. They trained for it in the Service: how to walk a rope line ahead of the principal and find the faces of the agitated, the dangerous. It was the riskiest part of the job.

"Sometimes I don't think you appreciate how scary a dude you can be when you have your mind set on something."

"No," Nick said. "He was looking around. It was like he was scared to even be talking about it." Nick finished the coffee and looked at the cup. "This is really fucking good."

Delia raised her eyebrows. "I know." She pulled out her phone. "Eliot Hopkins?"

"He's a lobbyist. A partner somewhere." Nick checked his watch.

"You're going to lobby him?"

"Something like that," Nick said. "Can I borrow your car?"

"Sure."

He dropped off Delia in front of her apartment. Ten minutes later he was cruising toward Hopkins's office in Georgetown in a Subaru Outback with a "COEXIST" sticker on the bumper.

Delia called him on the way. "He's not at his office."

"How do you know?"

"I called and talked to his executive assistant. I said I was with the courier company and was sending over someone with docs he needed to sign for one of his clients. He's working from home."

33

IT WAS A blustery day in Chevy Chase, the old-money suburb straddling DC's border with Maryland.

In Eliot Hopkins's side yard, the garden gate slammed open, its hinge squealing as the wind pushed it back, again and again.

Hopkins stepped out of the front door of the Colonial Revival and walked toward the gate. He wore a black suit and a white shirt with no tie. His hair was close cropped and he had the drawn cheeks of a triathlete.

He shut and latched the gate and turned back to the house, ducking his head against the wind.

He froze. Nick Averose stood on the walk a few feet from him. Hopkins didn't look like one might imagine a lobbyist, a glad-hander in a shark-gray Italian suit and tasseled loafers. With his black glasses, he had the air of a scarily competent math professor. Nick guessed that made a kind of sense. This man could work Congress and the White House like a marionette, turn the government into a moneymaking division of his clients' enterprises.

"Hi, Eliot," Nick said.

"Jesus. How the hell did you get in here?" He looked around the yard, the high hedges, the automatic gate still closed across the driveway.

"Let's talk about Emma Blair."

Hopkins's blinking picked up. His shoulders drew in. That fear again.

"I told you I haven't talked to her."

"I know what you told me."

Hopkins swallowed and forced himself to stand tall. It was pretty typical of high-powered men. They weren't used to being afraid. It made them uncomfortable, and they would try to bluster and domineer their way out of it.

Hopkins reached into his pocket and took out his phone. "You're on my property. I suggest you leave before I call the police."

Nick grabbed the phone out of his hand. Eliot took a step back and hit the gate.

"Do you know what I do, Eliot?" Nick asked.

The man nodded.

"Good," Nick said brightly, as if kicking off a meeting, and clapped his hands together.

Hopkins flinched at the sound.

"That will help us be more candid with each other," Nick said. He didn't like threatening people or implying threats, but this man was hiding something, and Nick had no time to waste. "Did Emma talk to you?"

"You're making a mistake. Do you know the kind of trouble you put yourself in by coming here?"

"I have so much trouble a little more doesn't matter."

He stepped closer and noticed the trembling in Hopkins's chin.

"Fine," he said quietly.

"Did Emma talk to you before she went missing?"

"I told her I didn't know anything. That I couldn't help her. That's the truth."

"Help her do what? What was she asking about?"

Silence.

Nick brought his face a foot from the other man's, stared him in the eyes. "Tell me," he said, his voice almost a whisper.

"The Fourth of July party at the Whitleys' country place. It was twenty-five years ago, and all of a sudden she's dragging it all up. She wanted to know if I was upstairs and if I saw anything. I didn't."

Nick knew the name. The Whitleys were a long-standing political dynasty in Maryland and Virginia.

"What happened at that party?"

Hopkins looked down and exhaled. "A woman died. Catherine Wilson. I went to Princeton with her, but I didn't really know her."

"How?"

"This is all public knowledge," Hopkins said, raising his hands as if declaring his innocence. "It was an accident. They had that party every year. Catherine came. Everyone was back for the holiday. She was younger than most of the other people there. She drank too much and went upstairs to pass out, but she fell in a bedroom. They found her dead in the morning. This was all open-and-shut decades ago. It was a fucked-up accident, and I don't think Emma ever got over it. Then for some reason she came to me a month ago and started dredging all of it up. That is all I know."

Nick took half a step back. Emma Blair wasn't a victim. She was a witness. "Why didn't you tell me when I first asked you?"

Hopkins gestured back and forth between himself and Nick. "To avoid exactly this kind of sketchy shit. I don't go digging around in past tragedies that happened in close proximity to the hundred most powerful people in Washington."

"Who was there that night?"

"Everyone. A bunch were still in college because of the youngest Whitley sister, but the older crowd was there, too. It was a kind of reunion. That party had been taking place since we were all in high school. A lot of people who'd gone to St. Albans, Georgetown Day, Landon, National Cathedral, Sidwell. Most of them were in their twenties, out of school, starting out on the Hill. Fourth of July at the Whitleys' was a tradition."

Twenty-five years ago, Nick thought. Families that prominent. The people at that house ran the city now.

"I told Emma the truth," Hopkins said. "I didn't see anything that night. I don't know anything about what happened to Catherine. I tried to warn Emma not to rake this stuff up, for her sake." He looked down. "And I was right. I have no idea what happened to her. I don't want to know. You ask why I don't want to be in the middle of this. Look at her."

"Who else did you tell that Emma came to you, that she was asking about this?"

"No one."

"Who was upstairs at that party?"

"I don't know," he said, underlining every word.

Nick put his hand on Hopkins's shoulder, didn't crush, didn't grab, but it was enough.

"I swear," Hopkins said. "If I knew something, I would have talked then. I'm telling you all this, I'm telling you the truth, because you should just drop it. Walk away. That's what I told Emma, because I was trying to protect her. If something criminal happened at that party, let it be. Those were the sons and daughters of senators, governors, heads of banks. You have no idea what those people will do to keep a secret—"

The driveway gate rattled and pulled back. Nick let Hopkins's arm go. A Porsche SUV rolled toward the house with a woman behind the wheel and a Bernese mountain dog in the back seat. The driver stared at her husband, cornered by a stranger on a winter day.

Nick started walking and went past her as she stepped out of the car calling out, "What is this? What's going on?"

Nick tossed Hopkins's phone onto the grass and slipped through the gate as it closed. He could have laughed. At the end Hopkins had been warning him off, telling him to stay out of this for his own sake.

It was too late for that. He looked down this perfect Washington street. He knew exactly what these people were capable of.

34

NICK DROVE BACK through the District, heading toward Delia's apartment in her car.

His hands tightened on the wheel, again and again, the anger getting the better of him now. He checked his speed, forced himself to slow down.

Emma must have seen something that night at that party. Did someone kill that woman? Did they go after Emma because she knew?

He called Delia. "I've got something," he said. "Are you at home?"

"Yeah. What is it?"

"I'll tell you about it when I see you," he said. "I'll meet you at—"

He heard three knocks over the phone. Delia let out a quiet gasp. "Someone's here."

"Are you expecting anything? Anyone?"

"No," she whispered. "The resident manager knocks sometimes. That's it."

"Don't go near it," he said.

A rustling came over the line, then the click of a door closing. "There's a car parked in front of the building." Her voice echoed. She must have locked herself in the bathroom.

"What make?"

"Chevy sedan."

"It could be the police."

Three bangs again, muffled now. He couldn't be sure if they were really the police or if they could be trusted.

"I'm a block away. I'm coming."

"But if they see you—"

"It's fine. Don't answer. That's entirely within your rights. What's the door code?"

"Nick, no."

"I'll be careful. What is it?"

"Seven oh four three."

A shout through the phone. "Delia Tayran. This is the Metropolitan Police Department."

"You can talk to the police," Nick said, "but you should have a lawyer. And I don't know if you can trust those men. I don't want anything to happen to you. I'm coming."

"Am I an accessory?"

"Did you believe I was innocent?"

"Believe?" She sounded shocked. He'd managed to make himself sound guilty. "Aren't you?"

"Yes," Nick said. "You weren't trying to conceal a crime. You did nothing wrong. You can do whatever you like, but right now I can't be sure those people are who they say they are. Just sit tight."

No answer.

"Delia!"

"I'm here," she whispered. He could barely hear it.

Nick parked illegally on the corner and climbed out. The sedan in front of Delia's apartment was an unmarked Chevy Impala with cop plates, DC 5930, and the low-profile trunk antenna of a detective's cruiser. It certainly looked like legit police, but he didn't trust anything or anyone anymore. If the people behind this were powerful enough to kill a former CIA director, they might have cops on the payroll.

He shielded his eyes from the sunlight and looked through the glass doors of the lobby. It was clear. He punched the code into the call box and entered. Delia's apartment was to the right on the second floor, so he went left, toward the farther stairs.

He raced up the stairwell, eased the door open, and slipped down the hall. The corridor came to a T and he leaned out. Two men in suits stood in front of her door.

If they were police, he couldn't imagine how they would have a search or arrest warrant for her. That was the only way they would break down the door. He watched and waited, heard them talk in low voices, the words indistinct.

If they went for that door, breaking it down or picking the lock, or if they went for their guns, he was going to stop them. He slipped his pistol out, held it by his thigh.

One man slammed the side of his fist against the door five times.

Nick's pulse drummed in his ears.

The man's shoulders fell.

They waited another thirty seconds, then turned and walked away.

35

THE ELEVATOR DINGED around the corner. The doors opened and closed. Nick waited until he heard the quiet hum of its descent and then walked down the hallway.

They were gone. He went past Delia's door to the end of the hall and a narrow window that overlooked the front driveway.

The Chevy pulled out. He didn't want to scare Delia with more knocks so he messaged her: "It's me. They left. I'm in the hall."

Her door opened as he approached it. She scanned the hallway, then led him in and locked the door.

It was a neat studio apartment, though in DC for some reason small units like this were often called "efficiencies," apt for a city of young strivers like Delia. The door was eight feet from the head of her perfectly made bed and the nightstand next to it, draped with a silk printed scarf. Her memories were arranged on top of the fabric: a blue-eyed charm from the old country to keep the evil away and a photo of her as a toddler with round cheeks and a two-toothed smile in the arms of her late mother.

The sounds of traffic filtered through the windows. With no bedroom or hall, the space felt public, exposed.

Her right hand rubbed her left, and she turned toward the kitchen. "I need some water. Do you want some?"

"I'll get it," he said, then went and filled a glass for her. When he came back, he saw her touching the lock on the front door, then pacing toward the window like a tiger in a pen.

He handed her the water, and she took a sip. The glass shook in her hand, ripples racing across the surface.

He went to her, steadied the glass, and placed it on the nightstand. She hugged him. He felt her breath even out, a trace of relief.

Nick had helped Delia's family resettle in the US. When he was in the marines, he had worked with her father, an Iraqi Army captain, and then sponsored the family's visas. Her mom and dad had passed away when she was in high school, and Nick had looked out for her. He had helped her put together her application for Carnegie Mellon, where she had finished her undergrad and master's in four years.

Despite everything Delia had been through, or perhaps because of it, she was a perfect overachiever, a scholarship kid. She never let the cracks show, never dropped the smile. Everything—the war she'd lived through, leaving behind all she'd known and starting over in the US in middle school—was an essay in the making, a challenge to be overcome and learned from. But now all of this threatened to take her life out at the knees.

"I'm sorry," he said. "I never should have brought you into this."

"I brought myself into it."

She'd had a hard-ass father, two older brothers, and a mind to prove that she could do anything the boys could. The toughness was a kind of armor as well. Her family had been under threat because her dad worked with the Americans. Militias had come looking for him one night, knocking on the compound gate while the family fled out the back. Delia had been a happy American kid, but she was also a daughter of war, with that middle-of-the-night fear woven into her nerves forever.

She sat on the edge of the bed and studied her hands for a moment. She took long breaths, seemed to savor the air. She was coming down off the scare. "I'm sorry, but this is just . . ."

He waited as her attention went to the door, then back to her hands in her lap, her nails. She felt like she was letting him down.

"Delia. You have nothing to feel bad about."

"Were those men really the police?"

"I think so. I will find out."

"But they could have been working for the people who killed Widener?"

"I'm not going to take any chances with that, Delia. You don't owe me anything, and I couldn't have gotten through this without you. If your dad could see you now . . ." Nick let the pride show.

That lifted her eyes up, and a hint of a smile touched the corner of her mouth.

"Thank you."

"I've had some time to think about it, in the daylight. I'm going to call Jeff Turner. He's done a lot more forensic work. He knows all the defense attorneys. I'm going to get some counsel on this. We'll make sure you're safe."

She nodded.

"Once I get the lawyer piece sorted out, I'll find someone for you to talk to, as well," he said. "I'll take care of everything."

"Thanks."

"Please. It's the least I can do." He put his hand on her shoulder. "Are you okay?"

"Sure," she said. "I have everything I need here. It's just . . . the door."

"I know."

Delia took a drink of water and ran her thumb along the side of the glass. "You said you've got something."

"Don't worry about that right now."

"What is it, Nick?"

He went over what he had learned from Hopkins, how Emma Blair might have been a witness to a decades-old crime, possibly a murder.

"I found a lead on Ali Waldron," Delia said. She went to her desk and turned the laptop screen toward him. "I wasn't able to track her cell, but I have this."

A black-and-white photo of Ali stared back at him, though she appeared about ten years younger. She was looking at the camera out of the corners of her eyes with a knowing smile.

"Is that a headshot?" Nick asked.

"I think so. She's an actress."

Playing a part. Of course. He looked over the windows on the computer. Delia had gone through everything—Google, Pipl, LexisNexis, TinEye, Facebook, LinkedIn, Instagram, Twitter—feeling for this woman's life through its online traces the way you would take an impression from an old grave with paper and pencil lead.

"Where did you get it?"

"It was a cached image. Google saved it as it crawled the web."

She clicked a link. The browser showed an error message. *404: Page Not Found.*

"The original is gone. Someone pruned Ali Waldron out of existence."

"This is great, Delia. At least we have a good photo."

She opened another window and showed him a list of addresses and banks, real-world connections to the anonymous shells.

"This is what I came back with on the truck registration and the shell companies. I was able to connect it to two lawyers so far, one in Grand Cayman and one in New York. They both have a specialty in corporations, structuring all these shells, setting things up offshore as necessary."

"Any clue about who the clients are?"

"No. Everything leads to another corporation, another veil."

He looked over the names. The lawyers who could do that kind of thing were hard to find. Their clients had to place great trust in them and would often go to them with other sensitive matters.

Nick thought about the kind of people who would have been at that party, the kind of people who lived and died by their reputation and would do anything to keep a secret. He thought of Ali Waldron, running toward the Capitol, and those black trucks. He thought of Emma in his home, looking at those photos on his wall of the politically well-connected, how that set her off, and made her think maybe she couldn't trust Nick. Political campaigns and committees needed to document their spending. They reported it all to the Federal Election Commission.

"Can you run those lawyers against FEC reports?" Nick asked. "I think they're all online. I want to see if they connect to any politicians."

"I can search it against all of the addresses and names I found, do a pattern match."

She chewed her lip and looked up at him, the concern back in her eyes. "Federal elections," she said. "How high up do you think we're talking?"

Federal meant congressmen, senators, presidents. "I don't know," he said.

"What if they're untouchable, Nick?"

He crossed his arms. What would it mean? He thought back to Hopkins's house, the fear he'd put in that man. How far would he go?

"One step at a time," he said. "I'm going to do this the right way."

36

GRAY PARKED HIS truck in an empty space in the underground garage, walked around, and opened the passenger door for Ali.

Nick Averose had escaped him on Capitol Hill, but that was fine. Gray had nearly let the rush of the hunt get the best of him. Killing Nick on the street would have raised too many questions. He didn't need a Lee Harvey Oswald on his hands. The plan from the beginning had been to kill Nick in that house with Malcolm Widener.

There was a certain story that had to be told. He wanted to take Nick cleanly, carefully, and needed to be able to stage his death just so.

It was difficult, but Gray had the advantage. Nick thought he was running from trouble, but he would get nowhere. The more pressure they put on, the more certainly he would fall into their hands.

As Ali walked just ahead of him, Gray's hand went to his pocket. Through the fabric, he touched a steel cylinder filled with a sedative. That would hold her if she panicked, give Gray time to prepare, to bring her out to the mountains and the place where people went away. Ali didn't know it, but she was here to audition for her life.

A door at the end of the garage opened. It led into the lower level of the house. Blakely stood there in a trim navy suit and an open-collared shirt.

Gray ushered Ali inside, and they followed David down the hall and then upstairs into a living area decorated with abstract expressionist canvases and streamlined bronze sculptures.

The blinds were already drawn. Two fireplaces commanded either end of the room. A white granite bar and a billiards room stood off to the side.

"Do you need anything, Ali? A drink?" David asked.

"Coffee, please."

David went to the espresso machine on the bar and started brewing two shots into a porcelain cup. Gray directed Ali to one of the couches. She sat as David returned with the coffee.

"Thanks," she said.

David put his hand on her shoulder. "You're safe now, Ali. We won't let Averose hurt you."

His eyes went to her bag. It was full, the change of clothes inside plainly visible. He could tell she was on the move. "Were you going on a trip?"

She took a sip, then looked up at him. "I didn't know what was happening. And after last night, everything with Malcolm Widener, I wanted to get someplace safe. I stayed with a friend."

"What about last night?"

"Sorry?"

"How did you know last night that something happened? It just hit the news."

"I drove by the house," she said, matter-of-fact. "I saw the police."

Gray's hand slipped into his pocket. David Blakely was careful with the company he kept. It was why he sought out women like Alexandra, no connections, no clout, a never-was actress with no family. No one would miss her.

"Ali, did you talk to anyone about the work you did for us, about trying to get close to Emma Blair, finding out what she knew?"

"Come on," she said. "No."

"Did you talk to anyone about how you approached Nick Averose yesterday?"

"Of course not."

"You can tell us. We look out for our people. We can protect you."

She put the cup down.

"Listen," she said. "You can stop talking to me like I'm some damsel in danger. You don't have to dance around it or try to see if I can handle all this. I know something went down last night. I don't need to know what exactly. I don't need to know what's going on with Averose. I just know he's a threat to you and to me, and we need him gone. Whatever it takes." Her eyes went to Gray. "I'm in."

Ali sat back and looked from one man to the other.

David tilted his chin up slightly, appraising her like a piece of fine art.

She reached forward and finished her coffee. "Is there a place I can wash up?" she asked.

David pointed to the side of the bar. She walked over

and went inside the half bath. The sound of running water came through the door.

David gave Gray an impressed look as he approached. Gray could tell that David liked her. She was hungry, an outsider like he'd once been. Alexandra was powerless, but her survival instincts were strong. She had been around long enough to know that if she tried to cross a man like David Blakely, he would destroy her, and the world would shrug. Her only choice was to double down.

"I didn't think she had it in her," Gray said quietly.

"I always hoped she did."

"And . . . ?" Gray said.

"We don't need to do anything precipitate right now." *Good,* thought Gray. "What should I do with her?" he asked.

"We can use her. I've gotten her close to Mac-Donough," David said. "She can lower his guard, help us make sure he's not cracking."

The bathroom door opened, and Ali came out, her face clean and damp.

She moved toward them with light steps, like a boxer crossing the canvas. "So?" she asked.

David put his arm around her shoulders.

"I want you to reach out to Sam. He's under a lot of strain. I need to know if he's handling it. Keep your eyes open. Let me know who he talks to. Do what you do."

37

NICK STAYED AT Delia's apartment until he was sure she was okay. They started looking for information on Catherine Wilson, the woman who had died at that Fourth of July party. He needed an obituary, and wanted to know the names of everyone else who was likely to have been there and how they might connect to Malcolm Widener and Emma Blair.

It was four in the afternoon. Delia forced him to eat something and heated up two trays of chicken tikka from Trader Joe's.

Once she was set up on the searches and had reassured him that she was fine, he headed out for Jeff Turner's office.

He left the car two blocks from Jeff's building and moved closer on foot. Jeff's Range Rover was in its usual spot. As Nick approached the building, he saw a sedan parked in a red zone out front, an Impala with the telltale bump of an antenna on the trunk. Jesus.

The cops were swarming him, talking to everyone who might have known where he was.

He thought of calling Jeff, but that wasn't a good idea if the police were in there. Better to wait and catch him in person. Nick turned the other way and ducked into a luncheonette. It was the last old-Washington building on the block, a four-story brick dump sandwiched between two shimmering towers. It would let him stay out of sight of those cops and still have a good view of Jeff's building.

He took the end stool and ordered a cup of coffee. The TV at the end of the counter showed a news helicopter shot of the scene at Malcolm Widener's home and then cut to something about a spending deal in Congress.

The murder was now public. He'd heard it on the radio on his way over, seen it playing on TVs through the windows of bars and restaurants as he walked. That was DC: news over the bar instead of sports, people rushing through solo meals glued to phones that surely were now ringing with *Times* and *Post* alerts about the death of the former CIA director. Nick's name and photo hadn't gone public yet, but that could happen any moment.

The waiter brought him a cup of bitter arabica, a comforting memory of every diner and every gas station he'd ever stopped in on the road, while he kept his eyes on Jeff's building.

The cops pulled out, two of them in the Impala.

He put a five down for the coffee, nodded his head by way of thanks, and left. Through a window he saw Jeff walk out of his office, heading for the rear exit. That would work.

Nick needed to talk to him, but he wanted to do it so that as few people as possible saw him and knew he was there.

The street was clear in both directions, as far as he could tell, but there still might be people watching.

He turned and started toward the alley.

38

JEFF TURNER HAULED open the door of his Range Rover and climbed behind the wheel. He started the engine and pulled out of his spot, a rented parking space behind a low-rise apartment building.

He turned right onto a one-way street.

"How long have you been waiting back there?" Jeff asked.

Nick hoisted himself up from the carpet onto the rear seat. He stretched his neck, eyes on the passing city.

"Just a minute," he said, and slid his entry set back into his pocket. Car ignitions were hard, but car doors were easy.

"I gather you saw the cops, then."

"Yes," Nick said. "Were they legit?"

Jeff looked at him in the rearview. "What the fuck kind of question is that? What are you into?"

Jeff still cursed like a marine, but the barrel-aged East Texas drawl had a way of softening it.

"How much did they tell you?" Nick asked.

"That Malcolm Widener was murdered, along with a guard. Your prints were all over the place. Your car was outside. You were stalking him, sending him threats, and are on the run."

He took a right turn, then fixed his eyes on Nick's in the rearview. "They said he had his throat cut." Jeff looked back to the road, staring straight ahead, cold, silent. Nick watched his face in the mirror.

He'd known Jeff Turner as a model the-worse-the-better infantryman back in the day, telling jokes that were filthy even by corps standards as they trudged under a broiling Mojave sun with ninety pounds on their backs, part of a long desert training exercise.

Nick marveled when he saw that kid he'd once known, now a successful DC contractor, wearing a well-cut suit as he worked the room at the Army and Navy Club or a security conference. Jeff's business was thriving, and it was all his own. He had toned down the jokes, barely.

There were moments, though, when Jeff's happy-warrior charm seemed put on, like he was doing an impression of his old self.

Nick would see something behind it—fear, maybe, the baseline dread that follows you back from war, that rings in your ears forever like tinnitus.

After the marines, Jeff had gone back to work as a contractor for a company that handled a lot of State Department VIP protection and other details in Iraq, Afghanistan, and Syria. Nick didn't know the full story, didn't even know where Jeff had been, but he had ended up in a gunfight. A trauma team in Germany had put his arm back together with four surgeries, and he had spent a year rehabbing it after he returned. Nick had seen that arm, the scars branching over the skin like aspen bark.

He had tried to feel Jeff out on it when he visited with him, but Jeff didn't bite, and Nick didn't press. Nick understood that; he never talked about the things he'd seen. Being there was enough. He'd catch Jeff sometimes when he thought no one was looking, lost in the dark, it seemed, or back in that truck as the rounds punched through the metal, and the guy would just shake it off with a smile.

Maybe it was too rough to talk about. Maybe Jeff's insane work schedule was his therapy, keeping his mind too occupied to drift back there.

Jeff and Delia. They were so different, but war had touched them both. That was what drew people to security work sometimes. It was a way to build up your defenses, to take back control.

He felt for the guy and had always wanted to protect him from whatever he was carrying. Now this shit. Police knocking on his door. Bodies close to home.

"Do you believe what they said about me?" Nick asked.

Jeff looked in the rearview. "Fuck you. No. Should I?"

"No," Nick said. "I was in that house on a job, a security audit. I walked into a murder scene. I checked Widener's vitals, but it was too late."

"What about the paperwork? The letter of authorization? All that?"

"It's gone. Stolen. Deleted."

"So it was . . ."

"A setup." Nick let out a low laugh. He knew how false that sounded.

They drove on. Nick looked to the right.

"Turn in here," he said, and pointed to a copse of bare trees along the Potomac, just north of the Watergate.

THEY PARKED AND climbed out of the car. Nick crossed the grass and started down a path toward the river while Jeff followed.

The sun dropped low in the sky, hidden behind the trees.

Nick needed open space. With each breath he could taste the fresh air coming off the water and the forests of Roosevelt Island.

He walked closer to the bank and looked down at a structure of rotting wooden beams. It was a remnant of the locks and canals that once stood there, a water gate near where Rock Creek flowed into the Potomac.

He turned and looked up at the Watergate complex, towering across the street. He and Karen used to come here to walk and picnic by the boathouses with a couple of sandwiches from the Italian Store in Arlington. She told him those ruins were how the building got its name. The curving facades and fountains and strange concrete teeth along the balconies had once been someone's idea of the future, but now, in this gray sunset, it just seemed dated and notorious.

Jeff stood a few feet to his left, his head turning slowly to take in the woods rising along the river on the Virginia side, the Key Bridge, the bluffs, the rocky islets upstream. Three Sisters, they were called, for the three granite stones. A hawk arced near the bridge and disappeared among the trees on the far side.

If you looked at it right, you could forget, for a moment, the capital that hemmed it all in.

Jeff turned to him. "What's your next move?"

Nick glanced at the path they had left behind. Two women walked by. He kept his voice low.

"I need a lawyer, but I need more proof of what really happened before I start thinking about turning myself in."

"What do you have?"

Nick had a few leads: the car registration, Ali Waldron's name and photo. He could point the police toward Hopkins. But with all the evidence against him, he needed more.

"Not enough," Nick said.

"You want to unpack that for me, bud?"

"No. For your sake, Jeff." The fewer people who knew all the details of this, the better.

"Nick, everything points to you."

"If I killed him, I would have done a better job."

Jeff winced. "Don't lead with that if you talk to the cops, all right? You're going to have a hard time convincing anyone without some serious evidence."

"I know. They got into everything I have. My safe at work. My computers." He thought of those messages that had been planted. They even knew how he talked: *No one is safe*. "It's like they're inside my damn head."

"How would you do it?" Jeff asked.

Nick crossed his arms.

"You're the best at this game," Jeff said. "Put yourself in the shoes of whoever's behind this. Frame yourself."

Nick looked down at the water. "Someone close," he said. He would use an inside man, a person Nick trusted, someone with access.

"Like who?" Jeff asked.

Nick rocked slightly side to side, his mind going too fast to stop. He thought of Karen. It was strange how she knew all the players in this. She'd gone to school with them. She might have been at that party where the woman died for all he knew. He pushed it away, felt sick for even thinking she had anything to do with this. The stress and lack of sleep had him seeing ghosts. He wasn't going down that road.

"Listen," he said. "You don't want to know the particulars. I think that's all part of why I was set up. I found out about something that serious people are trying to keep secret."

"Have you ever seen me scared?"

"No. That's part of the problem. I don't need you mad-dogging this thing. Don't worry about the why. I'll handle that."

"Then what can I do?"

"I need to find someone. I have her phone number. She's the only real connection between me and the people who framed me. Could I fix her location with that? I wanted to see if a trace was possible before I called her."

Jeff squinted. "Nah. That's police stuff. There are people you could pay off. Private investigators, bail bond guys. They have access to these data brokers who buy it all from the cell companies. They'll look someone up for the right price."

That meant having Jeff break half a dozen laws.

"I don't want you exposed on this, too."

"Get a lawyer and hire me through him. I'll do it for a dollar, and it'll all be privileged. I want to help you out here."

"You know someone good? If I'm going to fight this, I may end up going after some heavy-duty people. I need a major player, somebody who can run the whole battlefield, the media, the politics, someone who knows all the backroom shit of who's out to get who."

Jeff thought about it for a moment. "Ellsbury."

"You know Graham Ellsbury?" He was a fixed star among DC's constellations of power, the parachute you pulled in the midst of a career-ending scandal. His clients were all congressmen and celebrities and CEOs.

"I work for him all the time. This is about twenty thousand feet over your head. You're going to want somebody with juice."

"Can you get him quickly?"

"For you, sure. But you should lay low until then. He'll know how to approach the police the right way, and when."

"You think I can trust the police?"

"He can get you to the right people. If whoever did this can kill a CIA director, they could have some police working for them, too. I don't know. I wouldn't trust anyone or anything until we figure out a way to approach the law through Ellsbury. He's so high-profile that they couldn't risk icing one of his clients in custody."

Nick pictured it. A jailhouse assassination. Hanging

from the bars. A mysterious slip and fall and his lying with a broken neck beside the gang toilet.

"Sorry, man," Jeff said. "I'm not going to soft-focus this thing for you. It's bad."

"I appreciate it." He didn't want a shoulder to cry on. That wasn't Jeff's thing. He was answers and action, and that was what Nick needed right now.

"What else can I do?"

"Set the meeting with Ellsbury. If it's possible to do it without mentioning my name, that's even better. Just say it's for a friend of yours or something. I'll have more by the time we talk to him."

"Gun? Money? A place to stay? Name it."

"I'm set."

"Nick, let me—"

"I'm all right, man. You're doing plenty. Just drop me off near your office."

"Will do."

Nick looked south, past the Watergate and the Kennedy Center, watched the river flow like mercury toward the monuments.

"This town," Jeff said. "Makes you miss Baghdad sometimes."

NICK CRUISED OUT of DC in Delia's car. He had a plan, or the beginnings of one. He was building up evidence, piece by piece, pointing to the people who were really behind Widener's murder. Ellsbury was an unimpeachable lawyer. He would know what to do and who to talk to. It would let Nick get right with the police and start unraveling who was behind all this in a legit way.

He pulled over on a side street. If he couldn't trace Ali Waldron's cell, there was an easier way to get to her. He swapped SIM cards in his phone and dialed her number.

Three rings, four.

The line connected. No hello, just the faint coming and going of breath.

"Ali?" he said, upbeat, like an old friend.

No answer.

"It's me. Where are you?"

A slow inhale from her end, then the line went dead.

Nick looked at the phone. Had she recognized his voice? That was fine. Consider it a warning shot. He was getting closer. He would find them.

He changed the SIM cards back and took off.

Nick reached his neighborhood a half hour later. He palmed the wheel to the right, cruising past the houses, every stop and turn coming automatically, like a piece of music he had played a thousand times.

He saw families gathering around their tables, and parents coming home with shoulder bags stuffed with binders. He smiled and paused for a moment to savor the sheer normalcy of it.

Nick was up against Washington at its worst: the corruption and blood sport of high politics. It was so easy to forget the other face of the capital, the tribe of earnest wonks and civil servants—with their lanyard credentials and advanced degrees, their pleated khakis, Ann Taylor dresses, and tote bags stuffed with books— working to keep the government and the city's thousand other institutions running.

That was the real DC, as much as the graft, though a quiet job well done never made the nightly news.

Headlights flashed across Nick's vision as a car turned down a side street. He caught a glimpse as it passed: a black Chevy Tahoe.

It kept driving, heading out of the development. He needed to watch for any surveillance before he went inside his house, anyone lying in wait.

He killed the lights and pulled up to the curb down the block.

He had to check himself, to stop himself from completing the routine: pulling in, opening the mailbox with a creak, swinging open the front door, and calling for Karen, waiting for her voice, her touch.

Now he sat alone, gun at his side, scanning this quiet street like a thief.

Karen's car was in the driveway. The living room light went on and he saw her walk toward the kitchen. She was home early. She was safe. That was why he had come, to make sure.

But there was another piece. She might know about the woman who had died and what Emma Blair might have seen. She might have been at the party. He wanted to understand how she fit into all this.

Karen had grown up in that world of money and politics. Those were the people she worked for now as a communications consultant, testing, refining, and targeting their messages.

After Karen's first husband had died, she'd found out he had left her in serious debt after a string of failed investments. She'd had to go through a bankruptcy to settle it all. It devastated her, left her with almost nothing, but she still had her connections to that stratum where everyone seemed to know each other, loved nothing more than the name game: "Oh, Harvard? What year? Did you know . . ."

She was a master at it, connecting people, making connections for herself. By the time they had started dating she was already building her firm up from scratch into what would later be a DC powerhouse.

He had always been in awe of Karen's fierceness, her work ethic, her mind, but there was still something extraordinary about how quickly she had grown that business.

Nick checked his mirrors. No sign of the Tahoe. The street was clear. He got out and approached the house slowly, walked up on the lawn to check the backyard, and then went to the front door. He slid his holster back a few inches on his hip and went inside.

After he shut the door, he turned to see Karen in the hall, still wearing her dress from work. She stood still, her eyes wide, staring at him as if he were a stranger.

After a moment, she walked over and put her arms around him, held him tight.

"Are you all right?" he asked.

"The FBI was here, Nick. They were looking for you."

41

KAREN TOOK A step back. "I stopped by the house after a meeting in Tysons and they were here. Two agents. They needed to talk to you. They wanted you to come in safely."

She said "safely" like it was the most dangerous word in the English language.

"Why would they say that?" she asked. "What's happening?"

"It's a misunderstanding," Nick said. "Part of the job sometimes. I'm taking care of it."

He led her into the kitchen. She leaned against the table and put her cell phone down on a place mat beside a water glass.

"Where's your car?" she asked, looking toward the front window. She would have seen his headlights if he'd pulled into the driveway. Her eyes went to the keys in his hand, with the set for the Outback clipped on a red ring.

"I had to borrow Delia's," he said.

She shook her head, as if nothing was making sense. "They asked if I saw you last night."

Last night. The news about Widener's murder was everywhere. Of course she had put it together.

"Why were you asking me about Malcolm Widener and Emma Blair this morning?"

"Karen." He chose his words carefully. "You know I hate to keep things from you. And I know you can see right through me so I shouldn't even try."

She leveled her eyes at him. It was true.

"I would only ever do it if I had to. It's better for me to hold off on explanations for now. I'm going to talk to a lawyer. I'll work this out."

Her lips drew in. He could read the strain in her face. He was surprised she didn't press. Karen wasn't one to be kept in the dark, but she seemed to take it better than he had expected.

He looked like trash, he knew. She could see the desperation.

"I need your help," he said. "I'm close to something that could make all of this go away. Did you ever hear about a woman named Catherine Wilson? She died at a party at a country house that belonged to the Whitley family."

"I went to school with her. She was younger, though. Sweet girl, shy back then."

"Were you at the party where she died?"

"No. I was in Paris that summer. I've been to it, though, a couple of times, and I heard about Catherine. It was tragic. That party was always out of control."

"What happened to her?"

"She drank too much, blacked out or something, and

fell." Karen looked down at her hands. "It was an accident. Everyone was just gutted. All those families, all those kids had grown up together." Her eyes met Nick's. "Do you think there was foul play?" she asked. "What does this have to do with Malcolm Widener?"

"Was he there?"

"He could have been."

"Do you know who was there that night?"

"No. I know the people who usually went but it was big, maybe a hundred, a hundred and fifty people."

"Would there have been anyone there who is very high-profile today? Anyone who might be particularly concerned about his reputation? A political candidate? An appointee or judge up for a nomination?"

"Of course. Most of those kids came from prominent families."

"Who?" He picked up a pen and notepad from the counter.

"What?"

"Tell me all the politicians who would have been there."

"I don't know who was there that summer."

"Who would have been?"

"What are you going to do with those names?"

"Don't worry about that, Karen. Just tell me." The last few words came out louder than he intended.

"Nick, you need to get a good lawyer and contact the FBI."

"I am working on that. But I don't know if I can trust them or the police. And I need more. I need those names."

Karen leaned back, looking drawn suddenly, pale.

"Nick I'm not going to help you build a . . . I don't know what. There could be a warrant out for your arrest. This is the murder of the former director of the CIA, and you're still out there chasing down some theory that your flake ex-girlfriend told you about? Just stop, please." Fear edged into her voice. "Leave it alone. You're going to get yourself killed with this."

He put the pen down. Was she warning him away from something? "What do you mean?"

"I mean drop this. Whatever the hell was going on with Emma, whatever you're out there all night doing instead of being here at home with me. I don't know what's going on with you, but it seems like you're always looking for some excuse to go out and put yourself in front of a gun. Do you miss guarding? Is that it? Is this not enough?" She held her hands out to the sides, looking around their home, then gestured back and forth between herself and Nick. "Aren't I enough? If not, just tell me. I can handle it."

"No, Karen. Wait. That's not it."

"Then stop. It's already gone way too far."

He paced toward the doorway and looked into the den and then the living room, to the faces of Karen's clients and the shots of her and her school friends at their wedding.

Nick fought against the exhaustion, focused. Those photos had spooked Emma when she was here, when she came to Nick for help. She recognized how close Karen still was to all of those people from school who were now serious political players.

"Do you know something about what happened to the woman at that party?"

"No," she said sharply. "I told you."

"Are you trying to protect me? Are you trying to keep me from finding something out?"

She held her hand up. "This conversation is over."

"Are you trying to protect someone else? Are you afraid of someone?"

She looked down.

"Karen, whatever you do, you need to swear to me that you won't tell anyone, even law enforcement, about anything I told you now or this morning. About Emma, or Catherine, or Malcolm Widener. It's for your safety. That's dangerous information. Promise me you won't tell a soul."

"Nick . . ."

"Promise me that, please."

She shook her head slowly.

"What is it?" he asked. "You can talk to me."

"No, Nick. I can't. That's the problem."

He took a long breath in and thought about what she'd said, really thought. He could see how this all looked to her. The law had just come knocking on her door, asking about him like he was a fugitive, because he was a fugitive.

"I'm sorry, Karen."

She put her hand up. She wasn't one for theatrics or tears. "I can't do this right now," she said, her voice breaking. She turned away and walked down the hall. He heard the bathroom door open and close.

He had come in here and was about to start writing down politicians' names like some kind of hit list, talking about how he couldn't trust the cops and swearing her to silence. Of course he had scared her. And then he'd suggested she had something to do with it, that *she* was hiding something from *him*. He could understand if she wanted to throw him out the front door onto his ass. Nick leaned forward and planted his palms on the table. The people behind all this had put blood on his hands and made him look like a killer. Now he had seen that suspicion on the face of his wife. This nightmare was taking everything from him, threatening his home, his marriage. He brought his hands to the edge of the table and gripped it. Every muscle in his body drew tight, veins standing out, his forearms straining until they shook, the water glass rattling against the wood.

All he wanted to do was haul that table over, to give vent to this rage and the howl building in his chest. But that would only terrify her and make him look more guilty.

After a moment, he let go and brought his hands to his sides. He shut his eyes, breathed in and out of his nose, and pressed back the anger.

42

NICK WALKED TOWARD the front window. His phone buzzed in his pocket, and he took it out. Delia had sent a message, asking him to call her back. He couldn't talk to her now, not in the middle of this.

He looked down the hall and heard water running.

His eyes passed over the table. It was bare except for the place mats and the glass. Karen's phone was gone.

He took three steps toward the bathroom. The water had been going for a long time.

There was something odd about her bringing it in with her. She didn't use it to fill any empty moment, didn't hide in its screen. He liked that about her.

It didn't sound like she was calling anyone. But it was possible. Or she could have been texting. He watched the door.

He moved closer. Karen came out. She seemed better. Her eyes were clear.

She ran the back of her hand across her cheek. "Let's just take a step back, okay?" Her phone was in her hand. When he looked up, he saw she'd been watching him, tracing his gaze to her cell.

She offered him a bittersweet smile as she walked toward him. "Why don't we sit?"

She moved closer, looking up at his face. Verbena. That scent. It was the lotion she used on her hands. Fatigue and suspicion went around in his head like grinding gears. But behind that, overwhelming it, was something so simple. He needed her. He wanted to hold her.

Her lower lip turned up, all concern.

"I know this is a lot. Let me get you some coffee or something to eat."

It seemed odd to him, her sudden kindness after such valid suspicion. Had she contacted someone, and was she trying to keep him here long enough for someone else to come?

You're paranoid. You're losing it. This is your wife.

He forced himself to step away from her. His eyes went to the windows, but he couldn't see out. It was too bright inside.

"I shouldn't have come, Karen. I'm sorry I put you through all this." He needed to talk to Delia, and he knew he didn't belong in this house right now, if only to keep whatever was chasing him away from her. "I don't want to bring any of this closer to you. I'm going to go."

"Stay. Don't go back out there, Nick. I don't want anything to happen to you."

"It's for the best." He put his hand on hers, warm. Her hands were always so warm against his.

She glanced to the windows.

He pulled his fingers from hers, then dipped his head and started out, walking fast because he didn't trust himself to keep going.

43

NICK WENT OUT the back door, stepped off the deck, and moved to his right so he could get a view of the street. He stayed in the dark yard, turning slowly as he had been trained to do so long ago, eyes scanning from far to near, far to near, sector by sector, searching the still neighborhood.

He shook his head. He was standing out here in the night like a lunatic, swinging at shadows. He needed rest. He started walking, then halted.

It was the smallest thing: a flash from two houses down, a pinpoint of light hidden near the bushes between two of his neighbors' homes.

He slipped across the lawn, where the landscaping gave him some cover, and looked that way. A figure stood down the street, close to Delia's car. That person seemed to be waiting, watching, trying to intercept him.

He listened and heard only wind through the trees' bare winter branches and a car engine in the distance.

He looked for other surveillance. For every man you saw there were usually others hidden. He needed that vehicle. There were paths in the woods behind the houses, along the old creek bed and the drainage culverts. He could take them and circle behind the watcher.

He wanted to see how many there were, and if it was the police or FBI. If it wasn't, and if that was a lone sentry, he might be able to take him by surprise.

He went into the woods and followed the dirt path beside the creek, which right now wasn't much more than a damp depression in the earth choked with leaves. In a clearing to his left, there was a small playground.

His instincts pushed him to rush, but he forced himself to slow down. He didn't want noise. He looked toward the street and the lights of the houses. The figure was gone.

Nick took a few steps off the path.

He heard footsteps treading on the wet earth, coming toward him. It sounded like one person.

Nick ducked between the pines, going the other way, crossing the creek bed and the clearing, along the edge of the playground.

If there were others, Nick wanted to draw out this pursuer and get him away from his support. He took cover behind an oak and waited for his eyes to adjust to the dark, searching the woods.

His hand rested on his holstered gun, but he didn't draw. Not yet. There was a chance that it was a law enforcement officer. Nick wasn't about to kill a cop or force a cop to kill him.

Nick wouldn't shoot someone here unless he had no choice. He was trained to protect. This was no place to send bullets flying, with houses behind the target, children sleeping, no place to start a war.

The swings on the playground creaked softly in the wind. He and Karen used to stop here on their walks, sit and talk at the end of the day.

He edged around the tree, peered into the blackness. The white beam of a tactical light cut through the woods and hit him in the eyes as it scanned past.

It blinded him for a moment, left him helpless. He clamped shut his eyes and took cover again. Had he been seen? A cop would announce himself, but as he stood there he heard no call. That was one of the killers.

Nick drew his gun from its holster and looked around him, but all he could see was blackness and the streaking afterimage of that light.

He listened for movement, waiting for boots to drum the ground toward him. He picked up no noise but his own breath. It sounded so loud, and his heartbeat throbbed in his ears. He took a step to his right, his foot thudding into a root, then froze and searched the woods, gun raised, his eyes adjusting slowly but still only giving him shadows.

The wind pushed past him, and the branches creaked overhead. Had that person missed him? Moved on?

He turned, his vision better now, able to make out the lines of the trees.

Breath, footsteps—someone raced at him from the right, suddenly so close. Small lightning flashed in the dark, stabbing toward him. A stun gun.

Nick arched back and the electric spark buzzed by his chin. By its blue light he saw the man's face. Nick grabbed the attacker's collar with his left hand, dug his feet into the ground, and drove with both legs, hauling the man off balance, sending him stumbling and falling to the side. Something thumped in the dark.

Nick threw him so hard he lost his own balance and wheeled back. He put his hand out as he fell. White pain flared near his elbow as he hit something hard. He held on to his gun as he got up and spun toward the man, following a groaning sound, taking aim.

His eyes started to adjust. The light was better in the clearing. He saw a figure laid out on the ground, his head leaning against a railroad tie that edged the play area.

His jacket had fallen open, and a pistol hung from a strap holster on his waist. A suppressor was threaded into its barrel.

That was an assassin's rig. Nick took a step closer, kept his gun aimed at the man's face, and stripped the pistol from him with his left hand. That brought a stab of pain from Nick's left forearm. He must have cut it on the way down.

"Who are you?" Nick asked, each word measured, violence restrained for the moment. The grip of his pistol dug into his palm.

The man made a sound from deep in the back of his throat. His cheek lay against the railroad tie, head propped up, neck angled. Nick could break it so easily.

The wind blew between the trees. A swing stirred, the links of its chains complaining softly. He used to play with his nieces here. This was his home. The rage burned in him like a fever.

The man's eyes opened. He looked up at Nick with terrible fear, whimpered, and tried to get up, but his strength was gone.

No. No matter what this man deserved, Nick was no killer. He wouldn't become the lie they had made of his life.

"Who sent you?" Nick growled, and put his boot on the man's chest.

He tried to speak but could only manage a groan before his eyes closed and his head lolled to the side.

A noise like a whisper came from the ground just beside him: an earpiece. Nick put the man's gun in his jacket pocket, the suppressor jutting out, then took his radio and listened.

"Three minutes out," a voice said over the channel. "Do you see him? Wait for us to approach. You there?"

Nick keyed the mic. "He's gone," he said, low and fast.

"Copy."

"Where can I meet you?" Nick asked.

"Authenticate."

"Where can I meet you?"

"Authenticate. Copy?"

Nick didn't answer. They had some kind of system in place, a code word to confirm an operator's identity.

"Silence. Silence. Silence." That was the order to kill a network that had been compromised. Whoever was on the other end of that radio knew that their man was down. Nick watched his chest rise and fall slowly as he patted his pockets, both empty.

The man's eyelids fluttered, and he mumbled like someone talking in his sleep. Nick had no time for questions. He turned and ran toward the car.

44

FORTY-FIVE MINUTES LATER, Nick was walking down the fluorescent-bright aisles of a CVS. He'd already checked out but was circling back toward the bathroom.

He had called the Arlington County police using a fresh SIM card as he left his neighborhood and reported someone with a gun in those woods. He hoped they'd found the man Nick had fought. They would have plenty of questions about a guy laid out with a tactical radio setup, stun gun, and empty holster. At the very least they would stop anything else from going down on that street.

He held his left elbow to his side, hiding the blood-stain over his forearm. To everyone he passed he offered what he hoped was a pleasant, utterly normal smile, though he suspected that it, along with his general beat-to-shit condition, made him look like an escaped mental patient.

He entered the bathroom, locked the door, and pulled up his sleeve. A splinter as thick as a bamboo skewer was stuck into his arm. He covered it with soap and a splash of the rubbing alcohol he had bought. Then he looked up at the water-stained drop ceiling, grabbed the end of the wood shard, and pulled.

He leaned against the sink to steady himself, then dropped the shard into the trash.

A red gouge ran like a pocket under the skin, bleeding but not too heavily. He doused it in more alcohol, then opened a bandage with one hand and his teeth.

The knob turned and rattled.

He ignored it as he sealed the bandage over the cut and applied pressure. After splashing water on his face, he looked in the mirror, black circles under his eyes like a Halloween mask of himself.

He gathered his items and left, striding past the man waiting outside without looking at him.

A security guard with a salt-and-pepper beard checked his receipt on the way out.

Nick walked back to the car, searched it for any kind of tracking device, and then climbed in.

He lifted the prepaid phone and checked his messages. There was a voicemail from Jeff.

"We're on with Ellsbury tomorrow. Probably in the morning. I'll let you know. Get up early."

Nick owed Delia a call. He rang her through the encrypted app.

"Everything all right?" she said.

"Aces," Nick said, and scraped a few flakes of blood out from under his nails.

"Really? Is that why you sound like you swallowed a bowl of gravel?"

"Long day. But I talked to Jeff. I'm going to connect with a lawyer. I could use some good news."

"Did something happen?"

His wife might have sold him out, but he couldn't admit that and kept looking for ways around the evidence he had seen. He hoped it was the stress and lack of sleep taking his mind to that dark place. He shoved the thought away, like you would hide a box in an attic, and let the immediate tasks occupy him.

"I'll fill you in later. But don't talk to Karen. And let me know if she calls."

"Is she . . ."

"Later," he said.

"Sure. Well this might be good news. I dumped everything we have, the offshore shell corp and money stuff and the Federal Election Commission data, into a giant Neo4j graph database and tried a few things, but it really hit with a multimode network transform."

"English, Delia. I'm an old man."

"There are some political groups that made or received payments from one of the lawyers I connected to your LLC and mystery SUV."

"Where's the lawyer?"

"Grand Cayman. Though I may have found an office she's connected to in the US, in Delaware."

"What groups?" He grabbed a pen and paper from the console.

She read out the names of three political action committees. They all sounded equally patriotic and meaningless.

"Should I have heard of them?"

"No. They're basically just fronts, but they all seem to be connected to Sam MacDonough, the senator. They helped some other politicians, too, but if I had to bet, I'd say he's the common thread. He went to St. Albans with Malcolm Widener, and then Georgetown."

"With any of the Whitleys?"

"One of the boys was at both. They would have over-lapped."

"See if you can find out if they were friends—old newspaper articles, whatever you can find. MacDonough fits. He has his eyes on the presidency."

"Is that worth killing Widener?"

"I can't imagine what else would be. Are any of these connections rock-solid? Where we could point to a clear line between them and the LLC and the truck registra-tion?"

"No. It's all patterns. Overlapping addresses, law-yers, banks."

"All right. This is great, Delia. Thank you."

"What are you going to do?"

"Don't worry about that."

"Nick?" Her voice was urgent. "Where are you going?"

"I'll call you later, okay?"

"Be careful," she said softly, and ended the call.

He opened the browser on his phone. It took him two minutes to find Sam MacDonough's address.

45

NICK DROVE BY MacDonough's town house on Capitol Hill, not far from where he had chased Ali Waldron. A Capitol Police officer was walking on the corner, so Nick kept his distance. He drove around the block, where he pulled into an alley that led back toward the house and gave him a view of its front facade.

He parked and surveyed the white brick Federal-style home. He could see through the glass of the front double doors into the foyer. A couple in eveningwear walked out, and a handful of people lingered just inside the doors. It looked like the end of a dinner, something official.

He checked his surroundings, then pulled binoculars from his bag. He could make out more of the room reflected in a front hall mirror and saw a woman and two men talking.

Nick craned forward over the wheel. Sam Mac-Donough was on the right.

Emma Blair knew MacDonough. Nick was certain. He remembered one spring night ten years ago, when he and Emma were dating. She was in the kitchen cooking a Moroccan dish Nick had never heard of, and he had just gotten back from the store with a six-pack and a couple bottles of wine. They were having friends over at her place.

The news came on, and there was MacDonough, with his wife and two kids in pearls and plaids, announcing his run for the US Senate for the state of Virginia.

"Would you turn that off?" she said.

Nick asked her if she knew him.

"Just turn it off." She crossed the room and stabbed the power button.

Nick figured it was an old acquaintance of hers, just another hypocrite she couldn't stand to see doing the Norman Rockwell bit behind the campaign podium.

He wouldn't even have remembered it, except for the way she stood in front of the TV for a long moment after it was off, her fist held to her lips. She'd been quiet the rest of that night, all through dinner, when normally she would have been keeping every wineglass full, moving the conversation along with a joke here and a question there like a conductor working her way through an adagio.

Before they went to bed, he heard her crying softly in the bathroom. He asked her what was going on, asked her to talk to him.

"I can't," was all she said. "I can't."

What if she had seen Sam MacDonough upstairs at that Fourth of July party? What if he had played a part in Catherine Wilson's death?

Emma was always troubled, always hiding something, always so scornful of the people she had grown up among. Because she kept their secrets for so long.

She understood the dark logic of Washington. Some truths were too dangerous. They went too high and threatened the intertwined lives, the decades of shared confidences among the people who held real, hidden, permanent power, the ones you didn't see on TV and couldn't vote out.

Nick knew it from Emma. He knew it from his time in the Service, when he was duty-bound to see all while pretending he saw nothing. Behind the ivy walls and marble facades and porcelain-veneer smiles, the establishment families all had their secrets, their betrayals, their pacts. They'd spent the bulk of their lives in this small town, this ten-mile-square bog. They all knew too much, had seen too much. And if one man fell, who would go next? How many would follow? It wasn't blackmail. There was no handshake or bag of cash. It was deeper than that. It was the culture. It was the air they breathed and the blood in their veins.

Emma had seen enough to know that things didn't end well for women who tried to break that conspiracy of silence. The real power closed ranks. The capital destroyed you.

That secret had tortured Emma for decades. But in the end the tragedy was that she might have been right to keep it.

She'd tried to tell the truth. And now Widener was dead, and Emma was gone. The city was protecting itself, and now it wanted Nick, too.

A black Capitol Police SUV with a light bar rolled by and blocked part of Nick's view.

He needed some answers.

The right move was to get out of here, get some sleep at last, take cover until he could meet with a lawyer. But all those thoughts seemed so distant. He felt like he was watching himself move as he slipped the gun into one pocket and the suppressor into another, stepped out, and walked toward the house.

46

NICK STOPPED TWENTY feet out from the end of the alley, with a clear view of MacDonough inside the door. The last guests walked down the stoop. It looked like the senator was alone. He moved closer and could see half of the block in front of the house, and the Capitol Police SUV parked forty feet down, engine running, guard within.

An officer walked past the end of the alley, breathing fog in the winter night. That voice in Nick's head told him to run, but he drew closer, examining the senator's face, blue eyes and bright teeth.

His mind went to the mundane details of his work: locks and doors and windows, guards and blind spots, entry and egress.

Nick listened to the retreating footsteps of the officer on his rounds.

MacDonough. The man was a front-runner to be the next president.

Nick watched him as he locked the front door and retreated down the hall.

It felt so natural, the drive to slip right into that house, to put a gun in his face and get the answers.

He had spent a decade in the shoes of those guards, protecting VIPs, constantly searching for unreasoning men with guns, stalkers in alleys, killers as deranged as he probably looked right now. It wasn't all that strange to be on the other side. For years he had stopped threats by stepping into the role of adversary. He had played the assassin, and he felt suddenly cold as he realized he wasn't playing anymore.

Nothing was perfect. No one was safe. Not Senator Sam MacDonough, heir apparent to the Oval Office.

Maybe you can't bring people like that down with the truth, he thought. *Emma tried that. They can make the truth disappear. Maybe there's only one way to stop them.*

He watched until the lights went out, then stood in the dark feeling the weather settle into his bones, the gun weighing by his side.

No. There was a right way to do this. The evidence he had wasn't conclusive, but it was a beginning. He didn't know for sure that MacDonough was involved. He had to be careful. He wanted so badly to get back at the people behind all of this. It was warping him. He wasn't that man, that threat.

He walked back to Delia's car and started rolling through the alley. He looked in his rearview and saw the Capitol Police SUV pull up at the far end.

He drove off, took a few turns to make sure he was clear, then headed east on Maryland Avenue.

The next thing he noticed was the car veering over

the center line. Nick brought the wheel back straight. He was fighting to keep his eyes open.

He needed to rest, to crash somewhere. He had just rolled up on MacDonough's house with a loaded gun and no plan. He was losing control, stripped down to pure impulse. He'd been running too hard for too long.

He drove across the Anacostia, then along a highway until he found a Walmart parking lot. They always let people sleep in their cars. It was an old RVers' trick.

Dinner was three Clif Bars, an apple, and a banana that he had bought at the CVS.

He ate slowly, looking to his mirrors, then straight ahead. There were a few cars scattered across the parking lot, transients, people running from something like he was.

About a hundred yards off, a man with a beard down to his chest stood outside a Ford Taurus wagon. Cardboard covered the rear windows, scrawled with Magic Marker, quotes from the Book of Revelation. He was unloading cardboard boxes from the back seat, arguing with somebody Nick couldn't see and that Nick guessed might only exist in that guy's mind.

My people, he thought, and shook his head.

He imagined Emma out there in the night, running, living like this. Maybe she had gotten away, finally escaped this city.

Living. Please, just give him that.

He was meeting with Ellsbury and Jeff early. Tomorrow he would have more names from Delia of who was there that Fourth of July. He had the lawyer who would connect the shell companies. He was going to find someplace where records were kept, where the answers lay, someplace where he could break in and get the truth.

Or force it out of someone if need be. He knew what he was up against. He was getting closer, assembling the pieces. He would need proof, hard proof, the kind that couldn't be buried.

He rested his head against the seat. He had enough to start the counterattack.

47

SAM MACDONOUGH WALKED through the apartment bedroom wearing a pair of boxers and a V-neck T-shirt. After the dinner at his town house, he'd come here to meet Ali Waldron, to forget the campaign for a few hours.

He came up to the side of the bed and looked down into Ali's eyes, studying the curves of her face, the one dimple that appeared as she smiled.

She laughed and pulled the sheets up. "What?"

"Just looking at you," Sam said, and ran the back of his fingers softly across her cheek. She shut her eyes for a moment.

"Are you all right, Sam?"

He cocked his head. "What do you mean?"

"I can tell. You seem . . . troubled. Is it work? The campaign?"

He patted her shoulder. "You're sweet. It's a lot, but I'm fine. Much better now," he added, and smiled.

"Come back to bed," she said, and rolled onto her side. "For a while at least."

He put his hand on her side, felt her warmth through the sheets. "Maybe in a bit," he said, then turned and walked toward the door. "You want the light out?" he asked.

"Please."

He switched it off, left the door open a crack, and crossed the living area, the artfully matched rugs and sofa. It was a four-thousand-dollar-a-month furnished apartment that Blakely leased through one of his dark-money groups—off the radar, discreet.

Ali worked for David's political operation. She was on the payroll as an event manager, but she didn't do much party planning.

That was the beauty of keeping things like this within David's realm. He would make sure they stayed hidden. And with what he already knew about Sam, what was one more secret?

Sam's wife was down in Richmond, taking care of her mother. That was the official story, but she was sick of DC, the same faces, the same parties. She didn't like how Sam seemed to retreat into a persona as he prepared for his candidacy, how he wore the mask all the time now, even with her. They still loved each other, but not as they once had. The children were grown. It was a partnership now.

He walked toward the window. The blinds were down, showing only a sliver of the view down the street: the old Carnegie Library in the distance, a Beaux-Arts gem that had been turned into an Apple Store.

His mind went back to the image of Ali's still form, of her lying in that bed.

The election. The scrutiny. Ali was worried about him. She could see the strain he was under, the sins weighing on him, pressing down so hard he felt like he couldn't breathe. It was too much.

He put his hand to the molding beside the window and closed his eyes.

A woman lying still.

He was back in that country house that Fourth of July.

48

THAT NIGHT FOLLOWED Sam like a shadow for the rest of his life. The sick joke was that he could barely remember it. The party was held at the Whitleys' place on the Eastern Shore, more like a resort than a second home, a ten-acre estate with a main compound and two guesthouses, hidden on its own neck jutting out into the Chesapeake.

Fourth of July at the Whitleys' had been happening ever since they were in high school. It was an institution, and a drinking game called boat races was the main tradition. A hundred of Washington's best and brightest would line up on both sides of a long row of folding tables. They would start at one end with a toast. The facing players would have to chug from their cups, then flip them over with one finger before the next person could go, a race all the way down the line.

Everyone was bleary. That night Sam was twenty-five, out of law school and working a job on the Hill, but he could have been seventeen again, back in the glory days. The party hadn't changed. Roman candles fired off the end of the dock and at some point, John Carroll would always end up on the second-floor balcony in his American flag trunks and make the suicide leap to the pool.

Sam's friends just wanted to get hammered, catch up and smoke cigars by the water, but Sam spent half the night talking to a young woman, Catherine Wilson, after she was posted across from him while they flipped cups. She beat him every time.

She was still in college, Princeton premed, and had gone to National Cathedral across from St. Albans, though she was five years behind him. She was quiet, more so as the party got rowdier, though her laugh would come out suddenly, loud and unguarded.

Then Sam's old lacrosse friends called him over for a photo by the dock. Someone passed him a bottle of Haitian rum as a jangling Tom Petty guitar line blasted from the speakers. Catherine slipped away, and he lost track of time by the water.

He saw her go inside, later on, but by then Sam was feeling the liquor, and the night had sped up in his memories, the images strangely all black and white, jerky and incomplete, some moments missing and some suddenly clear, like a silent movie getting tangled in the projector's reels.

He saw her upstairs through a window, the blinds going down, the light going off. Bailing early. Premed. Lightweight. Sam's best prospect bowing out. More than that. He liked her.

He remembered going into the guesthouse later, lying on the couch, and then leaving, moving like a sleep-walker, his brain so clouded, at the edge of a blackout, his appetites running the show, prowling for more trouble, another bottle, someone up.

He was back in the main house, upstairs, his hand running over the floral-print wallpaper to keep himself upright. It seemed to breathe under his fingertips. He was in that room at the end of the hall where Catherine slept, her face so perfect in the faint silver light filtering through the blinds. He climbed into the bed, felt the curve of her body, the beautiful S, against him.

Then everything was in motion, who knows how long after he got in beside her. She was sitting up, her hands on him. She was pushing herself backward to get away, moving toward the edge of the bed, falling, hitting the nightstand, the floor.

He was on top of her, trying to keep her quiet. A low strange sound came from the back of her throat. He must have been afraid it would draw attention. Though maybe he was so far gone he was still trying to make it with her, a notion so shameful he would always shove it back as soon as it surfaced. His body weighed down on her chest, and his hand was over her mouth, lightly, so lightly, for how long he didn't know.

She was silent, still.

He raised himself on one arm.

"Cathy?" he said. She didn't answer. "Catherine?" Nothing had really happened, nothing unforgivable. That's what he thought at that moment. He'd been too drunk to go that far.

She wasn't moving. "Hey," he said, and ran his hand over her hair, then felt a sting of pain in his finger. He reached up and turned on the light, and saw the fine china shards on the floor, a dish that had been knocked off the nightstand's green marble top.

He'd nicked his finger, just barely bleeding, but as he looked down, he saw the red streaked across her cheek and lips. A few shards had scratched her neck.

He thought he might be sick but choked it back. He watched her chest, willing it to move. Reeling away, he looked to the door, then back. He was too fucking plastered to do anything but hurt her. He took a step into the hall, looking for help, or for an escape—he didn't know. There was no one.

He was trapped in this room with this girl with no breath. In that instant, even with his mind a black fog, he understood his life was over. Everything that had been handed to him, the money, the opportunities, the friends, the jobs—it was gone. He would be a disgrace, a stain on the family. His father was right, had been right about him his whole life. He wasn't worthy of the name. Born on third base and too soft to make it home.

He turned back into the room, his hands shaking, his own breath coming too fast, too shallow.

A voice came from behind him. "Sam, are you all right?"

David Blakely stood in the doorway. He saw everything: her body, her face. He would know, tell someone, tell the police.

"Sam?"

"I fucked up, David," he said, and held out his hands, one palm painted red. "I need your help."

David was calm. "Sam. I want you to go out to the guesthouse and go to bed."

"But what about—"

"Sam." David put his hands on his shoulders. "This is your whole life, this moment. I know you're drunk but you need to listen to me. Go down the hall, go out the back, go to bed. I will take care of this."

"David, I didn't mean—"

"Sam, go."

He left David in that room. They never talked about what he did. Sam had always mocked David behind his back, the Jersey boy, so hungry to be a part of this world, his dad some kind of construction baron who was always talking about what things cost at the parents' weekends. But in that room David Blakely risked everything for him.

Sam didn't know what kind of fucked-up world David came from that had taught him how to navigate a nightmare like that. But he was grateful.

In the morning one of the Whitley sisters found Catherine's body. No trace of Sam's blood remained, but there was a near-empty bottle of Stolichnaya on the floor. The scene in the bedroom told a story: a girl trying to keep up, drinking too much, passing out. Some combination of the blow to her head as she fell and the high blood alcohol fatally depressed her breathing and heart rate. It all looked like an accident.

Sam still spent the next six months waiting for the police to come for him, the knock on the door, the call that never came.

But Catherine's death was handled quietly. It was an embarrassment to her family. They knew the Whitleys. The Whitleys knew the local police. It was all done with tact, a cursory investigation and a sealed file. No one wanted a tox screen, to even open the possibility that drugs were involved, though they had been all over that party. Half of elite Washington had kids at that house and knew how a scandal could ruin lives forever, even the taint of it, even mere proximity.

It was a tragedy, and not the kind that makes for a moving speech. The families drew a curtain around it, and Catherine Wilson was snipped out of the story.

Even Sam let himself believe the official version, let the truth crumble like an old reel of film on a shelf. David Blakely never spoke of it. It had never happened, just faded into nothing with the rest of Washington's secrets.

But someone had seen him. Emma Blair. He didn't even remember her there, but she must have watched him go upstairs, or seen him go into the room or step out in those desperate moments after Catherine stopped breathing.

Emma had kept what she saw to herself all of these years. What changed? Did she watch Sam's face on the news as the early speculation about the presidential campaign picked up? Could she not stomach seeing the man from that night in the highest office? A month ago, she had begun asking questions, looking for corroboration, building her case. She was going to talk. So David Blakely had helped Sam once again.

The truth had been buried for twenty-five years, but it was worming into the light. Nick Averose was still out there. Half of the FBI Washington Field Office was digging into Widener's murder.

The past was coming for him now.

He didn't deserve the Senate, the presidency. He didn't deserve his life. He had taken that young woman's.

He hadn't spoken her name since that night.

"Catherine," he said.

49

ALI SLID OUT of the sheets and crossed the bedroom to the chair where Sam had left his jacket. She found his phone and took it out. She already knew his PIN. People tended to underestimate her because of her looks, to lower their guard, but she was always watching. David Blakely had taught her the value of information.

She unlocked Sam's cell and started scrolling through his calls, his emails, remembering the names, everyone he was talking to.

She put the phone back and moved toward the door, stopping a few feet shy, avoiding the dagger of light shining in from the living area.

She watched Sam, caught the haunted look he had now, the one he wore when he thought he was alone.

50

NICK GAVE UP on pretending to sleep and pressed the lever to bring the driver's seat upright. It was predawn on Saturday in the Walmart parking lot, reds and blues painting the clouds like the sky in a Titian.

He gathered the Clif Bar wrappers, apple core, and banana peel from the car, then walked toward the trash can, twisting from side to side to work out the knots in his back.

The promise of sun and the sharp air lifted his spirits. As he tossed the garbage, he saw a newspaper in the bin.

"Few Answers in Death of Former CIA Director." He reached in and lifted it a few inches. There was no new information, no mention of his name.

"Hey."

He spun. His car-camping preacher stood twelve feet to his left, hands clasped gently in front of him. Nick was ready for the beg, for the come-to-Jesus.

"Do you need something to eat?"

The question stunned Nick for an instant, then he looked to the trash can he had just reached into, and it made perfect sense.

"No, thank you. I'm fine." He gave the man an appreciative dip of the head and started back to Delia's car.

"God bless you."

"You too," he said. He was going to need it.

He checked his phone in the car to make sure his face wasn't all over the news. The other papers didn't have any more substantive information about Widener's killing. Law enforcement must have been keeping a lid on it. A CIA director dead under suspicious circumstances would have the cranks swarming.

He started the car, but before he could pull out, his phone rang.

"Jeff," he answered. "Is it still on?"

"Yeah. Now, if we can make it."

"Where?"

"His house." Jeff read out the address.

"I'll be there in thirty," Nick said.

"I'll meet you out front."

51

NICK ROLLED THROUGH a neighborhood of plane trees and pines. He could tell the houses were out of his price range because none of them could be seen from the street. About half of the driveways had gates and call boxes.

As he made the last turn, he saw Jeff's Range Rover and parked across the street. Jeff gestured to the passenger side. Nick walked around and climbed in.

Jeff slapped him on the knee. "You ready? I have the gate code."

"Can we trust this guy?" Nick asked.

"What do you mean?"

"I mean he's super connected politically. Did you ever hear of him working with Sam MacDonough?"

Jeff frowned, concentrating as he considered it. "The senator? Did you trace it to him?"

"I think so."

"What do you have?"

"A lot is circumstantial, but it's enough to paint a picture. I have some dark-money movements, LLCs within LLCs."

Jeff nodded and looked out the window to his left. He breathed out through pursed lips. "I hope that's not who we're up against here," he said as he turned back. "MacDonough didn't send him our way, that's for sure. I chased Ellsbury down. I had to beg him to get this meeting. And he doesn't even know who you are. But if you're feeling off, we don't have to do it."

Nick peered at the hedges, trying to get a glimpse of the house. "What do you think?"

"I say talk to him. Start working this the right way. But it's your call."

Jeff's eyes narrowed and he looked past Nick out the window.

Nick turned his head. "What is it?" he asked, examining the hedges, the long shadows cast by the rising sun.

"Nothing."

He turned back to Jeff. Suddenly, he saw a small aluminum canister with a spray top aimed straight at his face, inches away, held in Jeff's hand. Nick flinched back with a sharp inhale of breath. It felt strangely cold in his lungs, like gas escaping under pressure.

"What the *hunnhh* . . ." The last word froze in his mouth as Jeff's hands moved toward his chest, bracing him against the seat like a protective parent. Nick went to throw the other man's hands off, but his arms barely moved, hung like wet rope from his shoulders.

He wanted to shout, but his mind was trapped inside a dead body, like he'd been caught in some hypnotist's trick. Jeff's face filled his entire field of view, eyes looking deep into his own, checking them like a doctor. Then it split in two as Nick's vision doubled, and drew back, at the end of a long tunnel, a diffracted star, a pinpoint in the black, and then nothing.

52

DAVID BLAKELY WALKED down the aisle of the Gulf-stream. A man emerged from the stateroom at the far end of the jet wearing a Henley shirt and a pair of black jeans. This was Alan Ambler, heir to a media fortune, chair of the party's finance committee, and David's most important ally in locking down the nomination for Sam MacDonough. He was the ringleader in the money primary. David's day was stacked, so he was meeting Ambler here early, parked on the tarmac outside the private jet hangar at Reagan National Airport.

Through the open stateroom door, David caught a glimpse of a woman reclining in a lounge chair, beautiful enough to make the breath catch, something vaguely catlike about the corners of her eyes and her retroussé lips and the way she perched as she flicked through some endless loop on her phone.

It wasn't Ambler's wife or his daughter. David didn't judge. He had protected him on that front before, and it was proving helpful now as Ambler rounded up the other donors for Sam's candidacy.

Ambler moved with loose-limbed ease as he walked between the white leather chairs. He sat and took a Vitaminwater from the flight attendant before she returned to the galley.

"How was Miami?" David asked.

"Debauched," Ambler said. He tilted the bottle back and drank the entire thing in one go. "All the other donors are happy. It was seamless."

"How close are you to bringing everyone around to a decision?"

"I think I can get them tonight. The others wanted to know how much skin you're willing to put in the game. What's the maximum you'd be willing to contribute for Sam's presidential run, primary and general? I need your real ceiling. What's he worth to you?"

"I can go one hundred."

A smile pulled at Ambler's tanned, too-tight skin. A hundred million would be a record. That amount had been pledged to a campaign once before, in 2016, though that donor ultimately gave only twenty-five.

"Is that just to leak to the press, or would you really go that high?"

"All of it," David said. A hundred million was still only a tenth of what a presidential campaign would cost. David needed the whole party behind Sam, the endorsements, the data machine, the delegates, and the infrastructure in the primary states. But with David willing to prime the pump this much, the other donors would realize that the smart move was to bet with him.

"Why are you so invested in him?"

"I don't need to give you the speech again. Bottom line: we go back, and he's our best shot at the White House. You saw the polling. He's won every election he's ever contested by a landslide."

"I know," Ambler said, leaning in a little closer. "How do you do it? Win with the margins you guys put up? I mean, every other candidate you and Sam throw your support behind ends up on top. You never lose."

"We have a good model."

"Everyone has a good model. What's the magic sauce?"

"You get your people to go in on Sam and I'll share it with the whole party."

Success brought scrutiny, and David was ready. He had a whole script. He would talk about psychographics and data mining and social media targeting, going on and on with some TED talk bullshit about exploiting the deep psychology of voters.

In truth, David was at the absolute frontier of all the dark, but legal, political arts: suppressing votes, spreading dirt on opponents, pouring dark money into statehouses and judicial campaigns to tilt the battlefield in your favor, redrawing districts, packing and cracking them.

But winning sometimes required him to go further. It meant getting inside the opposition's networks, stealing their polling, sending out spies like Ali Waldron. At the extreme it meant making someone disappear.

All of that didn't make for a particularly rousing after-dinner speech at a fund-raiser, though. Why was David so invested in Sam? Because he owned him 100 percent. David wasn't proud of what he had done that Fourth of

July, but he was proud of what he had done with it since. Covering for Sam then and now was a massive risk, and he would do anything it took to protect that investment.

David had kept evidence from the night Catherine Wilson died, evidence that would condemn Sam Mac-Donough. He had never had to use it. He had never thought he would. Sam knew what he knew. It went unsaid. If David Blakely got this done, he would have power over the most powerful man in the world. Sam would be in charge of the FBI and the Department of Justice. They would be untouchable.

"Come on," Ambler said, and swatted David's shoulder with the empty bottle. "What's the secret?"

David leaned in and waited a beat to up the suspense. "Shitloads of money," he said.

Ambler grinned and sat back. "Fair enough. The other candidates are making moves, but that breakthrough on the spending deal will help him. We need to get him out front. I'm talking to the rest of the donors today. And I'll need to meet Sam one more time, a look-him-in-the-eyes thing."

"Tonight?"

"Tonight's great. And he'll be ready to announce?"

"Any moment. He has all the key staff lined up."

"There's nothing else to worry about here? No problems?"

"None," David said.

"Good. If we can get him out first, he'll be unstoppable, but we should move today."

"What's your gut?"

"With the way he's tracking, I'll just say I have a good feeling about it."

David put his hand on Ambler's shoulder, gave it a

squeeze. "That's my man. The White House is only the beginning."

Twenty minutes later, David was walking away from the hangar, back to his Audi.

Tonight. He needed everyone who knew the truth taken care of by tonight, and now he had Nick Averose under control.

53

STRANGE DREAMS TOOK hold of Nick. Fireworks blooming across the sky over the Mall, lighting up the worn stones of the Lincoln Memorial and the Washington Monument. It was a memory from ten years ago, Fourth of July. He and Emma had biked down the Virginia side of the Potomac and found an empty spot beside a grove of oaks where they could lay out a blanket and see the show.

He remembered watching the exploding lights shine across her face, her eyes wide and, for a moment at least, untroubled.

In the dream he looked at the fireworks overhead, like burning willows, and then back to her. She was crying, and suddenly she was gone, and a sick feeling overwhelmed him.

The vision dissolved. Reality pushed in, the hiss of gas, the dull ache in the center of his forehead.

A figure passed in front of Nick, but he couldn't see

clearly. Everything was blurred, slowly coming back into focus.

Voices to his left. What looked like a fireplace ahead. There was a mattress on the floor. He was inside a house. Something was on his face, covering his nose and mouth. The rush of a ventilator. The rhythmic ping of a heart monitor.

He was seated at a table. His wallet lay on it, alongside two books, a gun—his gun—and a photo: Emma looking over her shoulder, wearing her beat-up Orioles cap and smiling.

His wrists were bound to the arms of the chair with duct tape over towels. It was nothing, yet he could barely move. The monitor was clipped to the tip of his finger.

A hand emerged and placed an orange pill bottle on the table, then tipped it over. White tablets skittered across the surface.

"Those restraints won't mark him up?" It was Jeff's voice.

"Not with the sedative."

Nick looked down at the strange breathing apparatus over his mouth and nose. It reminded him of something he had seen at the dentist.

A man stepped into view, preparing something on a stainless-steel tray. A scar showed on his neck, running out from under the collar of his shirt.

He seemed so familiar, South Asian or from the Gulf, Nick guessed, about six-one and built like a bricklayer.

Nick's eyes went back to the titles of the books. Cicero. *De Officiis.* Plato. *The Trial and Death of Socrates.*

Tyrannicide. Suicide. The drugs left his thoughts murky and disordered, but he forced himself to focus, to understand. Those were fit subjects for a madman who had just killed the former CIA director. They were staging his death, making it look like this was where he was hiding out. He hadn't been meant to survive on that first night.

The beeping picked up. His own heartbeat echoed through the room.

"Gray, he's awake."

Jeff crouched over him. He wore surgeon's gloves.

Why was the other man calling Jeff by the name Gray? Nick's mind moved slowly. Gray. It was Jeff's alias. Jeff was working with the killers. He was one of them. "Jeff," he whispered. "What are you doing?"

He didn't respond.

"What happened to you?"

Jeff picked the gun up off the table and checked the brass.

He stood in front of Nick and looked into his eyes. "You get used to anything," he said.

He sealed his lips together and turned to the side. "Singh, let's get this over with."

The other man slit the tape with a scalpel—a disposable blade in a plastic handle—and Jeff put the gun in Nick's hand.

Nick's heart rate jacked up, and the monitor screamed through the room like a fire alarm. He tried to push back, but he was so weak. Jeff's hand guided his own, as if he were teaching him: the finger through the trigger guard, the barrel swinging up. The muzzle of the gun flashed at the edge of his vision and pressed in, tenting up the skin under his jaw, pulsing against his carotid.

His heartbeats merged into a continuous cry.

54

ANOTHER SOUND FILTERED into the room: sirens, getting louder and louder. The gun pulled back from Nick's throat.

"What the fuck is that?" the other man asked. Jeff had called him Singh.

Jeff listened carefully. "Those are police," he said. "Stay here. I'll check. We might have to take him out the back."

Jeff walked out, the gun in his hand, and Singh took a dozen steps behind him, looking out the window, trying to see what was going on. A door opened and closed near the front of the house.

Nick was alone in the center of the room. He inched his free hand forward and pinched the tube feeding him gas.

He lowered his jaw so the mask no longer fit properly and he could pull in fresh air around its edges. He took in long clean breaths, burning off the haze of drugs.

In the mirror over the mantel, he could see Singh

standing behind him, near the door, peering at the edge of the blinds. Nick recognized him now, one of the attackers from Malcolm Widener's house.

As he turned back, Nick let go of the tube. He held his breath against the sedative as Singh approached. Nick remained still, savoring the clearing feeling in his mind, the way his body began to feel once more like part of himself.

He held his eyes unfocused as Singh loomed over him and moved closer. He could feel his warm breath.

Still. Wait.

He kept his body limp, even as the adrenaline primed every muscle to move.

Hold. Closer.

Singh held the mask to adjust it, and leaned in to check Nick's pupils.

Nick shot his head forward, slamming into the bridge of his nose with a crunch.

Singh reeled back, stunned, falling along the edge of the table, his hand grabbing desperately and slipping through the pills. He landed on the floor, his head slamming down.

Nick peeled the tape and monitor off to free his left hand, forcing himself to concentrate, to move his drunken fingers. He stood, legs unsteady but able to walk, and scanned the room for a weapon.

His cheeks hurt, and he realized he was smiling like a lunatic, pumped up on some artificial joy that was now slowly dissipating. There was fear, but it felt so distant, lost in the exhilaration of drugs or escape. Singh pushed himself up, with one hand held to his face, squinting, disoriented. The scalpel gleamed in his hand, flashed toward Nick. Nick dodged to the right and the blade brushed across his shoulder.

The man had lunged too far, at the edge of his balance, still dazed from the blow. Nick shoved him to the side, toppling him, then closed in, hand on the table to steady himself. As Singh raised himself off the ground, Nick lifted his right foot and dropped it, slamming his head into the stone floor.

A hollow concussion filled the room, and Singh flopped down. Only the whites of his eyes showed. He was out, for now.

The scalpel had snapped against the floor. Nick grabbed the small blade and tried to fit it back onto the handle, but the attachment had broken off. He slipped the razor-sharp bit of metal into his pocket and moved on. He quickly searched the man for a gun or another weapon but found only a set of keys.

He took his wallet from the table—Jeff had his gun—then heard movement to his right. From the echo, he guessed it was a kitchen, so he cut left, through a dining room and past the back stairs into a mudroom, looking for a weapon as he ran.

Nick pressed himself against the door frame and scanned the backyard: a long lawn, going up a hill, hemmed in by thick stands of trees on either side.

He twisted the doorknob, metal creaking slightly against metal, and slipped into the backyard and the morning air. Jeff's Range Rover was parked in a driveway beside the house. Nick darted left, to the trees closest to him. They would give him some cover. As he entered the shade of the trees, he saw a brick wall topped in sandstone to his left.

He kept going, away from the house and the sound of sirens. He didn't want to go to the police, not if he could help it, not with the murder still hanging over him.

He heard the sound of a door opening and closing.

Jeff or his guards were coming for him, searching the yard. He moved as quickly as he could, picking his steps, quiet along the wall. It seemed to belong to the adjacent property, not this one. He looked for a break ahead, hoping that the woods at the top of the hill led to a road or a way out.

As he neared the top of the hill, he heard footsteps approaching. He stopped short and ducked behind a tree. A long shadow bobbed to his right. It wasn't coming straight at him. It seemed to be moving along a path that would bring it about six feet to his right, then past him.

The figure moved closer, rustling through the downed leaves. It didn't make sense that Jeff or Singh or anyone from the house could have gotten this far this quickly, and he hadn't heard any sounds of the police coming from this direction.

Nick's breathing picked up, sounded like a steam engine to his own ears. *Slow. Take it easy.* He lifted the keys he had taken from Singh, gripped them in his right hand, the blade of the long key sticking out like an ice pick. That was his best weapon. The piece of scalpel was too small to hold. He got ready to lunge.

The figure stepped into view.

It was Ali Waldron. Her hands were empty. No gun. He waited in silence for her to pass, so he could get around her and away without raising an alarm.

Her head turned his way, and she stepped back with a start. She looked at his face, the fresh cut on his shoulder, her eyes wide with shock. If she let out one cry the pursuers would find him.

She didn't make a sound, simply mouthed, "Are you okay?"

NICK APPROACHED HER slowly, step by silent step. She didn't retreat. Didn't shout.

She swallowed, pressed her lips together, dry mouthed with fear, of him, certainly, but her head kept turning back toward the house, the men pursuing him. She held her right wrist loosely with her left hand.

"We have to get out of here," she whispered.

Why hadn't she cried out to Jeff? Did she think she didn't have time? That Nick would hurt her before people could arrive?

He looked at the wrist and saw fresh bruises, then faced the house. She couldn't have come from there. No. She had been back here, watching.

"*You* called the police."

She nodded.

Something rustled in the trees between them and the house. He started walking and beckoned her toward the wall. They took cover behind another oak, shoulder to shoulder.

"My car," she said, pointing over the lawn. "It's that way."

"You didn't come with them?"

"No. On my own. I was just trying to find out what the hell is going on."

He peered around and surveyed the property, saw the road in the distance. They couldn't cross the lawn that way. Jeff would see them. If they wanted to reach that car, they would have to get out of here and work their way back around to it. Nick looked up. The wall was eight feet high. The cover was good here, the trees thick.

He bent his knees, wondering how much strength the drugs had stolen. The adrenaline still burned in his muscles. He took a long stride toward the wall, jumped and planted the toe of his boot against the brick, kicked up, and caught the stone at the top.

He hauled himself up to his chest, lying on the wide sandstone cap, staying low, ignoring the pain from the cut.

Ali looked up at him. She had brought him into this. His instincts told him not to trust her. He couldn't even be certain it was she who had created the distraction and saved his life.

"Come on," she said, and held up her hand. "They can't find me here."

He looked to the woods beyond the fence, then back, and stretched his fingers out toward her.

She clasped them, and he helped her up. She dragged her shoes down the wall, fighting for traction; gripped the top; and pulled herself up beside him.

He pointed toward a tangle of brush and leaves on the far side, and she eased herself down and dropped.

The last thing he saw was Jeff stalking through the trees, gun drawn. Then Nick leaped down behind her.

"What now?" she asked.

He scanned the trees and saw a path along a stream ahead. The adrenaline amplified every sense. The woods were a Technicolor riot in the morning light.

He pointed west, toward the stream.

"Run."

56

THEY RACED THROUGH a park that looked like it had once been an estate. The trail wasn't much more than a thin line of dirt hidden by rotting leaves. As the rush backed off its peak, Nick felt shaky and sick, and fought to focus on each step to keep from stumbling.

There was a good chance that Jeff would be watching the road that led back to her car. It was the most obvious escape from the house. He would have to come at it from another direction.

After they had put distance between themselves and the house, Nick looked back, slowing as there was no sign of the pursuers. He slipped off his jacket. The sleeve of his shirt was already torn from the blade. He ripped it off and wrapped it around the wound.

He eased the jacket back over the injured arm, hissing as the cut burned.

"Why were you at that house?" he asked her as they walked.

"I knew something was happening there," she said, each word deliberate. "I was worried that it would be bad, so I came to check. That's it. I just don't want anyone else to get killed."

"Like Malcolm Widener?"

"I didn't know anything like that was going to happen. I swear."

He wanted to interrogate her about who she worked for, about everything she knew, but his priority was getting away.

He turned, and they worked their way through the woods toward the road where Ali had parked. Branches scratched at their arms, their faces. They had made it far enough through the park that they could come at her car through the woods, not the street.

He stopped near the edge of the trees.

"There it is," she whispered, and pointed to a Toyota Avalon with Virginia plates parked a hundred yards down. She stepped forward.

"Hold on," he said, and looked down the street, trying to see if they were waiting, observing her vehicle. "How did you find out something was happening at that house?"

"From the people I work for."

"But no one knows you were there? No one knows you knew about it?"

"Yes. I was careful. If they found me there . . ." She swallowed. The fear got hold of her. Her eyebrows knit together, and her mouth tightened, the corners drawing down. He watched her, trying to figure out whether this was an act, some kind of elaborate ploy. He needed to go slowly, avoid any traps.

"Listen," she said, defensive now, as if she'd picked

up on the suspicion in his face. "I was helping them. I was their spy, their actress, whatever they needed. That was my job. And now I just want to find out what I'm in the middle of, what the hell they're doing, and how I can get out of it. They might kill me because of what I know. I think they were going to do it yesterday, but I managed to convince them I was loyal. Jesus. That woman disappears, and then Widener dies, and then I went to that house and saw whatever the hell they were doing to you. If they find out that I—"

"Disappeared?"

"What?" she asked.

"Who disappeared?"

"I didn't have anything to do with that."

He moved closer, towered over her. "Give me the name."

"Emma Blair. They—"

A black SUV rolled slowly down the street, searching. Nick waved her toward him as he stepped behind a tree for cover. She followed and stood by his side.

57

THEY WAITED IN silence. Nick listened to the truck's engine, waited for it to stop, for the hunt to begin.

All the while her words ran through his head. She knew about Emma's disappearance.

The sound from the truck grew faint, and he saw it turn a corner at the end of the street. It hadn't slowed down near Ali's car. The searchers must not have recognized it. He stepped out and started moving toward the Toyota.

"Keys," he said. She didn't move. "If they come after us, it's better I'm driving."

She handed them over. Nick absorbed every detail of the neighborhood as they approached the car, looking for static surveillance, likely hides, finding nothing.

He opened the driver's door and got in. Once Ali was in the passenger seat, he told her to turn off her phone. He pulled a U-turn and brought the car up to thirty miles an hour through the neighborhood, fast but not drawing attention. The car was well used but spotlessly clean inside.

He worked the mirrors as he drove, looking for any signs of pursuit.

"Who do you work for?" Nick asked.

She held the door handle and looked out the window. They'd gotten away, and the panic she'd shown earlier seemed to have subsided. She was calculating now.

"Is it a man they call Gray? He was driving the Range Rover and had the gun inside that house."

"He's part of it," she said. "But I don't work for him."

Nick waited, but she didn't say anything else.

"Listen," he said. "I need you to tell me the truth. And I can try to tell you what I know about what's going on. That's the only way we're going to make it out of this."

She crossed her arms and looked at him, seemed ready to deal.

"Do you work for Sam MacDonough?"

Her head drew back an inch. That got her attention. "What makes you think he has anything to do with this?"

"I've put together some pieces here, Ali Waldron. I probably know some things that you would like to. So?"

"I work for David Blakely. He's MacDonough's patron, his main donor."

Nick nodded coolly, his eyes on the road. He had been desperate to find the answers to those questions, but he had to be careful. He still didn't trust her. Offering him that information would be the perfect bait if she were trying to lure him into something.

"What happened to Emma Blair?" Nick asked.

"I don't know."

"It sounded like you knew."

"I was just supposed to get close to her, to find out what kind of information she had. I would go to the same AA meetings with her. I'd get coffee after. I tried to get her to trust me."

"You knew she disappeared."

"I swear I had nothing to do with anything like that. I just talked to her, but she never gave me anything. I only found out last night that she was missing. It was after I learned about Widener's death. I was trying to figure out what kind of trouble I might be in, how deep it went."

"Why should I believe a word you say?" he asked. She had sent him to Widener's house, conspired in a murder, trapped him in this hell.

"Because I helped you back there. Because I had no choice. I didn't know what they were going to do to Malcolm Widener."

He jerked the car to the right, pulled into a cul-de-sac. His hands clamped on the wheel, and he felt the blood rise in his face. He knew what he looked like, the veins full in his neck, the strength coming out.

"Did those men hurt Emma Blair?" he asked, taking his time with every word.

"I told you I don't know." She shook her head.

"Don't fucking play games with me," he growled.

She pressed against the door. "It's the truth. Who are you really? Why are you in the middle of all this?" He didn't answer, saw the fear in her. "Why you?" she asked. "They wouldn't just take anyone and try to make him out as . . ."

A killer. Let her think it. His friend had just tried to put a bullet in his brain, a violation so grave that he was only beginning to understand that it had really happened, that it wasn't some drug-fueled delusion. At this point he didn't know what he was capable of.

"Are you accusing me of something?" he asked, his voice like steel.

He heard a car engine coming, throttle open, loud, someone in pursuit.

"They talked about you. They said you were dangerous."

He thought of that man whose head he had cracked into the stone floor.

"I protect people. I don't hurt them. Not until you dragged me into this."

The engine thrummed, closer now.

She glanced back at the road, then to Nick, perhaps measuring whether he was a greater threat than the men on their tail.

"They could see us here," she said. "We should go."

He didn't know how much of what she was saying was the truth, how far he could trust her, but for now she was his best chance. He needed what she knew.

He hit the gas.

58

THE ELEVATOR DOORS opened with a chime, and Sam MacDonough stepped out onto bare concrete. He turned his head as he walked, surveying the full floor of an office building, now empty, stripped down to the columns and aluminum studs. Footsteps echoed. They were hard to place, and he spun to see David Blakely walking toward him, past a bundle of Ethernet cables hanging from the ceiling.

"This is yours?" Sam asked.

"The whole building," David said.

Sam pulled the corners of his mouth down, impressed, then walked toward the windows. He was eighty feet over Pennsylvania Avenue, and his eyes swept from the Capitol toward the White House.

"It's safe to talk?" Sam asked.

"That's why we're here."

"Is Nick Averose still an issue?" Sam asked. David had told him it would be resolved by this morning.

"You don't want to get too close to the front on this."

Sam ran his toe over the floor, grinding the drywall dust under the leather sole of his shoe. "So, no."

"We have him covered."

"How?"

"It will be taken care of."

Sam laced his fingers together, held them near his waist.

"This is too much. We can't announce in the middle of all this."

"That's why we need it gone now. You think this is scrutiny? Wait until you declare."

"I'll be lucky if I stay out of prison. The White House? No. I should withdraw. Let this all die down."

"You could," David said. "But you still need to make this all go away."

"I never told you to do anything like this, anything this . . . severe." He shook his head.

David cast his eyes down, disappointed. He took a few paces and picked up a framing square, let it balance on one finger. The tool looked odd in his hand, so comfortable, so out of place with his slim-cut blue jacket and open-collared shirt.

"This all started with something ugly, Sam. I got my hands dirty for you. You never had to. Maybe you convinced yourself it never happened, but it did. And you can walk down to the police right now, get a good lawyer, try to make some kind of deal. Tell the truth. That's the right thing to do. It's a hard thing to do. I could never. You know me." He held the square in his fist, rubbed his thumb against the worn aluminum. "Whatever it takes to get by. I'd admire you for it, but there's no easy way out of this."

He put one foot up on a putty bucket and looked out the window.

"Are you ready for that? A six-month round-the-clock news cycle about who you really are. How you got here. What you did that night. Who knows—it would probably be a relief. But remember that the violence started with you. You made your choice that night when you asked for my help. Everything else—what happened to Malcolm Widener, what happens to Nick Averose—is just the necessary consequence of that moment."

Sam took a step toward the window. "How close are we with the donors?"

"I talked to Ambler this morning. He thinks we can seal it up tonight. The deal you made yesterday put you over the top. They can line up the whole primary, and they're coming together around you, Sam. We need to meet him one more time, tonight. We're close."

He walked in a circle, looking around the space. "This could make a nice campaign headquarters," he said. "If that's what you want."

Sam turned, took in the floor from one end to the other.

"I can get my arms around this, take care of Averose," David said. "I have ways to control him. It won't be pretty, but it needs to get done today. I can keep the past buried. But I need to know if you're still in, Sam. If you're strong enough to go all the way with this."

He pointed at the window down Pennsylvania Avenue. "That's yours if you want it, and once you're in that house, you're above the law."

"Tonight?" Sam asked, and brought his fist to his lips.

"Tonight."

Sam took a deep breath. David watched him. He knew who Sam really was. He knew how he had come this far, even as he disappeared into the mask he wore, the man he played before the cameras, even as he pretended none of it was happening. It was time for him to stop lying to himself. He wanted it. He wanted everything. Who was he kidding? He could never stop.

"Then make it go away. By tonight. And we'll meet with Ambler and I'll fucking close this thing."

NICK FELT A drop of blood run down his arm as he drove. He glanced at his sleeve, then pulled into a strip mall, an oddly low-rent patch of asphalt at the edge of Bethesda's affluence. To their left, a red-brick apartment block made a half-hearted attempt to look colonial.

He eased the jacket off and checked the compress, trying to tighten it with one hand.

"Here," Ali said, and leaned over to help with the makeshift bandage.

They were far from the house where he'd been attacked, clear of anyone following. The time and distance had put them both more at ease.

"All right," he said, "cards on the table. I can help you find a way out of this, but we need to put together what we know. What do you do for David Blakely?"

"I work for one of his dark-money groups. Technically it's a foundation, a nonprofit, but it's really a front, part of a big political slush fund."

"And what do you *do*?"

"Whatever he wants." She raised her shoulders. "Up to a point. Listen. I knew David wasn't a Boy Scout, that he played hardball, did anything it took to get a win. I helped him spy on people, get information. It wasn't the most ethical stuff in the world, but I wasn't breaking any major laws. I thought I was learning the Washington game, how the city really works. I was okay with it. But what happened to Malcolm Widener? Whatever they were doing back at that house? I didn't sign up for any of that shit."

Nick didn't say anything. He was beginning to fully appreciate what she had done: gone against her superiors. She hadn't simply been at the house where he was drugged and had an attack of conscience. She had gone out of her way to find out what was happening. She'd put her life at risk to save his.

"And Blakely sent you to spy on Emma Blair?"

She nodded.

"What were they trying to find out?"

"I had a whole script. I was supposed to get close to her, get her to trust me. Start talking about how I survived being attacked by a guy back in college. How traumatic it was. I said I always wanted to come forward, but I was afraid that no one would believe me. I told her I wished I'd written something down after it happened, or told somebody, kept some kind of evidence. I figured they were looking for dirt on someone, one of Sam's opponents, and that Emma had it. This is standard campaign stuff, digging up oppo."

Nick knew the term. Opposition research.

"That wasn't it," he said. "She had dirt on Sam. They were trying to find out what she knew about him and who she told about it. They must have been studying her so they could get rid of her cleanly and destroy any evidence of what she knew."

Ali rested her hands on the dashboard. "Did they kill her?" she asked softly, looking straight ahead.

"I don't know," Nick said. "They were specifically looking for some kind of evidence she had? Are you sure?"

"Yes. That was the target. What she knew. And if there was a record anywhere. They wanted me to steer her toward talking about any diaries or journals she kept."

"Did they tell you what happened to her? What she knew about? This incident they were digging into?"

"No."

"What did she tell you?"

"Nothing. I couldn't get anything out of her. She started to seem suspicious when I pressed, then stopped returning my calls, so I dropped it. It was one of a dozen jobs I did for David Blakely that month. I didn't think about it again until I saw the clusterfuck that the Widener thing turned into. I started going over everything I had done. I found out she was missing. I realized what I was in the middle of. That's why I went to that house where I found you. I didn't know it would go this far . . . I didn't know people were going to die. I don't need another murder on my head."

She leaned forward, elbows on her knees, holding her forehead, eyes closed. He didn't push her. She was starting to fully grasp that she was an accessory in two killings, maybe three, that her life as she knew it was over.

Sam MacDonough and David Blakely had gone after Emma because of what she knew. She must have been able to connect MacDonough to that woman's death twenty-five years ago.

He had suspected as much, but his mind kept going back to the diary. What if Emma had some kind of evidence?

It offered up a sliver of hope that she might still be alive. What if they had threatened her, and she had given them whatever proof she had? And then what? She ran, hid somewhere? There was a chance—a small chance, but he wanted to hold on to something—that Emma was still out there, that she might even be able to bring this all out into the light.

Ali sat up and looked out the window, her fingers worrying her temple.

"You okay?"

"'Okay' is a stretch. I'm dealing with it."

"Did you ever hear them talking about what happened to Emma? Hear them talk about a diary again?"

"No," Ali said.

"Did David Blakely have a place where he might have taken Emma or kept her? Brought her to ask her questions?"

"He has a country house. I don't know exactly where, but it's on the way to Camp David, near Catoctin Mountain I think."

"Do you remember him talking about it a month ago? That's when Emma disappeared."

"No. He could have brought her there. He doesn't use it often, mostly for VIP events."

Nick's eyes went to the mirror. A cop drove into the lot and pulled up in front of a bank.

"What is it?" she asked.

He raised his hand. She turned and saw the patrol

car. The cop stepped out and looked across the lot, then said something into his mic.

Nick started the engine and rolled toward the north exit from the lot, watching behind him.

He believed what Ali had told him. But right now, he had to get to a phone. They had taken his at the house and he didn't trust Ali's. Delia and Karen both knew Jeff and trusted him. Nick needed to warn them.

60

NICK PULLED INTO an Exxon with a mini-mart, went inside, and bought two prepaid phones. He walked out, keeping his eye on Ali in the car. He tried his wife first, pressing the cell against his ear as it rang so he could hear over the noise of the trucks going uphill on the highway.

"Hi, you've reached Karen. Please leave a message."

He was surprised how much just the sound of her voice affected him, that singsong greeting he'd heard a thousand times. It led him to pause a moment before he spoke.

"It's Nick. Call me back as soon as you can. It's important. And . . . I don't know how to say this, but watch out for Jeff Turner. Don't talk to him. Don't trust him and don't let him near you. I know it sounds crazy, but he's part of this. I'm sorry for leaving like I did yesterday. Just call me, okay?"

He gave her the number for the prepaid cell, then

disconnected. His fist closed around the phone, and he pushed out a breath through tight lips. He had done everything he could to keep his voice even during the call. He didn't want to scare her off or sound like he had lost control, but just mentioning Turner's name sent rage pouring down his back. He couldn't stop picturing Jeff's face in that house as he wrapped his hand around Nick's and so placidly raised the pistol to his throat.

That man had sat across from him at so many dinners in his own home, had smiled along with everyone else as Nick and Karen walked down the aisle. His friend. His brother in arms. A fucking Judas.

The hate felt like something rotting inside him. He longed to give in, let it consume him, turn him into a tool of pure revenge. His hand ached for a weapon. He wanted to put Jeff on the wrong end of a gun. Going after him would be a true test. Jeff knew him so well, how Nick thought and how he hunted down a target. But Nick would find a way. Ali might be able to help him get close to the people behind this. He had to be careful, methodical. He couldn't let the fury get the best of him and warp his judgment.

There was only one consolation in finding out that Jeff had betrayed him. It relieved him of the suspicion that Karen was part of the conspiracy against him. It was Jeff who had led him to those doubts about her—*someone close*—when Jeff was their inside man.

A gas truck pulled in, beeping as it reversed past the open pumps. Nick waited for it to stop, then called Delia.

"Hey," she said.

"You all right?" he asked.

"Yes, why?"

"Is your phone secure?"

"Yes."

"Jeff Turner is part of this."

"Wait, what?"

"I'll explain it all later, but stay away from him. Don't trust a word he says. We were right about MacDonough. He's behind this, he and a man named David Blakely."

"The donor?"

"Yeah. He's the money behind MacDonough."

"What are you going to do?"

"I might have a way to get to them. I'll call you back."

"Be careful."

61

NICK WALKED BACK to Ali's car, parked by the air pumps on the side of the gas station. She was sitting inside the Toyota and stepped out as he approached.

Ali shut the door and leaned back against the car. "So the evidence you put together, is it enough?" she asked.

"To take them down?"

"Yeah."

"Not yet," Nick said. "And no one will believe it coming from a murder suspect. MacDonough and Blakely have the whole town wired. I was trying to do this the right way this morning, and I was nearly executed in that house. I have no idea who I can trust. What about you? It sounds like you know more than your boss thinks you do. How does that work?"

"I didn't want to be just some errand girl, always in the dark and easily discarded. I kept David's secrets. Over time, he used me for more and more sensitive tasks. I paid attention."

"You spied on him, too," Nick said, shaking his head. "Were you going to blackmail him?"

"No . . . I don't know. I wanted to understand what I was involved in. I knew information was valuable. He showed me that. I might need it to protect myself. I might need it for leverage. It was cash in the bank. That's David's real power, knowing people's secrets."

"And he used you to get them?"

"Sometimes."

"How close were you to Sam MacDonough?" he asked.

She looked at him warily, her eyes upturned. Nick saw he had struck a nerve. "Very."

"You got him to trust you?"

"As much as he trusts anyone."

"Did David put you up to that?"

"It was a way to keep tabs on him, to get leverage."

"Do you have anything solid we could use against them?" Nick asked.

"I could tell my story. They'd probably kill me before I could get anyone to believe it, though. That's what Emma was doing, right? Trying to tell the truth. To get the word out. And at least she seemed to have some kind of evidence."

"You don't?"

"No. Blakely's careful. There's nothing written down. Everything is in person or over a secure phone line."

"Why would they take such a risk now? Going after me and Malcolm Widener this way?"

"They don't have a lot of time. Sam MacDonough is about to kick off his public campaign. They need anything that might hurt him gone before that. A clean slate."

"When does he announce?"

"Once he locks up support for his nomination. That could happen as soon as tonight. They can't have any loose ends, anyone who knows about what happened to Widener. Like us."

It wasn't just them. Delia knew. Karen knew part of it.

Ali held her right hand with her left. Nick noticed it was shaking. She shut her eyes.

"Jesus. What was I thinking? I'm going to fucking die."

"I won't let that happen."

"We're not going to get away from these people. They're too powerful."

"I don't want to get away from them. I want to get them in a room and lock the door."

She looked up at him. "You're just going to get yourself killed."

"They're going to kill me anyway."

"You're out of your mind. The police are looking for you. You think you can just get to anyone, anywhere?"

"That's what I do."

Nick could use her help, everything she knew. He didn't think the people back at the house had seen her as she and Nick escaped. They didn't know she was there. The men she worked for still might not suspect her. She and Nick could turn that against Sam MacDonough and David Blakely.

He glanced at the bruise on her wrist. He wouldn't push her into danger, and he wasn't going in on anything with her until he was sure he could trust her. He would offer her an out and see what she did.

"They didn't see you at the house," he said. "They

may not even know you crossed them. You said you convinced them you were still on their side."

"Yeah. I did a whole performance last night to make it seem like I was all in. Reliable. I thought they were going to kill me in David's fucking man cave. It was terrifying, but I sold them on it."

"You're a hell of an actor. I should know. I need your help, but I'm not going to force you into anything. You can get in that car and go back to them, right now. You can pretend none of this happened. You'll have to live with yourself, but you might live."

He had his wallet, plenty of cash to make it into the city. He was going after them with or without her.

"It's your choice," he said.

She opened the driver's door and looked inside.

Ali was probably right. Going straight at them was madness. He wouldn't blame her if she walked, if she went back to Blakely and MacDonough. It could be the right choice. Maybe Emma should never have tried anything as dangerous as telling the truth. Maybe that was the only way to survive in this town, by giving in to power.

Ali climbed into the driver's seat, shut the door, and started the car. Her hand closed on the wheel, squeezing into a fist.

She leaned over and threw open the passenger door.

Nick got in.

"What's the plan?" she asked.

"I need to make a few stops."

62

JEFF TURNER SAT behind the wheel of his Range Rover down the block from Nick and Karen's house. Two kids on BMX bikes rolled by. He watched her through the kitchen window above her sink.

Steam built and ebbed on the glass. She was cooking something and had earphones in, hooked up to her phone.

Nick had tried to call her. Jeff knew that, but her phone never rang. Nick's voicemail never arrived.

Jeff opened a laptop on the passenger seat and scanned the screen. He had been set up on her phone for days. All it took was sitting out here with a stingray, a device that let him spoof a cell phone tower, and he was able to plant malware on her device. After that he had full control, could screen any calls going to her, delete voicemails, and even use the phone's camera and microphone to spy on her.

Listening in on her communications would help him

find Nick. It would also allow Jeff to keep her in the dark, unsuspecting, or stop her from calling for help.

He checked his mirrors. Would Nick come here now? He didn't know. He was a stoic and despite everything might not want to bring the danger back near his wife. But he was desperate, too.

Karen walked through the house, and he tracked her: bathroom, bedroom. He had lost Nick, sure, but that didn't mean he couldn't control him. His friend was a man of simple drives: to protect, and protect what he loved most of all.

He watched Karen slip her sweater over her head and then pull the blinds.

If it came to that, what was one more death? There was a certain grace in his sins. He was already so far gone his only choice was to keep going.

63

SAM MACDONOUGH OPENED the door to the apartment and stepped inside.

"Ali," he called out.

He took his jacket off and hung it over a low chair in the living room. He heard soft footsteps from the bedroom and walked over. Ali stood in the doorway.

"There she is," he said, smiling.

If there was ever a day he could have used a break, it was today. He needed someone like her, part of that world he shared with David, someone who wasn't scared of a little darkness. This thing they had would be over soon, too risky after he announced. He would miss it.

He went to her, took her hand, and put his arm around her waist. Something was wrong. Her body felt a little stiff to him for some reason.

"What's going on?" he asked.

"Sam," she said. "I need to talk to you about something."

He took a step back. He didn't need more problems. Not this week on top of everything else. This place was through the looking glass. He would meet her here and forget the campaign for a moment, forget the ceaseless pressure of the secrets he kept. His whole life, at home, in public, was under a microscope, but here he could be free.

"What is it?"

"You know you can tell me anything," she said.

He crossed his arms, not bothering to hide his annoyance.

"I'm worried about what's happening," she said. "I'm worried about David Blakely. I'm worried you're going down a path that will hurt you in the end."

"Ali, this is all above your pay grade."

"What happened to Malcolm Widener?"

Sam felt his teeth grind together, the muscles in his cheeks standing out. He took a breath, regained control.

"What are you talking about, Ali?"

"What has David Blakely had on you for all these years? It doesn't have to be like this. You can get out from under him. I can help you."

Sam felt the doubt working its way in. She was in his head. He would do anything to be free of Blakely, of that one stupid mistake, one moment of weakness twenty-five years ago he could barely recall. Why should he pay for it for the rest of his life?

But Sam was careful. He couldn't let the doubts show, couldn't let her know she was getting to him. His face was his mask, his instrument, his livelihood, and now he turned it. He wore it neutral, bewildered. Was it a setup? Was she taping him?

"Ali, you're not making any sense," he said. He moved

closer, and she retreated. "What is this?" he asked. His voice was calm, but the anger flashed in his eyes as he grabbed for her.

A hand clamped on his forearm, squeezing the bones like a hydraulic press. His head turned.

A man loomed over him: Nick Averose.

64

NICK HELD A gun between them and let Sam's arm go. The senator took a long step away, his eyes frozen, his mouth drawn tight in a grimace even as he let out a short, shocked laugh. He retreated until he backed into the dresser.

"Are you out of your mind?" he said. "You know who I am?"

The battle cry of the privileged. "That's why I'm here," Nick said.

Sam swallowed, licked his lips and pressed them together. Ali backed out of the room, her eyes on the gun.

This trap had been Ali's idea, a way to lure Sam to a place where he would lower his defenses. Now they had him.

Sam MacDonough watched her walk out of the room and turned to Nick.

"Just put down the gun. You can't do this to a senator. This is suicide. You know that."

Nick nodded. He tried to stay calm, despite the sweat building on his palm. He gripped the pistol. They'd bought it using Ali's driver's license at a sporting goods store in Virginia on their way back to the city, along with some clean clothes and a first-aid kit.

It did feel like a death wish, going after a man like this. Not an exercise this time, the real thing. But he was already dead if they caught him, in prison for life if the police found him. And as he thought of all the pain this man had caused, the fear and the doubt disappeared.

"Emma Blair. Where is she?"

Sam held his hands up. "I don't know."

"She knew what you did, and you hunted her down. Tell me what happened."

"I don't know what you're talking about," Sam said, almost pleading.

"What did she know?" Nick asked. "What have you been hiding all these years? What did you do to that woman?"

"What woman? What are you talking about?"

"Catherine Wilson. Fourth of July twenty-five years ago. The Whitleys' country house. Emma had evidence that connected you to her death."

"You're not making any sense," MacDonough said. "Just tell me what you want. I can help you."

Nick glanced to the right. Through the door he could see Ali in the living room, though she was hidden from the senator's view. Nick had already disabled the security cameras.

Ali reached into MacDonough's jacket pocket and took out his phone.

Nick moved closer to Sam. "You're used to lying without consequence. But think carefully about every word you say. If you lie to me again, you will die in this room."

MacDonough nodded twice, fast.

"Where is Emma Blair?"

"I . . . I don't know."

Nick straightened his arm, leveled the gun. "Don't."

"I . . . listen . . ."

Nick pressed the muzzle to his forehead.

"Please . . . ," Sam said.

"Tell me the truth."

"I can't."

The man's whole body started to shake. Nick could barely remember the fear he had felt the first time he was on the wrong side of a gun, looking down the barrel. He'd forgotten the way it paralyzed him, the way the terror shut the mind down. Year after year of hard training had taught him to control those instincts. But he knew that fear, called it up now. He needed to make MacDonough taste death, because he didn't want to pull the trigger.

He wasn't a killer.

Nick saw it all again: the pistol coming toward his throat that morning, Widener dead in a chair with his blood streaking Nick's hands. As he looked at this man and weighed what he had done, Nick realized he had no idea who he was anymore.

"Three," Nick said, and tightened his grip. "Two." MacDonough closed his eyes. "One." A moan, but no words.

Nick's finger curled around the trigger. He felt the spring push back. A whimper escaped MacDonough's throat.

But Nick didn't pull.

The senator opened one eye, just barely, risked a glance up at him.

Nick looked at Ali, standing now in the other room, waiting for him. She had put the phone back in the jacket pocket.

Nick sidestepped away from MacDonough, toward the door, keeping the gun between them as he backed into the living room.

Ali started walking toward the apartment entrance.

Boom boom boom.

Three hard knocks at the front door. She retreated and stood beside Nick.

"Senator!" someone called through the heavy door. "David Blakely sent us. Open up."

Nick stepped back. The only way out was the window. He gestured Ali toward it with a flick of his head.

MacDonough looked at him from the bedroom. "Just put the gun down," he said. "No one needs to get hurt."

"Senator? Hello? Open the door!" someone shouted from the hall.

Ali unlocked the window and shoved it open. The sound of traffic poured into the room.

Boom. The door strained against its hinges as someone battered it from the outside.

Ali climbed onto the windowsill, then lowered herself down the exterior wall.

Nick kept the gun on MacDonough.

The door shook again with the sound of splintering wood.

Nick moved backward, climbed onto the sill, then leaped out. He hit the ground hard, rolled over his shoulder, and came up running.

65

NICK'S SWEATY SHIRT stuck to his back. His eyes darted to the rearview. His hands grasped the wheel like he was wringing out a rag. A car raced toward them from behind and cut into the lane to their left. He looked at the driver.

"Nick!" Ali cried from the passenger seat, her hands stretching out toward the windshield. A car ahead had come to a sudden stop.

He slammed the brakes, and the car shuddered as the antilock system kicked in over screeching tires. He came to a halt five feet from the other car's bumper and then saw the rare open parking spot that the guy had stopped for.

The car to his left raced forward, and he saw the chrome aftermarket tailpipe. It was an old Crown Vic on custom rims.

Full of kids.

Nick pulled around the car in front. They were in

Ali's Toyota, which they had reached after a minute of flat sprinting away from Sam MacDonough and his men.

"Did you get it?" Nick asked. "His phone?"

"Yes." Ali held up a small blue device, about the size of a thumb drive. She had plugged it into Sam's phone while Nick was in the bedroom with MacDonough.

Before they had gone to MacDonough's apartment, Ali and Nick had met with Delia, and she had given them that bug. It would allow them to set up on Sam's phone, listen in on his conversations, track him, maybe more.

They needed to get the truth out of Sam Mac-Donough, to find some evidence they could use to take him down. Ali had tried kindness. Nick had used threats. But Nick had known that MacDonough was careful, that even a gun in his face might not be enough to shake him.

So Nick had played their own tricks back on them: spy, hack them, get inside.

Nick wanted to rattle MacDonough, see who he called and where he went next. He wanted him on tape incriminating himself. It wouldn't stand up in court, but it would still be something solid Nick could use to show a lawyer or the press.

He drove on, fast and slow, turning without signaling, on highways and quiet residential streets in Brookland, working methodically to spot or lose any tails before he met up with Delia to start exploiting Sam's phone.

He crossed the Anacostia and quickly turned toward the local streets. They passed under a bare canopy of trees, heading back toward the river and the wetlands that surrounded Kenilworth Park and Aquatic Gardens. Beside the park there was a miles-long stretch of swampy riverfront, and he could count on it to be empty out of season.

He pulled down a side road of cracked asphalt, turned on an access path, and parked along a low rise, with a view of the Anacostia and the hills of the National Arboretum across the river.

"Are we clear?" Ali asked, her eyes searching through the surrounding trees.

Nick had good lines of sight on every approach. He sat back and took his first full breath in an hour.

"Yes."

66

JEFF KNEW KAREN was home. He'd been watching. He knocked twice on the front door and waited, listened to her footsteps shuffling through the house. She opened the door a few inches and peeked through, her face wary. She smiled as she recognized him, opened the door wide, and gave him a quick hug around the shoulders.

He turned slightly, so she wouldn't feel the pistol on his belt, then she led him inside and shut the door. Jeff was able to screen her calls, delete any voicemail, but he was still alert, ready to act, wondering if her husband had found a way around him, a way to talk to her directly.

"Any word from Nick?" he asked as she ushered him inside.

She shook her head.

"And how are you holding up?"

"One foot in front of the other," she said.

"What can I do for you?"

She brushed her hair back behind her ear. "I'm not sure yet. I'm glad you're here."

A buzz sounded from the rear of the home. A clothes dryer.

"Give me a second, okay?"

"Of course."

She turned and walked down the hall. He strolled through the house, moving closer, step by measured step, silent along the runner, watching her from behind. He pondered that dancer's neck. Such a fragile thing.

He passed the dining room, remembered the nights they had all sat around the table. He didn't want to do it, to see Karen afraid the way Emma Blair had been. But this whole thing was spiraling out of control. Nick was on the loose, and now he knew who Jeff truly was. He had to be brought in.

Karen trusted Jeff. She was on his side, for now, and she would be useful one way or the other. Jeff had to be careful with her. She was smart, sharp enough to threaten everything.

He paused in the hall, watched her through the crack of the laundry room door, her back to him, her hair shining in the light like summer wheat.

How many had he killed in futile wars? How many to protect and enrich the corrupt? He'd lost count. He had always been a gun for hire, though now, finally, he was getting paid what he was worth.

That was Jeff's gift, his detachment. Kill enough and it becomes mechanical, as thoughtless as slicing steak. He had learned to switch off the hardwired human sympathies. At first, he was startled by how easy that was for him. He had to hide it. It made people afraid. But some of the men he contracted for recognized it and rewarded it. It was rare to find someone with that skill who could also camouflage it, move unseen through the everyday world. That was what made it so lucrative. It had earned Jeff a life like those of the men he'd once served.

His mind went back to the day one month ago when he'd come for Emma Blair. It was a quiet home like this one, a sun-filled parlor. He needed her and the journal that she kept.

He'd brought her to David Blakely's country place, the guesthouse in the back, hidden and secure. He'd leafed through the pages of that diary and read about what she had seen upstairs on that Fourth of July twenty-five years ago.

It turned out that Emma Blair kept many secrets, and now Jeff knew them all. They were as valuable as they were dangerous. He had to be careful, to pick the right moment to make his move and use what he had learned as leverage. If he handled it right, he could become a real player instead of a button man.

In the end, Emma refused to give in, to stay silent. She fought back that day. Jeff once again saw her eyes locked on his as he closed his hands around her throat.

"Jeff?" Karen's voice startled him out of the memory. His hands shot forward an inch before he checked himself. "Is everything all right?" she asked.

"Of course," he said, and pulled his face into a kind smile.

67

NICK AND ALI sat in her car, still parked in the woods along the Anacostia River. She leaned forward, peering through the windshield at the kudzu and trash at the end of the road.

Her face was ashen. She had gone against Mac-Donough, head-to-head. There was no turning back. The reality of it was sinking in as the adrenaline ran out.

"Are you all right?" he asked her. She didn't answer, just clenched her teeth, shut her eyes, and took a long breath in through her nose. He wondered if she was going to break down. He wouldn't blame her. But after a moment she straightened up and opened her eyes as if nothing had happened.

"I'm good," she said, and turned toward him. She looked at his shoulder and frowned. "You've got to let me clean that up."

He followed her gaze to his arm, where blood stained the fabric of his new jacket. It was where Singh had cut him, and it must have opened up as he hit the ground getting out of MacDonough's apartment.

He'd felt it burning but hadn't had much time to give it thought.

He nodded and slipped off his jacket while she reached into the back seat and grabbed the first-aid kit they'd picked up at the sporting goods store. He pulled up his sleeve and she eased off the old bandage.

He watched her work, getting her hands dirty, all down-to-earth competence as she cleaned up the cut. She now looked like the opposite of the woman she had presented to him when they met in his office two days ago.

"How did Blakely get to you?" Nick asked.

"I got to him," she said, and dabbed at the cut.

She looked at Nick's face. "You were expecting something else?" She shook her head. "No. I wanted to be a part of this game. I just didn't know how ugly it really was.

"I used to see Blakely at the private clubs around DC. I was an event planner, part-time. I had a lot of different gigs. At those events, I would see all these guys schmoozing, cutting each other in on contracts, just raiding the government for millions, lighting money on fire. It killed me, because I was smarter than most of them. I worked ten times harder.

"I was poor my whole life, and I was tired of being broke and powerless, at the mercy of guys like that, all the shit they get away with, the things they do to women who don't matter. I wanted to matter.

"I knew David was the real deal. I went up to him at the club one night, Chevy Chase. I told him I wanted to work for him, flirted a bit. He saw through that, but he also must have seen something he could use. I was good at playing a part."

She pulled two Steri-Strips from the kit and peeled them back.

"He used me, and I used him. I learned how he got information, control, influence. There's something about the people in DC; they all seem a little lonely, immature, lost outside of work, especially the guys. It's so easy to get to them. Their world is virgins and whores, day and night, home district and capital.

"So I made myself indispensable to him, his darkside secretary. I was going with it long enough to learn the game, get away from him on my terms."

Ali laid the strips across the cut, tugging them to seal it closed.

"I know escorts who work the bar at the Hay-Adams, and I know the society ladies in Georgetown in their Chanel jackets. The difference is a divorce and a degree, going to the right schools, knowing the right people. That's what I wanted, to be on the inside, to have my own piece of it. I thought I was learning about how power worked. I guess I did. I had no idea how fucked up it would get. I'm sorry. For whatever happened to Emma. For what I did to you."

"You're on the right side of this now."

"I better be," she said as she took out a bandage. "They're going to try to get rid of everyone who knows the truth about them."

Nick tapped the device she'd plugged into Sam MacDonough's phone. "So you're only helping me because you think this is going to work?"

"I don't even know if it will. But I think you're going to stop them one way or another. You got away from

Widener's house. I saw you in that room with Sam. You were so close. I know what you're capable of."

"You just switched teams, then, looking for a better killer, looking out for yourself?"

She snugged the bandage down over the cut. The pressure brought a stab of pain. "What else would I do?"

Car tires ground up the gravel road. Ali watched over her shoulder.

Nick got out, looking for someone coming, but only heard the low whine of an electric vehicle, out of sight, getting quieter. Delia came walking up the hill, her bag over her shoulders. She'd taken a Lyft to get here—her car was still back at the house where Jeff had ambushed Nick—and had it drop her just out of sight.

Nick met her on the path. She hugged him close.

"Did you get him?" Delia asked.

Nick handed her the device. "We got him."

She swung her pack off her shoulder. "Let's get to work."

BEHIND A LOCKED door, unmarked and unremarkable, on the third floor of the Capitol, Sam MacDonough collapsed into a Windsor chair, a glass of bourbon, neat, in his hand. He took a long sip. In the daylight it seemed to burn particularly bright on his palate, but as he choked it back, he could still smell the gun oil, still see down the barrel of Nick Averose's pistol.

His foot shivered against the ground like the needle of a sewing machine. He forced it to be still.

He looked around at the mahogany built-ins, the marble fireplace, the views straight down the Mall to the Lincoln Memorial. That fireplace was where, according to legend, the British had lit their torches before they burned this whole mosquito-infested town to the ground.

This was Sam's hideaway, a second office given to senators, known only to them and a few select staffers, where they could disappear to work or hold confidential meetings while staying close enough to the floor for votes.

This was the same place where he'd met with Malcolm Widener, where he first understood that the truth of that night was coming for him.

He looked into the empty fireplace. His dog rested beside him. He ran his hand over the sleek muscle of its back but found no comfort.

Afraid. He was afraid. Of Nick Averose. Of David Blakely. What did David really have on him? There had to be a way out.

Sam knew how the game worked. It had served him well. You look out for your donors. They look out for you. Someone had shown him the numbers once. For every dollar a company spends lobbying, they make an additional two hundred. David and the other moneymen had made hundreds of millions off his back, and in exchange they'd paved the way for his rise. He was a bagman with pomp. All of it was lawful as long as they avoided the quid pro quo. Everything was unspoken. Everything was perfectly clear.

The scandal wasn't the corruption but how much of it was legal. That was the real business of the Capitol, finding enough money to get reelected, spending 90 percent of your days dialing for dollars from corporations, donors, and interest groups and then voting accordingly.

The Capitol, this massive edifice of steel and stone around him, was for sale. He knew because he had put up the sign, but that didn't make it any less bitter. All of the pageantry—the bald eagles and wigged statues and Columbia holding aloft her flags—was a cover story for the oldest grift, turning wealth into coercion and calling it by the best names: divine right, mandate of heaven, social contract, whatever.

He stood, walked toward the window, and looked out through the Corinthian columns. He saw David Blakely's building, a shining block of glass, and the cranes beyond. There was so much money flowing through this city now. Once you at least had to pretend it wasn't all about cash, but now everything was so blatant. People ran for Congress as a stepping-stone to a job lobbying or contracting, selling influence, the real wealth, the real sway.

He would need one billion dollars to win the White House. That was what a campaign cost. Next to that a few lives were a rounding error, his soul some loose change.

But he wasn't going through all this to end up as another man's servant. He and David looked out for each other. That's what he told himself, but now, with everything coming into the open, he had to face it. David was in control because of what he had seen that night twenty-five years ago, because of the secret he held.

Blakely was always in the right place, always showing up uninvited. His old friend, he thought, curled his lip, and took another swallow of bourbon.

No. He couldn't stand the kid back then. He was always trying too hard at school with his flashy clothes, dressing up like some Ralph Lauren ad, paying for everything, a pretender buying his way into Sam's world. His father had been a serious player in New York and New Jersey construction, got rich by steering state government contracts to his companies, and he'd sent his son down to DC to work his way into the heart of Washington. He figured he could level up and get in on the federal action. David's whole life was a long con, a play for access, and it had worked beautifully.

He was an operator, and Sam had watched him transform, leaving behind that hungry kid from New Jersey. David was always looking for the right hand to shake, the right chance to get leverage. He'd seemed to trail Sam his whole life, prep school, then college. Sam had no idea how David had ended up outside that room on the Fourth of July.

But David had found his moment. Sam had sold him his soul over a dead girl's body and had been trying to buy it back ever since.

He put his hand to the worn stone of the window frame and looked toward the White House.

He was so close. He'd done unthinkable things to keep the past in the past, to get here, to this day. And that was what made his stomach turn. He would have everything, and he'd still be under David Blakely's thumb.

He laughed, long and loud, the sound echoing around the empty hideaway. It felt good, broke through the dread.

The dog cowered.

How had he let himself get so twisted up about this? He was the fucking candidate. That was going to be his house. He was in charge. There was a way to get back control.

He took a breath and drained his glass. "Sorry, David. This is my show."

He lifted his phone. It was time they had a talk. David answered on the third ring. Sam told him he wanted to meet him in the quiet place where this had all begun.

69

NICK DROVE ALONG the Anacostia Freeway, weaving through traffic, while Delia worked on a laptop in the passenger seat. A map was open on the screen, tracking MacDonough's position. Her bug had worked.

"I'm up on his audio now," she said. "If anyone calls, we can listen."

"Did you get anything else?" Ali asked.

"Just the location data. I'll start pulling down his texts and emails."

"They were careful about writing anything—"

"Hang on," Delia said to Ali, and narrowed her eyes to focus. "He's talking to someone."

She pressed a button on the laptop. A voice came over the speakers. "I've got this, Sam."

"No, you don't. Nick Averose had a fucking gun in my face."

"I'll meet you there. I can get you someplace where

we'll both be safe until this is over. We'll get through it. He'll be under control."

"How exactly does that work?"

"I'll tell you in person. But this is going to end tonight."

The call finished, leaving only dead air coming from Delia's speakers, like the soft rush of a stream.

"That was David Blakely," Ali said. "But that's not enough. They didn't say anything."

"Can you hijack his mic or his camera?" Nick asked.

"Not with that phone," Delia said.

Nick turned to Ali. "Will there be anything in his texts or emails we can use?"

"Maybe, but I doubt it," Ali said.

"Where is Sam now?" Nick asked.

"The Capitol," Delia said. "But he's moving. He must be headed out. What do you want to do?"

"Sam and David will be together. We'll know where. We can get to them."

"What does that mean?" Delia asked.

"I can stop them," Nick said.

"How does that work?" she asked while Nick checked the mirror. "You just, what, kill them?"

Nick pushed the gas down and passed the car ahead. "It's protection. They're not going to stop until they've gotten rid of everyone who knows what they've done."

Delia looked from him to Ali, who just nodded her head. "He's right."

"We're inside," Delia said. "We can find something."

He clenched his jaw. He was tired of questions, of waiting, of putting all his faith in the truth like it was some old idol. There were other ways to stop them. Nick knew how.

"That's not you, Nick," Delia said.

It hadn't been. But a lot had changed in the last two days.

"They'll slip," Delia said. "They'll give us something. We can do it the right way."

There wasn't enough time. Nick couldn't stop thinking about David Blakely's calm reassurances over the phone, about one word: "tonight."

"Tonight?" Nick said. "How could he end this tonight?"

"I don't know," Delia replied.

"If they got enough leverage on me?"

"Oh, god." Delia saw it too. "Karen."

There was one way they could get control of Nick—if they had something Nick loved, someone Nick would trade anything for, even his life.

The car jumped forward as he pressed down the accelerator and forced his way into the left lane. He was going home.

Nick's phone rang in his pocket. He answered it.

"Nick." It was Karen, her voice strained. "Where are you?"

70

"I'M DRIVING," NICK said. "By the Anacostia. Are you okay?"

"I think so . . . I don't know, Nick," she said, her voice thoughtful.

"Are you safe?"

"Why wouldn't I be?"

"Where are you?"

"At home."

"Did you see anyone outside? Is anyone watching the house?"

"I haven't noticed anything."

"You need to go. It's not safe there."

"Why not? What's happening?"

"They could be coming for you. I'll meet you some-where."

"Nick, please. Just go to the police. I can meet you there."

"Karen, I know how this sounds, but I can't trust the police. I can't trust anyone. Did you get my message?"

"There was no message. I didn't even see you called. Let's just get together and talk, okay? What about—"

"Karen, no." He realized that if Jeff and the people he worked for were able to intercept calls and delete messages, they could listen in as well.

"What?" she asked.

"Don't say where. They might be listening. Stay away from Jeff Turner. Don't believe a word he says. You need a new phone. This isn't secure."

"Who's listening, Nick?" Her voice sounded desperate now, a whisper. "You're scaring me with this."

The traffic slowed, and Nick cut over into the right lane.

"I'll meet you. I'll explain everything. Is there a place that only you and I would know? Is there a way to tell me so anyone listening wouldn't be able to find it?"

Silence.

"Karen?"

"Sancerre," she said.

Nick thought for a moment, back to when they first started dating.

"Do you remember where that was?" she asked.

"Of course. I'm on my way."

Silence.

"Karen? Karen!"

"I'll be there," she said.

The line went dead.

71

SAM MACDONOUGH POWERED up the hill through the exposed roots and drifting leaves. He put his hand to the rough bark of a beech tree for balance and saw the low concrete platform beside the stream. David Blakely stood at the edge, his back to him.

David didn't seem to notice Sam's arrival. Then he turned and raised his hand.

"I don't remember this being that steep," Mac-Donough said as he approached him, though he was barely breathing hard.

"It was. We just got old."

Sam climbed onto the platform. "God. It hasn't really changed. I should have picked up a bottle of J&B. Remember that?"

"What swill," David said.

"We didn't have much choice."

"People's dads must have had some better liquor."

"We didn't know what was what."

David moved closer, tilted his head slightly as he looked into Sam's eyes.

"Are you okay? I'm sorry my guys didn't get in there earlier."

"I'm fine."

He walked to the edge of the platform. This was where he and a group of friends from St. Albans would come after practice, to hang out and drink stolen scotch. A few would smoke weed they bought near the canal when Georgetown used to be seedy, the last traces of its life as a port town. The others would always let the joint pass them by—booze was fine, but no drugs. They were fourteen and fifteen years old and already thinking about security clearances and future campaigns.

They would walk down here from their school on top of Mount Saint Alban. There the National Cathedral towered over the whole city, and the Bishop's Garden, designed by Frederick Law Olmsted, stood perfectly arranged at the center of the elite precincts of upper Georgetown.

Sam remembered when Malcolm Widener came to him while they were stretching before lacrosse and told him that there was a construction crew getting ready to pour concrete near the hangout, which meant they could leave their mark on this place forever. It was a refuge from the McLean backyards with their putting greens and fieldstone fences and fathers looming over. Those boys would inherit the city one day, if they survived the papered-over family strife and impossible weight of expectations.

Sam brushed away some leaves with his toe.

"Is it still there?" David asked.

Sam nodded as he looked at the names scrawled in

the concrete. There was Ambler's. And his own. And there, at the bottom: *Malcolm.*

Sam crouched down and touched the letters, tinted red with the last sunlight. He remembered the boy, all sinew back then, dragging his finger through the wet concrete. He thought of the words he had spoken to David about Malcolm Widener: *"I need you to handle this."*

With that vague phrase, Sam had ordered his death. The memory filled him with nausea, but he pushed it away. He'd gotten very good at that.

And there was David: *DB.* Sam didn't remember ever inviting him down here, but somehow he'd always shown up. Now he was part of Sam's life forever, set in concrete.

"Are you all right?" David asked.

Sam nodded and rose, stayed calm even as David's gaze lingered on his face. There was dampness along Sam's neck and back, the sweat going cold now, but Sam put that mask up, hid the fear.

"This has all gone too far," Sam said. David's stare unsettled him, but he moved closer. "You should never have gotten rid of Malcolm Widener."

David remained still, except for a slight narrowing of the eyes. Sam waited, felt a quiver working into his calf.

David raised one corner of his mouth and looked up slightly.

"But don't you remember, Sam? You, Sam Mac-Donough, killed Malcolm Widener two nights ago."

Sam stepped back, raising his hand. "No, no." He was at the edge of the platform, but David kept coming. Blakely brought his face close to Sam's and then looked down.

"Can you hear me, Major Tom?" he whispered, and then sang it in a strange tenor. "Can you hear me, Major Tom?"

He crossed his arms and scanned the woods in every direction.

"I guess no one's coming, then," he said, and held out his hand. Sam angled his hip back a quarter inch. The motion was barely noticeable, but David slipped his hand into Sam's jacket pocket. He came out with a small digital recorder with a red light glowing at the top.

David turned off the device, then examined it.

"Come on, Sam," he said, the words like a razor over ice.

Sam started moving to the side, scanning the trees, looking for one of David's killers, but David grabbed his arm before he could get away.

"SAM, YOU'RE FINE," David said. "It's not like that. No one is coming. There's no one else here." He let his arm go. "You think I'm going to hurt you? After everything we've done?"

Sam kept his weight on the balls of his feet. He wiped his hands together, trying to dry off the sweat.

"Did you talk to anyone? The FBI? Justice? Any lawyers?"

Sam cleared his throat. "No, this was just for me. I wanted insurance."

David bounced the recorder in his palm. This clearly was no professional job, no FBI wire. "I like you trying to soften me up with the nostalgia. That was good. Who have you talked to about what's going on?"

"No one."

"And what? You get some evidence, and then you look for a bigger fixer? Some crisis lawyer? Lanny

Davis? Randy Mastro? You put it on me and say I free-lanced the whole thing?"

"I haven't said a word. I was taking precautions."

David tapped the recorder against his palm like it was a pack of cigarettes. "I understand, you know. You thinking you can throw me under the bus. That's DC. That's logical. But since you decided to take the gloves off, let me tell you that it will never work.

"You have blood on your hands, Sam. I saw it. I cleaned it off the floor of that fucking room. We are in this together. We live or die together. All right?"

This was what Sam feared, what consumed him as he stared at the ceiling in the early morning dark.

Sam and David had gone for decades without the full terms of their arrangement ever being spelled out, an unspoken pact.

David was always out there, working on his behalf without even being asked. Everything always seemed to turn in Sam's favor. A golden boy. He never wanted to probe too deeply into what David did for him, in order to insulate himself, but also because he never wanted to face this fact. David had evidence of what had happened that night.

That was why he'd invested so much in Sam's rise. Because he'd owned him ever since that Fourth of July. Now he could use Sam to turn the executive branch into his own personal criminal enterprise if he wanted.

"What do you have on me?"

"Everything. But that route doesn't end well for any-one. That's not what's happening here. I'm not leverag-ing you. I'm protecting you."

"You can drop the good-friend shit. I know what this is."

"I can understand why you would feel desperate after what Averose did to you. We're almost through this, Sam. You may not see it. But this"—he raised the recorder—"is how everything falls apart. Nixon was getting away with it. He won in a landslide in 1972. He would have been fine except for the paranoia and the panic and the tapes. Always the fucking tapes. Look at everything the Kennedys got away with, and now they're saints. No one wants a scandal. This city heals itself. Everyone knows not to go digging because everyone has something buried. You are within hours of having the party behind you. The whole machine—the money, all the officials, the real power—will have your back."

Sam took a few steps along the platform. "But Averose is out there. And Ali Waldron. She knows way too much and now she's working with him."

"I have that under control now."

"How?"

"So far we've been measured." He raised his shoulders. "But the clock is ticking. There is a way to get our arms around this tonight, before we close with the donors, and before you announce."

"I want to know what you're going to do."

"We need to get a little rougher," David said.

Sam kneaded the bones of his right hand with the fingers of his left.

David held up the recorder. "I like this hardball shit, Sam. I like that you're ready to do what it takes.

"Forget optics and insurance, okay? This man is trying to fucking kill you. This is what he does. He gets to people. We need to get you someplace safe, out of the city, someplace he can't touch you. We meet with Ambler there. Everything stays on track."

"And Averose?"

"Once we're protected, my man makes this all go away. All of it. We go to war."

Sam looked at him and felt strangely calm. David had proof. David could destroy him. What Sam had feared for twenty-five years had finally been spoken aloud. There was relief in knowing at last, so clearly, that he had no choice.

73

SANCERRE. IT WAS a French wine, but for Nick and Karen it could only mean one place: the hidden stream valley of Dumbarton Oaks Park, where they had gone on their first night together.

He walked down a dirt road with an old stone wall rising high to his left. The sun was down, the last traces of blue gone from the sky. He was in the heart of Georgetown, a neighborhood of centuries-old town houses, Middle Eastern money, and establishment families, of endless crowds buzzing the luxury shops of M Street, and yet here, only a short walk from the main drag, it all fell away in silence.

A family that combined a political dynasty and a patent-medicine fortune had built up the Dumbarton Oaks estate, once home to Vice President John C. Calhoun, into a little paradise of gardens and a world-class Byzantine art collection, all now run as a museum and research library by Harvard. The valley behind the Oaks, a pastoral landscape of small waterfalls and pools, had ended up in the hands of the Park Service, mostly forgotten and open to all—if they could find it.

The entrance was at the end of an old lovers' lane, a dirt road, all so out of place in the middle of DC's congestion.

He walked along the gravel. A white sign hung from a post outside the Dumbarton Oaks Park entrance. The park was closed, but he pushed apart the gates, the chain rattling as he squeezed through and entered. The trees arched overhead like a cathedral.

They had left Ali's car in the neighborhood, the closest spot they could find, and Delia and Ali were acting as lookouts at the foot trails leading into the park. A cheap pair of earbuds hung from his right ear, hooked up to his phone so he could stay in communication with them.

He moved deliberately, gliding through the shadows in silence and listening for Karen, or an ambush.

They'd come here on their first date, though this place was the last thing he'd expected that night. He had first met her through a friend of Emma's he used to play softball with and would run into her on the political scene in DC: she with her husband, Nick with a gun, guarding. She was always friendly to everyone, with none of that attitude a lot of VIPs had, where anyone on the payroll was treated like a servant and anyone who wasn't in a position to do them a favor may as well have been invisible.

Years after her husband died, Nick had run into her again at the Safeway on Wisconsin Avenue. Many of the Safeways in DC had a joke nickname that locals used, and this Georgetown outpost was known, true to form, as the Social Safeway. They ended up talking for fifteen minutes in the produce aisle, and he finally screwed up his nerve to ask her out.

He wanted to impress her, so he made a reservation at Citronelle, the best spot in Georgetown at the time. While they had a drink at the bar, waiting for their table to open up, she looked around the room. To Nick the place was a well-earned luxury, but he later understood what it must have looked like to her: full of loud, laughing lobbyists with their personal reserves of wine, and well-cured Washingtonians in their bow ties and pearls looking as if a new century hadn't started and Perle Mesta might pop over for dessert.

"Can we go?" she asked, and Nick started trying to figure out how he had managed to screw up the date that quickly.

"Sure. Is everything okay?"

"It's fine. I just—" A cackle as a man in a collarless shirt insisted the sommelier try his wine. "I could use some air."

Nick put down cash for the drinks, and they stepped out.

"Sorry," she said as they went down the sidewalk. "That just felt a little stuffy. I grew up here. Sometimes you see those characters, the look-at-me power stuff, and it kills me. I deal with them for work nonstop. You probably think I'm crazy, but can we just walk?"

"Of course," he said, relieved, actually. He'd spent more than enough time in Washington power lairs like that, though usually he was standing by the wall, on guard and going hungry.

He and Karen walked north. Georgetown still had a few head shops and fake-ID places and thrift stores back then.

She pointed out a modern cinder-block house, standing out against the Georgian and Federal mansions. "Joseph Alsop's. You know, Kennedy, the night of his inauguration, is at the White House, a little buzzed, and Jackie goes to sleep, and he's in that huge house all alone, and he just walks out, comes up here, and knocks on his friend's door, looking for a drink and a bite to eat."

"Is that right?"

"That's how I heard it," Karen said. She always went with the most colorful version of an anecdote. "Sometimes you just want to drop all the pretense and raise a glass, you know?"

They went into a wine and liquor store, where she said she used to come with her fake ID and buy cheap beer for her and her friends from National Cathedral before they went to hang out after school.

But tonight, she picked out a bottle of Sancerre from the fridge. "Trust me on this one, okay?"

He bought it, and a couple of plastic cups. They walked down this dirt road, and sat on the stone footbridge over the stream, and he poured them each a glass.

He remembered how the wine tasted, like a summer picnic that had stretched out lazily until the sun went down and the sky turned red. They sat like that, talking until midnight, when a flashlight came down the trail from the Wisconsin Avenue side, some poor guard, and they ran off like two kids who had just dingdong-ditched a house, trying not to laugh, her hand in his as they cut through the trees.

NICK WALKED THROUGH the empty park. He heard movement to his right and stood still, searched the darkness. Two eyes flashed toward him like glowing coins.

A raccoon. It ran past him and disappeared in the undergrowth. He watched where it had come from, trying to find out if something had spooked it. There was no sign.

He went to the intersection of the trails that led into the park, his best vantage. High fences and walls surrounded most of the park, separating it from the museums and embassies all around.

A soft ring emerged from his headset. He had barely placed it in his ear so he could hear his surroundings better. He clicked the button on the cable to answer the call.

"I talked to Ali a second ago," Delia said. "We're clear."

"Good. Hang tight."

His nerves turned every rustle of wind into someone approaching. He held his pistol by his thigh and watched the trail behind him, shifted his weight from one foot to the other, tried to keep at bay the worst of his imagination: that they had taken Karen, too.

In the distance, a figure seemed to materialize out of the dark. The moon was the only light in the park. Karen came into the far end of the clearing.

He started toward her. She took three more steps and stopped, but he kept approaching. She looked devastated, and he hated himself for bringing this threat down on her.

Her eyes went to his right, to the darkness. He looked, and heard footsteps coming through the leaves in that direction. His phone rang in his ear—he was so focused it barely registered, but he clicked the mic button. Delia spoke as he scanned the woods.

"There are men heading for you, Nick. Down a side path, the way you went in. I don't know where they came from. You need to get out of there."

"Karen," Nick called, and waved her toward him as he raised the gun. "We need to go."

Her face changed. There was no panic or shock. She already knew that someone else was there. And even as he grasped what was happening, he couldn't overcome the instinct to protect her.

"Karen, come on!" She stepped back, three paces, without turning away, her face stricken with an awful blend of pain and guilt and pity.

"Get out, Nick!" Delia said.

His hand was still held out to his wife. "I'm sorry," she mouthed, and stepped back into the dark. He let his arm drop as he heard the men moving toward him from both sides, then he turned and ran.

75

NICK SPRINTED ALONG the path, then stopped, leaning back hard to check his momentum. They would expect him to run. They would be waiting, would sweep toward him, close in on all sides.

He needed to do what they wouldn't expect. He slipped silently to his right, where almost no light fell, toward a tree growing over the stream, just beside the footbridge where he and Karen had sat that first night.

They were doing a careful search, closing in on him. He didn't know how many of them there were; at least four from the sound of it. He needed stealth for the moment, needed to stay out of sight until they passed, to get behind them so he could get away or take them silently one at a time.

He stepped into the water, so cold it burned, then waded in as flashlight beams moved through the park, flickering between the trees. His phone was on silent, and he tucked it out of sight on one of the stones under the bridge.

He lowered himself into the stream down to his waist, felt the water soak into his clothes, his skin and muscles tensing against the chill, heels slipping into the muck of the streambed.

He crawled back, under the bridge. The light shot across the surface as the sound of men running grew louder. The beam came around the bridge, to where he was crouched. He lay back, took a long breath, and sank his head below the water.

Boots pounded the earth. Voices above. Below the surface they sounded like murmurs. The light flashed by, warm red through his closed eyelids, and then black again. He waited, lungs squeezing, air running out as his heart raced. Each beat boomed like a kettledrum in his submerged ears.

He brought his face closer to the surface, and the light returned. He sank down.

Hold. Calm. Hold.

The darkness returned, and he risked a breath, brought his face above the water and filled his lungs.

Thump . . . thump.

One man on the footbridge overhead, pacing slow. Nick rose, his wet clothes weighing him down. All he wanted to do was move, act, rush, but he forced himself to go inch by inch, to stay silent. He felt for the underside of the span and twisted his head to get a glimpse of the man above.

He was facing the other way, holding a pistol fitted with a suppressor. He halted. The light shone into the water on the far side, then turned Nick's way.

Nick came from under the bridge, snatched him by

the legs, and hauled him to the side. The man dropped hard, striking the stones with the sound of a well-hit line drive.

The flashlight fell, cast a half circle along the path and through the trees as it rolled to a stop. Nick stepped onto the bridge as the man rose on one knee.

Nick punched him in the jaw, twisting his head to the left. He sprawled unconscious on his stomach.

Nick grabbed the pistol from his hand, then killed the light.

Had the others heard? They must have seen the light. He jumped down to the side of the stream and retrieved his phone. The lights were deeper in the park now. He had made it behind them and might have a path to the exit.

He cut through the woods, closer to the museum fence line, with its brick walls and wrought iron gates. The flashlights turned his way, but he was far from them now, hard to spot in the brush. He ran, the air freezing against his damp skin, back to the gate where he had entered and the dirt road.

The gate was too obvious an exit, so he slipped along the fence toward a neglected corner of the park thick with undergrowth. He ran hard at the wall, jumped, and planted his foot against the brick, getting his hands up over the top, his palms grinding into the old stones. He pushed himself up, stayed low, and dropped toward the sloping dirt on the far side.

He ran back to the street and saw the glow of a dome light down the block: someone getting into an SUV. He stayed close to a brick wall and ran toward it, a Chevy Suburban. He could make out Jeff's profile through the back window. Karen sat next to him.

He kept the gun at a low ready as he closed in, fifty feet away. She held her hand out and placed it on Jeff's shoulder. A few words passed. No fear. No threat.

Nick ran as the truck pulled out, a hundred feet off now. There was no way to shoot through the glass at this distance without being as likely to hit her as Jeff. The red glow of the truck's taillights disappeared over the hill.

If he had been trying to find some way not to believe what he had seen in the park, to not believe that she had betrayed him, there was no hope now. It left him in shock, as numb as his fingers.

76

DELIA WAS CALLING. He put the headset in his ear and answered.

"Are you okay?" she asked, her breath rapid, the words clipped.

"I made it out. Where are you?"

"On the move. R Street. They got Ali."

"What?"

"Two men. I saw them throw her in the back of a car, a black Suburban. She fought them, and god, one of them punched her in the head so hard. She just dropped. It was . . ." Delia cursed under her breath.

"Did they see you?" he asked.

"I don't know."

"Go toward the car. I'll find you."

He was already running down the brick sidewalks, the quiet tree-lined streets, sprinting as hard as he could, his lungs burning.

He raced on, dodging a car as he shot across an intersection, and then saw a woman moving, away from the streetlights. Delia.

He crossed the street. She turned toward him, her face full of fear, and then a sad relief.

He led her south toward the car. "Which way did they take Ali?"

"Toward Wisconsin Avenue. But they have too much of a lead on us now. What happened to Karen?"

"She . . ." He couldn't get into it. "What's the last location you got on Sam MacDonough's phone?"

"I just checked it," Delia said as they crossed the street. "They were heading northwest into Maryland, way out of town."

"Ali said David had a country place out there in the mountains. On the way to Camp David somewhere. It's secluded. It sounded like it could have been where he brought Emma Blair."

"I can pull up Sam's location when we get to the car."

"David said he and Sam would be together. Someplace safe."

"What are you thinking?"

"If I can get to them, I can put an end to all this from the top down."

They kept going past the mansions and row houses, all cobblestones, narrow streets, and alleys here. He stopped at the corner beside a high brick wall covered with ivy and leaned out, peering toward the car. He wanted to check if the attackers had found it, if they were lying in wait.

As he searched the dark, Delia's fingers drove into his forearm. She pressed against him.

He turned to see a man coming at them from behind.

The gun in his hand shone dully under the streetlights as he raised it and aimed straight at them.

Nick threw his arm around Delia's shoulders and brought her into his chest, twisting away from the gunman and covering her with his body as he drove them both forward around the corner.

Tss. The bullet sounded like a knife on a sharpening stone as it flew past and he took another step.

Tss. Chunks of the brick wall blew out to their left in a red cloud. Bits dug into his neck. He held her and pushed on, fully around the corner now. He pressed against the wall, taking cover, his left arm around her shoulder, cradling her against him while he raised his own gun and faced the corner, waiting for the man to come, ready for his shot.

"Nick," Delia said as she pushed him away from the wall.

Snap. Her body tensed against his. She cried out in pain.

HE TURNED, SWUNG the gun away from the corner, and saw a second figure coming toward them with a pistol in his hand on the street where they had taken cover.

That man's bullet had struck Delia.

Nick took aim and squeezed the trigger. The gun flinched in his hand and spat white from the end of the suppressor. The man fell.

Nick felt blood on his arm, and he saw the flat terror and pain in her eyes. "No no no." He said it over and over.

He supported her as they walked toward Ali's car. She grew heavier, weaker with every step. "Just hang on, okay? Hang on."

He scanned the street behind them as they walked, sweeping it with his gun. A figure emerged near the corner, pistol in hand. Nick fired two shots, opened the passenger door, and helped her in.

He ran to the driver's side, still covering that corner, then started it up and gunned it out of the spot.

She was still breathing, her heart still going, her hand over the wound. It was high up on her chest near her shoulder. She had slipped her backpack onto the floor.

Her eyes closed, and she fought to open them, then shut them again. He reached and pressed his hand over hers, putting pressure on it, on her fingers so cold. She whimpered, ground her teeth together.

"Delia, it's going to be okay."

She shut her eyes, tilted her head back, and took long, slow breaths through pursed lips.

The moment when she'd been shot kept replaying in his head. Nick had her covered with his body, but she had tried to push them both out of the way, had exposed herself to save him.

He maneuvered the car with one hand, flying through the side streets, racing toward Georgetown University Hospital.

"I'm cold, Nick."

"One more second, okay? Just stay with me."

"How'd I do?" she asked.

"Great, sweetheart. You did great. You saved us both back there." He could barely talk, seeing her there so small, holding out against the pain, silent, still. "Your mom and dad would be so proud."

A faint smile touched her lips, then disappeared as her head slipped to the side.

78

NICK STOPPED THE car outside the ER and jumped out to help Delia from the passenger seat. A nurse marched toward them, and they eased Delia onto a stretcher.

He had called ahead as he drove and said he had a gunshot-wound victim, using all of the priority language he remembered from his Secret Service days. He spoke like a first responder and wanted them ready. He dropped the call before they had a chance to ask for his bona fides.

He walked in beside her and handed over Delia's wallet, with her ID and insurance cards. He needed to forestall as many questions as possible, standing here in damp clothes, looking like a psychopath. The gun was in his jacket pocket, the suppressor now removed, too big to conceal attached.

"And you are?" the nurse asked.

"I found her on Water Street. I don't know what happened. She was on the ground, bleeding."

This was the closest hospital to the attack. Nick knew that this would most likely end with him in the hands of the police or the killers. It didn't matter. All he cared about was whether Delia, her fingers like ice, would make it.

He moved with the nurse quickly down the corridor, out of the waiting area. Over his shoulder he noticed a uniformed cop.

Delia's eyelids were just barely open, showing only the whites as the nurse checked her airway and they rolled toward the treatment rooms.

"You'll have to stay out here, sir," the nurse said, but he couldn't let go, couldn't take his eyes off Delia's face, strangely serene in the middle of all this horror.

A hand pressed on his chest, and he turned to find himself facing another nurse, a guy maybe six foot two, with deep-set eyes and heavily muscled arms sticking out from under his scrubs.

"It's for her sake you can't go in," he said. Nick stepped back. He saw the cop again, and the intake receptionist, armed with her clipboard. He pressed against the wall and noticed a side corridor.

Two doctors strode past him, looking serious, heading for the room where they had taken Delia. The first nurse had disappeared, and in the reflection on a glass partition on a desk, Nick saw her talking to the police officer.

He needed to be here in case anyone came for her, but getting thrown in jail wouldn't help them. He would have to find a place out of sight where he could stand post. He looked for his moment, then slipped down the hall and into the night.

He took a spot outside near the exit with a view of the main door and the entrance to the parking lot, rested his hand on the pistol in his pocket, and waited.

79

NICK PACED, FIGHTING to stay warm. How long until Jeff and his men found out that she was here? He saw the headlights of a truck pulling into the lot and gripped the gun.

As it came closer, he could make it out: a white pickup with a college-aged woman driving. He relaxed slightly and turned toward the hospital doors as they swept open.

It was the cop from the waiting area, backed by two hospital security guards, both armed. Nick weighed his options, decided in an instant. He had already seen the patrol car parked a hundred feet up the sidewalk. There was only one cop. That was good.

He wasn't going to kill three men just for doing their jobs, and if they tried to detain him, the easiest way out was to get locked up in the back of that car. He stepped to the side, ditched the gun and suppressor discreetly in a bush, and walked away from them.

"Hey, sir!"

He kept walking.

"Stop!"

It was a direct command from law enforcement. Playtime was over. He stopped and turned.

"Were you with that woman who came in? The Water Street incident?"

"Is she okay?"

"She was shot."

"Is she okay?"

"How did you find her?"

"I don't want anything to do with this. I found her. I helped her. That's it. Can you tell me how she's doing?"

A light shone in his face. He knew he looked like a drifter.

"What's your name?"

Nick had left his ID in Ali's car. He didn't want to show up on any system, didn't want to lead the men hunting him here. Surely the police had his name, his description. Perhaps it was a good thing that he felt barely recognizable after being dragged through the silt.

"I don't want to get involved."

The light lowered. The cop stood a few feet away, right hand drawn back, hanging a few inches from the grip of his pistol.

"Do you have some ID?"

"No."

"Why not?"

Nick raised his hands, no threat. "Can you tell me if she's going to make it?" He wasn't sure if that was aiding his case, but he couldn't help it. He had to know.

The policeman appraised him. "Turn around," he said.

"What for?"

"Turn around." The cop put his hand on the gun. Nick complied. Cuffs wouldn't be too much of an issue. The bracelets closed on his wrists, and the cop walked him over to the patrol car, sat him on the bench seat in the back. The two guards walked off.

Alone. Good. The cop was calm. That was what he needed.

Nick sat against the vinyl, took in a shallow breath, the smell of sick and fear that always lingered in a cruiser's back seat. A steel cage separated the back seat from the front. The officer closed the door and sealed him in.

He saw him talking on his radio, standing a few feet from the car. The officer pressed his lips together until they disappeared. Bad news.

Nick just needed a minute alone. That man was the only officer on duty. He would go back in to question the nurses, find out more. There would be a chance.

The driver's door opened, and the cop sat down behind the wheel and started working on the mobile data terminal. It was turned so that Nick couldn't see it.

"So start at the beginning. How did you find her?"

Nick didn't answer. He could wait this rookie out. He kept his eyes on the driveway.

"There are just some simple questions and I can let you go."

No answer. The cop glowered at him and kept working on his terminal, searching. Nick watched the entrances and exits. This was not his first time working surveillance from a patrol car, though the cuffs were new.

Headlights at the top of the drive. Black Suburban.

It stopped near the other hospital entrance. Two figures emerged.

They were here.

It felt like his heart had ground to a halt in his chest. He leaned forward.

"I will tell you one thing," Nick said. "If she is still alive, she isn't safe. She told me that much when I brought her here. Whoever shot her will find her and try to kill her."

The officer looked at him in the mirror.

"She needs protection," Nick said.

"From you?"

"No."

"Is that why you're not talking? You know who did this?"

"They are going to kill her. Just go inside. Keep watch. They're coming."

Nick craned his head to the side, saw the glowing text of the cruiser's data terminal, read the messages scrolling down the side window. There was a call out, with a description. His description. And as the text scrolled by, he saw an image at the bottom: an old headshot from his time in the Secret Service.

"Please," he said, and ground his teeth together, trying not to slam his body against the barricade in rage and frustration, trapped here while those killers closed in on Delia.

The officer swallowed and looked him in the eyes.

80

JEFF STROLLED DOWN the hospital hall, his shoes squeaking slightly against the linoleum, utterly at ease. Doing high-end security often involved working with the police, and he knew how to copy their mannerisms, that unmistakable bearing of the law. There were always cops waiting around in emergency rooms. They would have to get an arrestee checked out at a hospital and given a clean bill of health before he could be transferred to custody.

He carried false credentials, too, just in case, but no one tried to stop him as he walked past triage and up to the nurses' station.

"Hey, I'm here about the GSW."

"Trauma three," the nurse said.

"She going to make it?"

"You should ask them."

"Did anyone come in with her?"

She opened her eyes wide and nodded. "Weird guy, looked like he rolled through the gutter."

"Where is he?"

"Disappeared as soon as he dropped her off," she said.

Jeff scowled. "All right. I'm going to be hanging out outside the victim's room." He pulled a pad from his coat, jotted down a number, and tore out the page. "If you see that guy again, call me immediately. That's my cell. He did this. He may come back and make sure he finishes the job. Don't let anyone else back there."

"Okay," she said, and took the paper, her lips pressed into a flat line. Nurses were tough by necessity, but that kind of cruelty got to her.

He pressed his hand against his pocket, where he carried a small kit with a fourteen-gauge needle and two vials. "Don't worry," Jeff said. "I'll look out for her."

He tapped twice on the desk and started down the hall toward the treatment rooms. He passed the trauma room—empty—and then found her in a bay. He pulled the curtain closed.

Delia's head was to the side, but as he got closer, he saw her chest move, saw the bandage poking out from under the gown. He looked at the heart-rate monitor. It seemed like they had gotten her into a stable condition. An intravenous line ran into her arm.

He traced its plastic tubing and saw what he needed, a small port in the IV that could be used to inject medicine.

After pulling on a pair of latex gloves from the box on the wall, he took the syringe out and looked at the two vials.

Jeff chose the one on the right and filled his needle with a faint yellow liquid.

He slipped the syringe into the port on the tube, put his thumb on the plunger, and poured the liquid into her arm. She moaned softly, turning her face toward him, and he sealed his hand over her mouth. Her eyes fought to open and now stared into his.

"It's okay," he whispered, pushing down as she struggled weakly against his weight. "It's okay." He said it over and over, in that soothing bedtime-story voice, until her eyes closed and she fought no more.

81

NICK STARED INTO the cop's eyes. The man's cell phone warbled, and he answered it, then stepped out of the car. He talked for a moment, looked at the patrol car and the hospital, and then walked toward the entrance.

Nick watched him until he stepped inside and then rolled onto his side. He took a deep breath, relaxed his shoulders, and eased the cuffs around, under his legs. He barely had room in the confines of the back seat, but he managed to pass the restraints under his feet and brought his hands in front of them. The chains on the standard Smith & Wesson cuff gave him slightly more latitude than the cuffs that Delia had shown him two days before.

He thought of her, of her half smile as she said "yoga." He pictured the killers moving toward her now, imagined her gone, her young life ended, never another word, and it filled him with a rage like a high fever, left his mind empty of all but a simple drive to close in on and destroy Jeff and anyone else who got near her.

He dug his fingers underneath the armrest and tore it off. Ten wires ran to a plastic harness inside the door near the window control. Four were cut. That was how they disabled the back windows in police cruisers. He pulled them all from the harness and started connecting different wires, looking for power.

He heard the whine of an electric motor deep in the door, but the window didn't budge. That must have been the switch to put it up. He touched another pair together and the windows slid down. Fresh air streamed into the car.

Nick grabbed at the roof and hauled himself out. He crouched low, using the car for cover, and then ran to the bushes and retrieved the gun, holding it in front of him, his hands still cuffed.

He started moving toward the black car parked near the other entrance. Its lights turned on, so bright he could barely see someone going toward it: a man pushing a wheelchair. Nick ran along the side of the hospital, sticking close to the landscaping for cover. Shielding his eyes as he moved closer, he saw the man carrying a small figure into the back of the truck. The interior light shone on their faces. It was Jeff and Delia.

The truck's door slammed shut as the driver pulled out and sped through a quick U-turn. Nick's feet pounded the concrete as he sprinted after, flying over the ground. The red taillights grew smaller in the distance as the SUV neared the exit. He pushed faster, lungs tightening, thighs burning, heart hammering in his chest, but he had no chance now as the truck pulled through the exit, barely slowing as it turned onto Reservoir Road.

Nick stopped and nearly collapsed as the dread overtook him, an awful weight low in his gut. She was gone.

82

DAVID BLAKELY PULLED open the oak front door of his country house.

Alan Ambler stood outside.

"Come on in," David said, and waved him across the marble foyer. Normally, David didn't answer his own bell, but there was no household staff working this evening. Tonight's conversation would be closely held.

The first floor was a cavernous open space with sweeping views of the mountains that hemmed in the compound. It looked more like a clubby resort hotel than a private home. Modern chandeliers hung from the cathedral ceilings, filling the space with soft yellow-orange light.

They turned down a side hall, and Sam MacDonough walked out to greet them.

David ushered the two men into the library, all blond wood and Alvar Aalto originals, and left them to talk as he went behind the bar for a fifth of Pappy Family

Reserve. He slit the foil on the five-figure bottle. To-night they were celebrating. He poured three glasses and joined Sam and Alan in the sitting area.

He watched Ambler leaning in closer, inch by inch, while Sam eased back in his chair. It was Sam's final audition for the presidency, and he looked as relaxed as a guy sitting at home on a couch watching a ball game.

David's second phone vibrated in his pocket. He quieted it, then slipped the screen out for a glance. He stood and left the room. He'd been waiting for this call.

He headed for the rear of the house and raised the phone to his ear.

83

JEFF SAT IN the passenger seat of the Suburban as they drove northwest out of the city. He looked over his shoulder, where Singh sat in the back seat beside Delia's limp body.

Her chest rose and fell in a deep, artificial sleep.

"Is she stable?" he asked.

"For now. The gunshot went through her chest muscle. It didn't enter the cavity."

Jeff lifted his secure cell and called Blakely.

"Where is Averose?" David asked.

"He ran."

A cold silence.

Jeff looked at Delia and the rust-colored blood staining the bandage near her shoulder. "But we have Delia Tayran," he said.

It would have been cleaner to simply eliminate her—the fewer people out there who knew the truth, the better—but now they might need her as leverage on Nick.

"Bring her here."

"Are you sure?"

"She's close to Averose?"

"Like family."

"Would he give his life up for hers?"

"Without a second thought."

"Then we use her to get him under control."

"Are Ali and Karen there?"

"On the way. The others are bringing them."

Jeff had handed off Karen to two of his men after the ambush so that he could go after Nick. He told her she needed to stay with them, that it was just a way to keep her safe for a while.

"We have everyone who knows except for Averose," David said.

"The guesthouse?"

"Yes. Keep her out of sight and come in the back way. I'm about to close this, and I can't have any loose ends."

84

NICK SAW A patrol car pacing him two blocks back, so he turned right. He kept on, driving the exact speed limit, waiting for the cop to come, for the flashers to light up. But it drove straight past him. The escape from Georgetown left him with his face flushed.

He was driving Ali's Toyota. Delia's pack full of gear was on the floor in front of the passenger seat. He'd gone into it for a pick and opened the double lock on the cuffs.

He pulled over in Friendship Heights and checked Delia's computer. A photo of David Blakely was up on the web browser. The malware they had planted on Sam's phone was still reporting his location. It was stationary now, in the mountains outside Frederick.

He switched the map to a satellite view and zoomed in on the address. It was a compound, ten or fifteen acres, with a massive main building that looked like a retreat center and a guesthouse in the back. Sam was there, and David had said that he was going to keep him

close, take him somewhere they would both be protected. That house fit the bill.

Nick pulled out. He didn't know if Jeff would have
taken Delia and Ali there, too. But there might be a way
to find out. Nick reached into Delia's bag and pulled out
one of the prepaid phones.

He dialed a familiar number and listened to it ring as
he gripped the wheel. The call connected, and he heard
the voice of an old friend, Jeff Turner. "Who's this?"

"Is she alive? Delia?"

"Nick." He was startled for an instant, but then he
kept on, calm. "She is."

"What do you want?"

"Come in. You can protect her. Protect all of them if
you play this right."

"All of them?"

"Delia, Ali, Karen. We only want you. We want this
all to go away. You come in, and they'll be safe."

A trade. His life for theirs.

"Where are you?" Nick asked. He heard faint voices
in the background.

"No, Nick. I know you. I know what you're thinking,
but coming after us is hopeless. If you give yourself up,
they'll be okay. I swear. I'll set up a place where we can
meet."

He found himself wishing it were true, a simple sac-
rifice. He would have taken the deal in an instant if Jeff
hadn't betrayed him twice, hadn't destroyed and cor-
rupted everything he loved. No, he wouldn't hand himself over to die, because he knew the others would die
with him. Ali was right. Jeff now had everyone who
knew the truth. He was drawing a circle around this,

burying the past. They could get rid of everyone who knew about Malcolm Widener's death.

Nick didn't answer. His tires beat a steady rhythm on the road.

He had no choice. There was no deal. The clarity washed over him like a shower after three days' march. He wouldn't die for nothing, for a traitor's promise. If he was going to give up his life, he would do it by going straight at Jeff and the men he worked for.

Coming after us, Jeff had said.

"You're with David Blakely and Sam MacDonough," he said. "They need you to protect them."

A disdainful laugh from Jeff, but he laughed an instant too late. Nick knew him so well; he had thrown him. Nick was right.

"Don't get them killed thinking you can fix this." There was cross talk in the background. "I'll call you back. Keep your phone on."

"I'll call you. It'll be a different number."

He smashed the phone down on top of the wheel, cracking it in half, raining plastic shards into the foot well. He dropped it onto the seat beside him and pulled out the board. Of course Jeff wanted him to keep it on. They would try to track it.

Nick pressed down the gas pedal. He was going to that house. He wasn't 100 percent certain, but it was enough for him to plan his next moves.

Jeff had taken Delia, and Nick had to assume he was at that country house or on his way. Sam was there, and most likely David. If Nick got his hands on those two, he could get the answers he needed in any case. He could put an end to all this. Cut off the head and kill the snake.

He moved by instinct: the simple draw of revenge, of protection. It burned in him, made the skin of his face feel hot and tight, made his heart pump too fast, but the clarity of it brought a kind of solace.

This wasn't him. But he had no choice. He would become everything he hated: the threat, the assassin. David Blakely's estate would surely be locked down like the White House. David was careful, and Jeff knew how to turn a site into a fortress.

He didn't know how many guards they would have. Going after it on the fly was suicide. But that didn't matter anymore. He passed a car, his speed climbing, ordering the rest of the night in his mind, what he was up against, and what he needed, and where to get it.

Acetone and peroxide, maybe black powder, and something he could use to blind them all, to make himself invisible.

DAVID STRODE ACROSS the back deck of the main house. He ignored the wind running down the hills, cutting through the wool of his jacket as he watched the rear entrance to the estate.

A black Suburban pulled in and wound toward the guesthouse. David was bringing them all here. He had everyone in hand who knew the truth, and with them he would be able to control Nick Averose.

He could shut this whole mess down tonight. This property was safe, secluded, surrounded by guards and completely under his control. That was why he had brought Sam MacDonough here. Jeff Turner was arriving now. He'd known Nick Averose for decades. He could anticipate him, counter him, play on his psychology.

But David hadn't brought Sam here only for his protection. David had brought him here to protect himself. Sam had tried to make a move against him with that recorder, a predictable and understandable panic, but still a threat.

He wanted him here tonight under watch. He wanted him close and complicit for these final steps, so that Sam would be just as exposed as David was, so that he could never leave David holding the bag. It was a way to renew the unspoken pact they had made twenty-five years ago.

David watched one of his guards patrol the fence, then stepped back inside. He went into the library, where Ambler and Sam were talking, and closed the door silently behind him. Sam gave him a smile as David stood just inside, looking over Ambler's shoulder.

"One last question, Sam," Ambler said. "Your life is about to be under a microscope. Is there anything you need to tell me? Anything that might come out during the campaign that we need to prepare for? I'd rather find out now than on the front page of the *Times*."

Sam thought for a moment, his lips pressed together, then shook his head. "I'm an open book."

Ambler let out a breath. "Great. You wouldn't believe the shit I hear."

They rose, both understanding that their conversation was drawing to a close. Ambler walked toward the door.

"Did he pass?" David asked.

Ambler grinned. "I have to go. I need to make some calls from the car, but I think we're in excellent shape."

"I'll walk you out," David said. He strode with Alan through the foyer while Sam hung back near the library.

"So?" David asked Alan.

"I think you have this. I need to take a couple of people's pulses again, but I'm all in. I'll call you back in, say, a half hour or so and let you know the verdict from the rest of the committee."

"If you had to bet?"

"I'm confident. Start thinking about the best way to make the announcement."

86

NICK CHANGED CLOTHES and cleaned himself up in a gas station bathroom before hitting the first spot on his list: Sally Beauty. He bought a pint bottle of concentrated hydrogen peroxide—sold as a liquid developer to lighten hair—along with a tube of hair dye and a bag of cotton balls for show. He gave the clerk a compliment on her gels—a diamond on each finger—and walked out two minutes before the place closed.

He found an open armory. A bell rang over his head as he pushed into the store and the man behind the pistol case looked up. Nick nodded his head solemnly. There was always an air of unspoken violence and ugly but necessary duties in a gun shop.

He browsed long enough to not seem desperate and looked at a few pistols with the unrushed manner of a man indulging a hobby, not arming for battle. He still had the gun he'd taken from the man in Dumbarton

Oaks, though he hadn't been able to pick up the suppressor in the rush from the hospital. Nick preferred the other pistol, the one he'd bought before he cornered Sam MacDonough in the apartment. It was a striker-fired Smith & Wesson .357 SIG, the same gun he normally carried. All he needed was ammo—a hundred and fifty rounds of jacketed hollow-points—four extra magazines, a cleaning kit, and two mag holsters for his belt.

He eyed an AR-15 carbine, the weapon like a second limb from his time in the military, but buying a gun would raise red flags. He could do a lot more damage with a rifle, but that was fine. He would be in close anyway.

Next was Walmart. He moved with a cold efficiency, taking care as always with prep and gear. A bullhorn. A knife. Acetone. Blackhorn 209 powder. A little green box from the garden center. A few cheap metal thermoses. And as he checked out with the cashier, a young mumbler with gauges in his earlobes, Nick looked at the locked cabinets full of pregnancy tests and Sudafed and cigarettes.

"And a pack of Camel Wides," Nick said.

He threw his purchases into the back of Ali's car while scanning the lot, thinking about his preacher friend from this morning. If ever he needed a blessing, it was now.

He climbed into the driver's seat and headed for the mountains.

They rose higher as he drove. The highway began to climb and fall, tracing the first foothills, the ridges shadow upon shadow across the night sky.

He exited the interstate and wound along country roads, climbing through switchbacks, heading for the top of a long ridge. The trees grew so dense they blacked out the stars. He avoided the main routes. He had to come at them unseen.

A yellow sign warned of a sharp turn ahead, and Nick pulled into the narrow shoulder of the hairpin turn.

He could see the lights of an estate in the valley below. David Blakely's house.

87

IN THE GUESTHOUSE at David's estate, Ali stood as the door opened. She took a step back as two men walked into the suite where she was being held. She recognized one of them from outside Dumbarton Oaks. Singh, someone had called him, before he sent Ali to the ground with a vicious blow to her eye.

They carried a young woman, stumbling between them through the sitting room, moaning quietly in pain. She seemed to be drifting in and out of consciousness. Her head swung to the side and Ali saw that it was Delia.

Ali gasped, her hand rising toward her mouth. Singh led Delia into a bedroom. A moment later, Jeff entered the suite and watched through the bedroom door as the two others settled Delia on the bed.

Jeff's eyes went to Ali, and he strolled slowly toward her across the sitting room. The left side of her face was a mask of pain, and her balance was still off. She reached back and grabbed the arm of a chair to steady herself.

"Why would you go against us, Ali?" Jeff said, moving closer still, his eyes inches from hers.

"I thought it was the right play," she said, bottling up the fear, her eyes not wavering from his. She looked around the room. "Is this where you brought Emma Blair?"

"It doesn't have to be like that for you, Ali. The martyr thing."

He put his hand against her cheek, the skin of his palm soft and cool, and then he gripped it, hard, and the pain made the room spin.

"How much does Nick Averose know?" he asked, squeezing harder.

She cried out but didn't answer.

"Don't make me do this, Ali. Who else did you talk to?"

He let go and she took a stumbling step back, put her hand to the wall.

"Ali, please. There's a way out of this. It's up to you."

88

NICK WANTED HIGH ground. He wanted the weakest point in the estate's perimeter. He bumped along on a fire road, fighting the wheel as he climbed the hills behind the compound. A black line of clouds moved across the night sky, far to the north.

Just behind the ridgeline, he pulled over, leaned down, and tugged out the fuse for his running lights. The car was blacked out, and he went on by the moon's glow, barely crawling until he could see the compound below. He pulled to a stop a hundred yards from the power lines that fed the estate.

The main building looked like a luxury hotel with massive multilevel decks facing the hills and twenty-foot windows along a great hall.

Where are you? Nick thought. He wanted Jeff and David and Sam, and needed to know where they might be keeping the others. He lifted a brand-new spotting scope and scanned the windows and doors. Men in dark suits with military bearings guarded the entrances. Patrols moved along the perimeter. There were at least a dozen guards.

He looked over the fences. Along the front of the estate there were iron pickets, relatively easy to bypass but too exposed. At the rear of the property, down the hill from where he had stopped, the fencing was more secure: chain-link with barbed wire, all well lit. He'd seen worse. Razor ribbon would've been more secure but would have killed the refined air Blakely was shooting for.

The guesthouse, a mansion in its own right, stood near the back of the property between Nick and the main house. The guesthouse had a private pool, covered for the season, alongside a pair of tennis courts. He surveyed its rear facade and the windows along one side but saw nothing. All the blinds were drawn.

He and Jeff had once been like brothers. They had trained and fought side by side for years in the marines. Even under threat, pulses pounding but minds calm, they could operate without a word. They knew each other that well.

If Nick were down there, if he knew someone was hunting him and his client, he would have reinforced that guesthouse, set it up in advance so they could hole up if an attack came. It was three stories and seemed purpose-built for protection, a safe house, a fortress. Or a prison if Nick handled this right.

Nick had already loaded his gear into a cheap camping backpack and given the Smith & Wesson a quick strip, clean, and oil.

He checked the action on the pistol, then drove a magazine in and loaded a round.

He saw a light flash near the fence line: a regular patrol.

He had to be sure this was the right place. He had to know their location. He didn't have time to wait for his targets to appear. He needed to draw them out, to provoke.

Nick took out his phone.

89

JEFF TURNER WALKED through a hall on the ground floor of the main house. David Blakely came around the corner, pulled Jeff into a room lined with wine bottles, and shut the door. "So where is Averose?"

"I talked to him. I told him we would make a deal."

"And?"

"He'll bite."

"What did Ali say?"

"She had nothing solid on you. No real proof."

"And who else has she spoken with?"

"Just Nick and the woman he works with, Delia. We have everyone."

"That tracks with what we picked up from her digital trail." David's eyes flared. "All right. So we get Averose and we've got our arms around this thing. What will it take?"

"He's going to call back. Protecting people is his blind spot. With enough pressure, I can bring him in."

Jeff had seen Alan Ambler's Mercedes leave the property through the front gate as he walked back from the guesthouse. He knew the kind of stakes that David was playing for. Jeff had watched Blakely operate for years, but he still couldn't believe his confidence, locking down a presidential nomination in the middle of all this, never losing focus, step by step, as if it were all routine.

"Tonight," David said. "This is moving quickly. I need the problem gone. Every piece. All of them."

Jeff nodded slowly. "They're all connected to Nick Averose, and the law thinks he's a killer. There's a story there. It'll sell. We put the blame on him once he's gone. You want me to start now?"

"Yes. Get Averose. Use the others as leverage. Whatever—"

Jeff's phone chimed in his pocket. He lifted it. Unknown number.

He connected the call but didn't say a word.

"I'm ready," Nick said, his voice calm.

90

NICK STOOD OUTSIDE the car, looking over the estate and listening carefully as Jeff spoke. He could pick up the rustling of movement, perhaps someone else in the room. Jeff was in motion. Nick needed those sounds. He could use them to fix Jeff's location.

He narrowed his eyes and focused on every whisper coming across that line: the rush of breath, air moving across the microphone, the murmur in the background.

"Where are you?" Jeff asked.

Nick didn't answer. Every second was more information. There were black SUVs parked in the driveway. He thought Jeff was at the estate, hiding there below, but wasn't certain. He needed to be sure, needed to know where he had put Delia and the others.

He thought he heard a door close. The background noise grew quiet. Was he outside? Nick scanned the exterior of the main compound and the path leading to the guesthouse, but it was mostly hidden by landscaping, high hedges on both sides.

"Are you going to give yourself up? You can save them, Nick."

He stayed silent.

"Answer the fucking question," Jeff snarled.

"They could be dead already. You want me to trust you? I need to hear their voices."

The creak of a door.

"Here," Jeff said. Nick listened for the echo of his voice, a basement, a cell, but there was none. He studied the ground-floor windows of the guesthouse and the main building, looking for a light to change, for shadows to move behind the blinds, but saw nothing.

In the background, he heard a woman's voice and a man speaking in brusque commands. Everything on the call suddenly sounded boomy. Jeff had put him on speakerphone.

"What . . . what? Where am I?" The words were slurred, but he could tell it was Delia. She was alive. Hope filled him, felt like it was lifting him off the ground. *Careful,* he warned himself. Jeff knew him, knew how to manipulate him.

"She's still coming down off the meds, but she's stable. The shot was through and through, only muscle."

A few gruff words he couldn't make out came over the line, then the sound of footsteps.

"Nick?" It was Ali's voice, pitched high with fear. "I'm okay. And Delia's okay. Please just . . ." She sounded like she was reciting a script, being fed lines, but then her voice changed, quick and strong. "We're at David's place near Frederick. The end of Oak Hollow Road. There's a guesthouse in the—"

A thump, a strangled cry. He only made out one more word: "upstairs."

"You want more blood on your hands?" Jeff asked.

"Only yours," Nick said, and went to kill the call. Jeff's voice came to him, faint as he pulled the phone away, but clear enough.

"And Karen?"

Nick gripped the handset, and brought it back. "I know she's part of this. She's working with you."

"That doesn't mean she's safe. Just the opposite."

Had Jeff somehow tricked Karen? Coerced her? "Don't you—"

"Time's up. This one's on you."

91

ALI LAY ON her side on the silk rug, felt its cool weave as she raised herself up, then stood, fingers to the wall, trying to regain her balance after Jeff had knocked her to the ground. He stared at her, lowered the cell phone, and took a step closer.

"You shouldn't have done that, Ali," he said, his arms swinging slowly as he approached her.

Singh moved in from the other side as he spoke to Jeff. "Averose knows they're here. He'll come straight for them. You should have just killed her." He looked through the bedroom door to Delia. "You have to use her now. Make him understand the consequences."

Ali stepped in the doorway, put herself between them and Delia. The two men moved closer.

"Don't touch her," Ali said.

Singh raised his gun. She shrank from it, bringing her arms up. Her chest seized, and her knees started to bend, as if she could take cover against the threat.

She brought in a long breath and fought against the fear. Maybe this was the end; that thought alone nearly brought her down. But no. She took a step in front of the bed and stood tall. She was tired of calculating, of playing the angles. This was black and white. She wasn't going to let anyone else get hurt.

"Ali, don't be stupid," Jeff said.

She fixed her eyes on him as he moved closer, his left shoulder forward, his right hand down near his thigh holding a gun.

She didn't retreat. Jeff's hand came so fast she barely saw it, just felt the pain bloom in her cheekbone as her vision wavered and she stumbled back. He towered over her as she caught herself with a step to the side, and she held her hand to her cheek.

She stood again, her full height, face-to-face with Jeff as he raised his gun. Even as she felt a drop of blood trail from her swelling lip, and even so close to this killer that she could taste his breath, she smiled, a lunatic smile, as if feeling the pleasure of a free fall off the edge of a building.

"You don't touch her," Ali said, and moved toward him.

Crack crack.

White light filled the room. Ali felt the bullets enter her chest, the shock before the pain. She put her hand back and grabbed for the bed frame as she fell.

92

NICK WAS ALREADY moving, eyes fixed on the guesthouse. Something flashed twice behind the blinds. Gunshots.

No.

He sprinted between the trees toward the estate's power lines. They ran through a narrow cut in the forest, a twenty-foot-wide strip with wooden poles every fifty yards. He crouched next to one of them and pulled out a travel mug from the side pouch of his bag, packed with a pint of black powder, enough to blow up a three-foot-diameter tree stump. It was a sturdy double-walled steel tumbler, and he attached it to the pole with two long strips of duct tape as the smell of old creosote filled his nose.

He took out the pack of Camels, tore the foil, and tapped one out. That would be his fuse.

He lit the cigarette, tasted the bitter smoke.

It was better he go in this way, for everyone. The odds were bad, but if they killed him or took him, they wouldn't need to do any more harm to the hostages to try to get to him.

His heart was going hard, a faint nicotine high over the anger flooding his body. So strong. He felt like he was boiling over.

He tore off the filter and eased the unlit end of the cigarette through the mouthpiece of the mug. The wind was steady, east to west, and the red ember burned down evenly.

The clock was ticking. He took off downhill, toward the lights of the retreat.

93

JEFF MARCHED TOWARD the main house, head forward, arms out to the sides like a man wading into a brawl.

Ali was dead. That was fine. He had gotten everything he needed to know from her, and it was time to start rolling all of this up.

Nick knew where they were. Based on what Ali had called out to him, it almost sounded like he already knew about this estate. He might be close. Jeff had to warn David, to get him into a secure room at the guesthouse. The main building had too many ways in.

Nick was coming. Nick, who had always played the assassin. Nick, who would never cross the line to the dark side. Now he would be ruthless, bent on killing, the real thing.

Jeff clenched and unclenched his fists, felt the flush along his neck and temples, the adrenaline driving him now.

He and Nick had been sparring for so long. Now the true fight was coming.

94

NICK HIT THE edge of the woods and looked across the clearing to the fence and the estate beyond. He dropped to one knee, the blanket of pine needles beneath him as soft as sponge.

From his bag, he pulled the bullhorn, laid it down, and then brought out a small green plastic device, about the size of a cigar box, with a circular opening on one side.

He thumbed down the trigger on the megaphone and bound it with tape, moving carefully, knowing that the slightest rustle would be amplified into a roar. He placed the box just behind the microphone.

He checked his bag one more time, acetone and peroxide splashing in their bottles, then lifted the backpack onto his shoulders. The rubber floor mat from the car was tucked into its straps.

The lights of the patrol moved away far down the

property line. He looked at his watch and eyed the sprint to the fence, the three strands of barbed wire running along the top.

Nothing is perfect. No one is safe.

He crouched, ready for the last sprint. The charge on the power lines would blow any second.

95

DAVID BLAKELY WALKED into the library, his phone to his ear. Sam stood.

"It's Ambler," David said, and put the call on speaker.

"Hello, Alan," Sam called out. "What's the news?"

"We are in business, gentlemen."

"We have it?" David asked.

"It's yours," Alan said. "Everyone is on board."

Sam threw his arm around David's shoulders.

"All the major donors, the whole damn party is in."

"I know how much work you put in on this," Sam said. "We'll remember that when the time comes."

"With you out front, and with the support that David is bringing, it was open-and-shut. The president is vulnerable. This is a lock as long as we avoid a messy primary, none of this circular-firing-squad shit, so we're going all in on Sam. The endorsements are lined up. The only question is how soon you can announce."

"You name it," Sam said. "Everything is ready. We could do it at the events we have set up tomorrow night or Monday if we need to."

"We want it soon. We're going to blow you out with support at the launch, make it a united front."

"Thank you, Alan."

"I'll get to work coordinating the announcement. Tell your team to send me what you have."

"We will," Sam said.

"Congratulations, folks. Enjoy it. But the hard work is just beginning."

"We know it," Sam said.

Alan ended the call.

Sam paced the room, brought his hand to his forehead, then down. David just smiled at him as it sank in. They'd done it. Sam's eyes went down as the joy gave way to calculation. He stopped and faced David. "Jesus. This is going to work."

"You're fine," David said. "I'm handling it." People always said the truth will out, but David knew that was bullshit. The truth decayed like everything else, faded until it was gone. Dust to dust.

"So what do we need to do before we announce?" Sam asked.

"We need you clean," David said.

"What about Averose? And Ali?"

"We're close to getting Averose, and we have everyone else who knows about this in hand."

"Where?"

"Not far," David said. "But I'm not going it alone this time. You tried to make a move against me, Sam, and I need to make sure you're not playing a double game here, that you won't try to put this all on me. So I need to hear it from you, with open eyes this time. Are you ready to make it all go away?"

"There must be some easier way—buy them off, make a threat."

"No, Sam. They disappear. Do you want this hanging over your head for the rest of your life? I can tell the right story, make it perfect, put it on Averose. It's easier than you think. We can end this tonight."

"With everything else we have going on?"

"It only gets harder after you announce. None of this can be connected to you or me. But I'm not moving until I know you're in. You do this and you're free. Once you're in office you'll be above the law. The FBI, the attorney general, they'll answer to you. It's yours if you want it, but you have to make the choice."

David watched Sam rub his hands together slowly, staring into empty space. He knew Sam wanted the Oval, even if it meant that David would own him. But if this indecision was an act, it was a damned good one.

Sam dipped his head, then looked up. The blue eyes flashed.

"You do whatever it takes," he said.

David put his hand on Sam's back. "I'm proud of—"

Boom. A low concussion shook the room. It was powerful but far-off and muted, like a jet breaking the sound barrier in the distance. It hit the gut, not the ears. The room went dark, and a shrill note pierced the air, building higher and higher, like steel scraping glass, until it couldn't be heard at all.

They stood in the blackness. "What the hell is going on?" Sam whispered.

The door banged open, and Jeff walked in with a

flashlight, moving with an infantryman's determination. David strode toward him and leaned in close.

"We need to get you out of here," Jeff whispered.

"What is it?"

"It must be Averose."

"Perfect. Take care of him. Where is he?"

Jeff shook his head. "That's it—he's everywhere."

96

NICK HIT THE fence running flat out. The estate's lights were down, but they would be back soon.

The bullhorn had cried like microphone feedback when he turned on the green box. It was still going now, but he couldn't hear it. The device he had placed in front of the microphone was putting out an ultrasonic tone. It was a cheap garden tool, designed to repel pests, who had a higher hearing range than humans, but it could also play hell with motion detectors that operated in the ultrasonic range. The piezo speaker in the bullhorn was good for amplifying ultrasonics.

With the security they had up, they would know he was approaching—sensors always ran off a battery backup—so his only choice was to make it seem like he was coming from every direction.

He grabbed high on the chain-link, hit the top with two hard pulls of his arms. He ignored the pain in his shoulder, reached for the floor mat, and threw it over the barbed wire. He hooked his hands over it and hauled himself up, twisting over the top, then dropping on the other side.

He landed hard on the balls of his feet, keeping his momentum going forward, rolling over his good shoulder, and coming up in a crouch in the dirt.

He raced along the fence and saw the flashlights moving over the patchy winter lawns. A dogleg in the fence gave him partial cover, though it wouldn't last, and he was far enough around to glimpse the path from the main compound to the guesthouse.

"Come on," he whispered. "Come on."

"THIS WAY," JEFF said, covering the left side as he and the other guards moved in a quick march toward the guesthouse. They covered David and Sam in a diamond pattern, four men, all armed, close enough to take a bullet for the principals.

Jeff looked up at the windows of the guesthouse as some of the auxiliary power kicked in. Delia and Karen were secure in rooms on the east side, the second and third floors. He would have Sam and David hole up in the suites on the other end while the guards hunted down Averose.

He dipped his card at the side entrance. It was one of three ways in, all secured by steel-cored doors. The windows were reinforced and made from shatterproof glass.

"East, south, north," he said, pointing to the guards in turn. Each would take an exit. "And give me your access cards."

"What? Why?"

"In case he kills you, I don't want him getting in."

Jeff held his hand out and twitched his fingers, and the three men obliged.

"If you need in, you radio me. The duress code is 'all right, just fine.' If I hear those words in that exact order, I'll know you're a hostage, so watch what you say. Now get to your posts."

Jeff stepped backward into the guesthouse, scanning the grounds with his gun out, then slammed and locked the door.

98

NICK CREPT ALONG the edge of the tennis courts, covered in the narrow gap between the hedges and the green windscreen woven into the court fences. He paused at the end and surveyed the guesthouse. There were three entrances but none on the side facing him and the back of the property. It was a long set of facades with no doors.

No one was watching it, because it offered no way in. He looked at the six AC units, the pipes and vents running from the back wall on the ground floor. There must have been a boiler or utility room of some kind.

He pulled the acetone out and opened the cap on the thermos. The solvent's fumes dizzied him. He poured it into the steel canister, filling it three-fifths full, and then took out the plastic bottle of peroxide.

He took a deep breath to steady his hand and eyed the run to the back of the house for the last time. The guards' lights swept the property in relentless arcs.

Nick poured in the peroxide and heard the liquids hiss as he cranked the metal cap down on the thermos. He sprinted for the back of the house.

Acetone peroxide puts out about 75 percent of the power of TNT and is one of the most unstable explosives on earth. You only ever mix it cold and let it breathe, because the last thing you want is for it to be hot and under pressure during an uncontrolled reaction.

The metal creaked and strained, growing warm as he shoved it through a dryer vent. He sprinted to his right and ducked for cover behind one of the AC units.

He was still moving, dropping into a crouch, when the blast hit like someone slamming him in the back with a phone book. His whole body tensed, instinct pushing him to take cover, but he stood instead.

Shrapnel rained down. The boom echoed from the hills. The guards' flashlights whipped toward him. He was already racing, pulling a water bottle from the side of his bag before he ditched the pack and ducked into the smoke.

After a long last breath, he doused his head and face in water and disappeared into the fire.

THE BLAST HAD blown a hole in the stucco and wood of the exterior wall and Nick rushed into it. A stud slammed against his arm, then let go with a splintering sound. He pushed past the shattered framing and drywall within, pressing on blindly through the dying flames into the house.

He tripped over something and caught himself with a long step. The heat pressed in against his lips and burned at his neck as the water cooked off. He opened his eyes a millimeter and saw light ahead.

He kept going and made out two pairs of washer-dryers on his right and a wall covered in electrical conduit. Something crashed behind him, and burning embers spit past him. He turned in the doorway and saw that part of the wall had collapsed into the flames, blocking the way he had come in.

He was in a custodian's room. He looked down and saw a glowing patch of orange spreading up the sleeve of his jacket. He slapped at it twice, and the embers went black. Ducking low, he risked a shallow breath, then rose up and opened the metal service panels attached to the wall. The first held the circuit breakers. The second he had to pry open with the tip of his knife. It was the multiplex system for the alarms and doors. He ripped out the wires from the harnesses.

Smoke stabbed at the back of his throat, but he held on until he had severed the last connection, then he turned, his lungs aching in his chest, starving for air. He stepped into the doorway and breathed. The walls seemed to sway. He didn't have time to rest, to get enough oxygen to stop his head from swimming.

He raised his gun, his shoulder stiff, the pain roaring. It felt like the cut had opened up in the chaos. He ignored it and stepped through the doorway, sweeping the hall.

Tss-boom.

A bullet sailed next to his head, blew out the wall in a puff of plaster. He dropped back into the smoke, cutting off his own desperate breaths, darted low to his right through the fumes, and came out on the other side of the expanding cloud.

He recognized the man's face behind the sights of a pistol—it was Singh—and then a light mounted under the barrel shot into his eyes, brilliant white, blinding him.

He arced left, made himself a hard target as he aimed into the white, where the man's face had been. One shot, two.

The light tumbled to the floor, and he heard a heavy thud. He'd found his target. He blinked and tried to regain his vision, closing in. Singh was gone.

A woman's muffled cry came from upstairs.

100

NICK MOVED TOWARD the sound of the voice. The main hall had stairs at either end and a mezzanine twenty feet up from the floor of black-and-white checkered marble.

Guards were pounding on the doors from the outside, the echoes booming through the house. He watched the door handle shake, but it didn't budge. Access was down.

He climbed the stairs, following his pistol as it tracked from threat to potential threat. Another call. It sounded like Delia's voice. He started down one of the halls that led off from the landing, passing through a small sitting area with twin club chairs and a Tiffany lamp. He caught his reflection in a glass-fronted bookcase.

The hallway was clear, and he heard the voice again, coming from the far end.

His throat burned, his mind and vision still clouded by the fumes. He fought the urge to run to her, even as he heard her voice, that muted cry. He counted six doors between him and the room, all dark, four partly open, and a side hall. It felt wrong. A setup. A shooting gallery.

He moved slowly, testing each step for the slightest sound that might give him away. More display cases lined the walls. Antique canes filled one, ceramics another.

With his back to the wall opposite the first door, he scanned inside the room as he passed. It was too dark to see every corner of the interior. He took a step closer to the threshold.

Something skittered on hardwood, and his eyes and gun went instantly to the noise over his right shoulder, back the way he had come. Silver and copper flashed, and a penny rolled on its edge.

A misdirection. He knew instantly, spun the other way and lunged toward the side hall to his left. The barrel of a pistol emerged and took aim. Jeff Turner's face was behind it. Nick's free hand shot out and seized the wrist. A white explosion went off a foot from Nick's eyes as the gun fired, so close it deafened him, sudden silence in the midst of this chaos, and then a high drone like a mosquito's. But he hadn't been hit.

Nick drove his fingers deep into Jeff's forearm and wrenched his arm to the side. The gun slipped from Jeff's hand, banged onto the hardwood behind him, and slid into one of the rooms. Nick twisted, bringing his own gun across his body to get a shot. Jeff blocked his wrist and then drove his knee straight up into Nick's elbow, bending it the wrong way with a crack.

The pain pushed Nick to the edge of a blackout, and

his gun dropped to the ground. Jeff reached down for it. Nick kicked it down the hall as his right arm fell by his side.

Jeff ran for Nick's gun, crouching and lifting it and turning in one smooth motion, but Nick was already sprinting at him. He dropped low and caught Jeff around the waist, pulled him in with his good arm, shoved with his legs, lifting them both high, in the air now. Nick hoped that he could slam Jeff, come down hard enough on top of him to stun him and gain the advantage.

They crashed into the bookcase near the top of the steps. The glass shattered and rained onto the back of Nick's neck as it tipped over. Nick landed on top of Jeff, who was stretched out on his back across the broken woodwork and open books.

Jeff groaned. He tried to raise the gun, but Nick knocked it away, out of his hand. The pistol slid across the hardwood. Nick watched it sail off the mezzanine and fall to the first floor, skittering along the marble.

Nick raised himself up, ready for another blow, but Jeff seemed barely able to move, his eyes on the ceiling and mouth open in a mute scream.

Nick's broken arm was pinned underneath Jeff. As he wrested it free, he felt blood and his hand brushed against a shard of glass that had dug deep into Jeff's back.

"Where are Karen and Ali?" he asked.

Jeff's eyes looked straight up. His mouth writhed in pain. He was out of the fight for now. Nick put his hand to the ground. He needed to move. All the noises around him, even his own voice, sounded like they were coming from underwater, some aftereffect of the blast.

"Help me," Jeff gasped.

Nick got up on one knee.

His head turned to the sound of someone coming up fast behind him, but it was too late. A flash of metal swung toward his temple. The world shook, tilted on its side, as Nick fell.

David Blakely stood over him, holding a cane with a brass grip in the shape of a horse's head. It whipped through the air again.

Nick raised his arm to block the cane, but the metal handle smashed into it, and made the limb drop, numb. The cane drove into his ribs, then his shoulder as he tried to cover up, pushing himself back on the landing, the broken glass crunching under him as Blakely struck him again and again.

The brass grip flew toward his head, and Nick shoved himself to the side, his heel slipping across the carpet, as he went over the top stair. He tumbled, sliding and rolling down the stairs, the room spinning, bolts of pain shooting through his body.

His head slammed against the floor as he landed on his back, knocking the wind out of him, fighting to breathe through paralyzed lungs.

He couldn't move, could barely keep his eyes open. He heard Jeff pleading with David for help, but Blakely simply stepped over him and descended the stairs, closing in on Nick.

101

SAM MACDONOUGH STEPPED into the hallway, his breath sawing in and out. David had told Sam to wait in this room on the third floor, but now the guards were gone, and David's head of security was nowhere to be found, and the house was a war zone: blasts and gunshots and smoke.

Sam heard the sound of someone trying to break down a door, somewhere close, and he knew he had to move. He wasn't going to wait in that room to die. He was getting out.

He crept down the back stairs, then paused. *Come on, Sam, get your shit together. Someone is going to hear you.*

He dragged his hand over his face, took a long breath, and kept moving, toward the second-floor landing.

He peered around the corner and saw a figure dragging himself along the floor, crawling toward one of the bedrooms. It was the man handling David's security.

Sam had only ever heard him called by a work name, Gray.

Sam's hand went to the wall to steady himself. A body on the ground in a country house. The wallpaper weave under his fingertips. The terror freezing him, making him numb. He was here, and he was back there, twenty-five years ago.

The man raised his head and saw Sam, beckoned him over. Sam took a few cautious steps toward him.

"How do I get out of here?" Sam asked him.

Blood soaked Gray's shirt, and he took ragged breaths. Sam followed his gaze into the bedroom, where a gun lay just under a chair.

When he looked back, the man's eyes were on his own. "Help me," he said, and reached for his arm. Sam pulled away by reflex. He heard someone moving upstairs.

"I don't have much time. You get me out of here and I'll tell you the truth about David Blakely," Gray said, sneering as he spoke the name. "You want out from under him? Help me."

"What are you talking about?" Sam said.

Gray eased himself back, sitting against the wall, his body trembling. He licked his lips and shut his eyes against the pain. "Emma Blair. I brought her here."

Sam moved closer, crouched down to hear the man's weak voice.

"I got rid of the evidence," Jeff said, and swallowed, fighting for air. "Her journal. I read it. David lied to you about that night at the Whitleys'. You didn't kill that girl. He did."

102

AS DAVID MOVED down the stairs toward him, Nick looked to the side, the edges of his vision fogged. The gun was down here. He had seen it slide toward the parlor.

David stopped on the bottom step, holding the cane back, his other hand forward, trembling. They were the shaky, charged movements of a man unused to the fight, whose adrenaline was surging just at the edge of control. He hesitated, six feet away, looking like someone facing off against a wild animal, although it was Nick who was vulnerable.

Blakely wasn't used to killing, but Nick watched his eyes. He saw them lock on and then empty out as David seemed to look through him. He knew that look, had been trained to catch it as the telltale of an attack.

Smoke drifted through the hall. Nick filled his lungs, fought against the vertigo.

He was barely able to move, let alone get the better of an uninjured man, but he had to try to make it to his gun.

David took three choppy breaths, clutched the cane, and came for him.

Nick put his hand to the floor and prepared to rise. David stopped and looked to his left.

Sam MacDonough was walking toward him with a pistol in his hand.

David Blakely turned, the cane hanging from his fingers, and watched Sam approach from the other end of the hall, the blue eyes now dull, wide open with shock, unblinking as he looked from Nick on the floor to David.

"How do I get out of here?" Sam asked.

David crossed toward him. "Sam, give me the gun." David didn't like the way Sam's shoulders rolled forward, how he held his head slightly down, showing his teeth but with no smile this time. He didn't like the hand so tight on the grip of the pistol, or Sam's eyes, how they drilled into him with hate.

"Who's outside?" Sam said.

"Sam," he said. "We can still make it out of this. I can—"

"Shut the fuck up!" Sam barked. "If I hear you talk about how you're looking out for me one more time I . . ." He held up the gun. "It's over. I know."

"Know what, Sam?" David said, his voice soft.

"Fourth of July. You killed Catherine Wilson. She was alive when I left that room. Was it just so you could own me?"

David moved toward him. "Sam, you're not—"

"Not one step closer," Sam said, his voice a low growl. "Twenty-five fucking years. Emma Blair saw what you did in that room. You weren't protecting me. You were protecting yourself. Your leverage."

David shook his head, and pulled his face into a mask of sympathy. "Sam, I don't know what you're talking about, but I—"

"I wasn't a killer," Sam said, his voice quiet now, as if talking to himself. He raised the pistol.

David took another step.

Sam's hand shook. The gun barrel jittered in the air like it was writing in cursive, then went steady.

David lunged toward him, hand out to seize the weapon. "Give that—"

Three shots. David reeled back and looked down at his chest. It felt like three slaps. No pain. So strange. Then pressure bloomed near his heart, burning more than anything else. He dropped the cane and touched his fingers to his breastbone as his legs gave out.

He hit the ground, and darkness moved in, his vision all black with a white spark here and there.

He was in that room again, that Fourth of July, and through the window he could hear the Roman candles firing off the dock.

He knelt over Catherine Wilson, looking for something he could use to clean up, to make this all go away. This was his moment, the outsider's chance. He would do whatever it took to earn himself a piece of this world and of Sam MacDonough forever.

Her eyes opened and met his. Her chest rose, the movement so slight he thought he'd imagined it. Before she could make a sound, before she could scream, he put his hand over her mouth. She was weak, so weak after she had struck her head. He barely needed to press. She was awake now. She would talk. She would tell everyone that he was part of it. Who knew how much she remembered? She might say he had attacked her, not Sam. It would be so easy for David to fall. He didn't belong here. He had no senator father.

But it was more than simply protecting himself. He knew how far Sam could go. He knew what this woman's life would be worth. He held her nose gently and pressed his hand over her mouth until her body went still.

103

AS THE SHOTS rang out and David Blakely fell back, Nick Averose raised himself and took three long, unsteady steps toward the parlor. The gun was there, resting against the fringed edge of a rug. Nick lunged for it with his left hand as he heard Sam MacDonough's steps lumbering toward him. Nick closed his fingers on the textured grip of the pistol and turned.

Sam stopped in the middle of the hall and brought his fists to the sides of his head, the right still holding the gun. He looked like a kid protecting his ears from some terrible noise. He shut his eyes. The muscles in his arms tensed, and his whole body shook as a hollow sound escaped his throat.

He was breaking. Nick kept the gun on him, still in his left hand, his weak side. He could have killed him now. But there had been enough death. He wanted the truth.

Sam took in a long breath and brought his arms

slowly to his sides. His body quieted as he regained control. He opened his eyes and turned to Nick.

"Sam," Nick said. "You can put an end to all of this."

Sam looked down at his own gun.

"Everything's going to come out, Sam. Don't make it any worse. Just put it down. That's not you."

"It is now," Sam said, his voice empty of all feeling. Nick saw his fingers tighten on the gun. He swept it toward Nick.

"Sam, no!" Nick shouted, but he had no choice as he pulled the trigger twice. Sam fell and hit the marble flat on his back. Nick felt the floor shake and strode toward him, keeping the gun trained on him as he kicked the pistol out of the senator's outstretched hand.

He looked down at Sam's eyes, open but unseeing, losing their light.

104

NICK CLIMBED THE steps to the second floor. David and Sam were both gone. The taking of life—no matter how justified, and even in the middle of all this noise and smoke—left him with the feeling of standing in an empty church.

He needed to get the others and get out of here. He turned on the landing and saw Jeff's body slumped against the wall. The sight filled Nick with a dark satisfaction tinged with nausea, as all the corruption and violence of this place weighed on him.

He kept moving past Jeff, his eyes on the door at the end of the hall where he had heard Delia calling for help. It was open. Someone had broken off the door handle to unlock it. He raised the gun and closed in. When he was twelve feet away, he saw two figures moving inside, turning toward him.

Karen stood beside Delia, with Delia's good arm draped over her neck. Karen's right shoulder was held forward. It looked like it was injured. Nick lowered the gun and ran to them.

"Nick," she said. "I'm so sorry. Jeff told me that he could help bring you in safely, that it was dangerous to go to that park alone. He said if you kept running, you might get killed. With what the FBI told me, and everything happening, I believed him. God, Nick, I didn't know."

The dread that had been rammed down his back like an iron pipe since before sunset was gone. They were okay. All he wanted to do was hold them close, but he couldn't yet, not until they were all safe.

"It's all right," he said, and scanned the room. "They had you upstairs?"

"I forced the door after I heard the gunshots," she said, her eyes going to her shoulder. "I was trying to get away when I heard Delia's voice in here."

"Was there another woman? Ash-blond hair?"

"Yes," Karen said, closing her eyes and tilting her head toward the bedroom.

Nick stepped toward it. Ali lay on the floor, staring at the ceiling, chest still. He'd seen it before on the dead, but it was still so strange: the look of peace on her face. Nick's throat tightened. The floor shook as the guards outside pounded on the main door. He went back to Karen and Delia. They still had a chance.

"Can she walk?"

Karen nodded. "I think they gave her something, a sedative. Is there a way out of here?"

Nick peered outside through the small slit beside the blinds. He saw the lights and the smoke.

"Did all of these guards know that they were keeping you here?"

"Only Jeff and a couple of his men, I think. It seemed like he was hiding me from the regular security. He said they were taking me somewhere for my safety, but by that point I knew it was all wrong. They put me in a suite upstairs and locked me in."

A boom shook the house. They were trying to break down that door. Nick looked out the window's edge and saw a small lot behind the pool where two black SUVs were parked.

They were close. There was a way out.

105

KAREN PULLED OPEN the east door of the guesthouse and walked out, guiding Delia.

A guard stepped toward them. "I've got her," Karen said. "There are more people inside, injured. He's in there. Upstairs!"

Nick pressed against the wall, just behind the door in the dark anteroom, gun held high by his chest as the lead guard pounded across the marble toward the center of the house.

He slipped around the door after two more men ran in, their attention fixed on the long hall and the bodies lying on the ground.

His arm was in agony with every step, but the cold night air felt like a deliverance. He moved through the shadows toward an access lane, covering Delia and Karen as they approached the black SUVs. He was ready to shoot their way out, but the guards' first objective was clearing that guesthouse.

Nick had taken the car keys from Jeff's body and given them to Karen. He scanned the grounds with his pistol as one of the Suburbans roared to life.

Nick came around the passenger side and climbed in. Delia lay in a reclined back seat. Nick pointed to the rear gate.

"There," Nick said. "Keep the lights off." Karen drove, gripping the wheel as the car leaped forward.

Nick kept the gun ready as they came closer to the exit. In the mirrors he saw lights converging on the guesthouse. One flashed their way, but the gate was already opening on its automatic sensor.

Karen hit the gas as soon as they could fit through, and they raced into the night.

Nick watched behind them, pointing Karen to the side roads that climbed into the hills surrounding the estate. He felt the pavement give way to gravel.

"Are they coming?" Karen asked as they neared the ridgeline.

Nick traced the narrow roads snaking toward them through the woods. No lights.

"We're clear."

He looked into the back. Delia's eyes opened slowly. He reached with his good arm and took her hand. "There you are," she said, and smiled in a merciful haze.

They drove on through the trees. A switchback gave them a view of the valley below. Smoke climbed into the air. Red and blue lights flashed through the forest, tracing Oak Hollow Road toward David's compound. The blasts that Nick had used to get inside were big enough to draw attention for miles. The police were on their way.

The men behind all of this had been so careful with evidence, laying out a perfect story, but that house would offer no easy explanations: David Blakely dead on the ground, Sam MacDonough twenty feet away with gunpowder residue on his hand. He was a senator, a presidential contender. This was too big to go away now. There would be questions, and there would be answers. There was no one left to cover it up.

106

NICK STEPPED THROUGH the door of his office, cradling a five-inch stack of folders under his arm. He dropped them on the table and flexed his elbow, rubbing it with his left hand.

It had been eleven months since Jeff fractured the arm at David Blakely's estate. Nick had finished all the physical therapy, but the joint still barked at him toward the end of long days when weather was coming in.

He heard Delia's voice in the back. It sounded like she was finishing a call.

Ahead, light spilled from the meeting room. As he came closer to the door, a chair pushed back. Karen rose, a half smile on her face and a roller bag beside her. Her computer was open on the table.

She walked toward him, and he wrapped his arms around her.

"I thought you were going to be in meetings all day," he said.

"I dropped the client. Life's too short."

"When's your flight?" Nick asked.

"I have a few hours. I thought we could all get dinner." She glanced at the stack of folders on the table. "Do you have time?"

Nick looked at the pile, then to her. "Always."

"Ray's?" Delia asked, standing in the door to the back hall, coiling a cable. That place was Nick's favorite, a no-frills Arlington steak joint that carved everything in-house.

Karen nodded.

"Deal," Nick said. "I'll drive."

He locked up the files, then took Karen's bag as they walked toward the door.

He and Karen were in a good place now, so far from that house, those desperate hours as they fled.

Jeff had manipulated Karen from the beginning. He came to her the day after Malcolm Widener was killed and said he was worried about Nick, that her husband might be having some kind of breakdown and might have been involved in the death. He needed Karen's help to get Nick into custody safely. Jeff told her he could talk Nick down at the park without anyone getting hurt.

They had framed him so well. Everything she had seen herself and heard from Jeff pointed to Nick as a murderer or a madman. He'd put a gun in a senator's face and refused to turn himself in, telling Karen not to go to the police, to trust no one but him. He understood why she believed Jeff, his old friend, when he came to her full of false concern.

She and Nick would never fully forgive themselves for what happened that night, even as they found a way to forgive each other.

He'd started reaching out to attorneys the morning after they escaped David Blakely's house. With Sam and David and Jeff gone, it was finally safe for Nick to come in from the cold.

His lawyer had once been the deputy head of the FBI criminal division and now worked for Williams & Connolly, the DC litigation and defense powerhouse. Nick knew how unlikely his story sounded as he laid it out beginning to end in a glass-walled conference room on the firm's seventh floor, along with all the evidence and leads he and Delia had tracked down.

It was a high-profile case, and high-risk, but the attorney saw that if he handled it well, he might earn himself a spot in the history books, up there with the Pentagon Papers and Watergate. He arranged for Nick to turn himself in at the federal courthouse in Alexandria and face charges. He talked about making a plea, once. But Nick would only accept the full truth, even if that meant a trial.

Piece by piece, Nick's account was confirmed as the FBI unfolded what had happened at David Blakely's country house. The forensics sketched out the disturbing scene—Sam MacDonough killing David Blakely and Jeff Turner shooting Ali Waldron, one of David's employees who was being held at the compound.

The evidence response team searching David's property eventually found a safe, and in it the insurance policy that David Blakely had kept for so long: a torn piece of fabric stained with the blood of both Catherine Wilson and Sam MacDonough. It was proof that something dark had happened on that Fourth of July twenty-five years ago.

They'd dropped the case against Nick by the end of

summer. Now he was a key witness in the congressional investigations into Malcolm Widener's murder and the other crimes that David Blakely had committed as he paved the way for Sam MacDonough to take the presidency.

Every so often a scandal breaks that is so brazen the whole town can turn against it, let it draw attention away from the everyday graft. Lawmakers were desperate to control the damage and show they were on the side of sunlight as the affair took over every front page and went wall-to-wall on cable news.

Men who a few months before had rubbed shoulders with David and Sam now pointed their fingers and read out somber statements to the press. It was easy enough. Sam and David were dead. They had no more favors to give or secrets to trade.

A bill was working its way through Congress to clean up dark money and campaign finance. They were piecemeal measures, not nearly adequate, though still more than Nick had expected.

He didn't know how deep the investigations would go, how far they would extend beyond Sam and David to others who had benefited from their tactics. The politicians and appointees might try to tell only half the story, to let those two carry the sins of the whole town.

That was the only good to come from all the bloodshed at David's country house—Sam and David had already paid for what they'd done. Their crimes had come to an end. Nick didn't have to count on Washington to bring justice. If they had survived, all of this might have been kept hidden forever.

Still, he wasn't going to stop until everyone who'd played a part in David's political machine was exposed, until Emma Blair's and Catherine Wilson's stories were brought into the light.

The truth rarely came as a revelation from on high, changing everything in one bolt. Nick knew that the truth was a long battle, an up-before-dawn daily grind. He was glad to play his part, to join all the others who got up every morning, fought traffic and crammed into Metro cars, trying to do something decent in this city in spite of it all.

Nick had already started handling different kinds of jobs at his shop. He'd spent so much time whiteboarding and drinking bad coffee with congressional investigators, FBI agents, and assistant US attorneys that it only seemed natural to volunteer his help after he was cleared. He began advising them on witness protection, cold cases, and public integrity investigations, using his talent for getting inside the head of an adversary and the law enforcement training from his Secret Service days. He'd always been more of an ops guy, more bullet catcher than investigator, but something had changed in him that night between the hospital and David Blakely's country house.

Karen let a lot of clients go and started focusing more on nonprofits and foundations. She encouraged Nick, as he went back to the law, to help find people who had gone missing and with crimes that had never been solved. Between the FBI and state and local police, there were thousands of them, reports filling archives and basements around DC and in Quantico, cabinets stacked with case file after case file. Every one might hold a hidden truth, a story that needed to be told.

At Ray's, they talked long after the plates were cleared. Karen had helped Delia through her recovery, and now the three of them would gather for dinner every Sunday, so close after all they had been through, family in all but name.

They dropped Karen off at the airport for her overnight trip. Nick carried her bag onto the sidewalk and then held his wife for a long time, at peace amid the passengers and planes and cars rushing by.

A light rain started falling as Nick and Delia drove back to the office and went inside. He sat at his desk, unlocked his drawer, and took out the files. Delia came in a few minutes later and put a cup of coffee down beside his laptop.

"I figured you'd be going late."

"Thanks."

She clapped him on the shoulder and stepped out.

The streets were quiet now, a cold night in Washington. Nick pulled up his chair and got to work.

ACKNOWLEDGMENTS

MY PROFOUND GRATITUDE goes out to my editor, David Highfill, whose insights absolutely transformed this novel, and to Dan Conaway, my agent, for his guidance, humor, and the extraordinary care he takes with his authors. Thank you to the incredible team at William Morrow and HarperCollins—Liate Stehlik, Tessa James, Kaitlin Harri, Andy LeCount, Rachel Weinick, Joe Jasko, and so many more—for all their support, and to Aja Pollock for copy editing the manuscript. Eliza Rosenberry works wonders in spreading the word about these books.

Thanks to Julian Sanchez, Matt Yglesias, and Tom Lee for the many years of poker, the welcome in the District, and technical advice. Tom introduced me to the hidden alleys and workshops of Shaw and shared with me his hacking know-how. And thank you to Delia Kashat and the rest of the SAIS crew for pulling back the curtain on so many DC worlds.

Thanks to Allison Archambault, Steven Davis, and Thea, and to Rick and Eileen Burke for the homes away from home. To KC Higgins and Peter Higgins for their encyclopedic knowledge of all things DC, and to Mona Lewandoski for her help with Senate details. Ray's the Steaks closed while the book was in editing, but I kept it in as a little send-off. And a special thanks to Cornell

Riley, Eileen Burke, Tisha Martz, and Lauren Carsley for generously taking the time to read the manuscript and give terrific suggestions.

Thank you to the red-teamers and security experts who've advised me on the books over the years and helped inspire this one: Deviant Ollam, Chris Gates, Matt Fiddler, and the folks at OnPoint Tactical. I did take a few liberties with tactics and techniques. And yes, Nick Averose's particular specialty is a real one.

One of the great joys of this work is sharing stories and scenes with my family. They are brilliant and hilarious and don't let me get away with anything, for which I am enormously grateful. My mother, Ellen, offered excellent advice over many drafts of this novel. My wife, Heather, saved the day on this one with her wisdom, love, and encouragement. You're the best, HB.